TENSION

E.M. DELAFIELD

BRITISH LIBRARY

First published in 1920

This edition published in 2021 by
The British Library
96 Euston Road
London NW1 2DB

Cataloguing in Publication Data
A catalogue record for this publication is available from the British Library

ISBN 978 0 7123 5393 9
e-ISBN 978 0 7123 6797 4

Text design and typesetting by JCS Publishing Services Ltd
Printed in England by CPI Group (UK), Croydon, CR0 4YY

Contents

■ ■ ■

The 1920s

■

◘ 1920: *Tension* is published.

◘ 1920 (**January**): Prohibition starts in the USA, banning the manufacture, transportation, and sale of alcoholic drinks. Campaigns for a similar prohibition in the UK are largely unsuccessful, though Edwin Scrymgeor is elected as Scottish Prohibition Party MP for Dundee in 1922, beating National Liberal candidate Winston Churchill.

◘ 'Homes for inebriates' are waning in the 1920s. Many opened in response to the Inebriates Act 1898, which allowed 'habitual drunkards' to be compulsorily admitted for one to three years, or longer for voluntary 'patients'. Between 1899 and 1910, 84 per cent of those compulsorily committed were women. The Mental Deficiency Act 1913 superseded the Inebriates Act, reclassifying 'habitual drunkards' as mentally ill. Many homes for inebriates were similarly reclassified as mental institutions by the 1920s, and it wouldn't be until the 1930s that alcoholism began to be recognised as a disease – for example, Alcoholics Anonymous was founded in 1935.

◘ 1921: According to the 1921 census, there are 1.75 million more women than men in the UK.

◘ 1921: The 1921 census shows 564,000 female clerical workers (up from 179,000 in 1911) – fewer than the 736,000 male clerical workers, though 89 per cent of people employed in typewriting offices were women.

■ ■ ■

- **1923:** The Matrimonial Causes Act 1923 makes adultery by either husband or wife acceptable as the sole ground for divorce.

- Throughout the 1920s, there was an average of 2,718 divorces a year in England and Wales. In 1920, less than a quarter of divorces were initiated by the woman; by 1929, this had gone up to almost 60 per cent.

- **1928 (November):** Radclyffe Hall's lesbian novel *The Well of Loneliness* is banned in the UK after an obscenity trial, following a campaign by the *Sunday Express*. Its most explicit passage is 'and that night, they were not divided'. The Obscene Publications Act 1857 remained in place until 1959, which introduced the idea that a work could be defended as being for the 'public good'.

- **1929:** *Marriage and Morals* by Bertrand Russell is one of the most prominent publications in the debate about free love and marriage, prompting protests and criticisms.

- **1929 (December):** E.M. Delafield's most famous creation, the Provincial Lady, makes her first appearance in serialised form in *Time and Tide*. The first volume of diary entries is published the following year.

◨ ◨ ◨

E.M. Delafield (1890–1943)

◨

E.M. Delafield was born Edmée Elizabeth Monica de la Pasture in 1890: her pseudonym was a play on words, replacing 'pasture' with 'field'. Her mother was a noted writer, as Mrs Henry de la Pasture, and her children's book *The Unlucky Family* was particularly popular.

At the age of 21, Delafield entered a French religious order in Belgium as a postulant (someone who has made a request to join an order and lives there for a period of time before admission). She left without joining but returned to nunneries and religious orders in several of her novels, including *Consequences*, *The Pelicans*, and her first novel, published in 1917, *Zella Sees Herself*.

Delafield worked as a nurse during the First World War and married Colonel Arthur Paul Dashwood in 1919. After two years in the Malay States, they moved to a village in Devon, which she loosely fictionalised for her most enduring work, *The Diary of a Provincial Lady*. It was initially serialised in the feminist magazine *Time and Tide*, of which Delafield was a director, and published as a book in 1930. It has never been out of print. This heavily autobiographical comic novel was followed by three sequels, which saw the Provincial Lady become a successful writer, travel to America, and carry out war work in the Second World War.

Delafield had two children, Lionel and Rosamund, familiar to readers of the *Provincial Lady* series as Robin and Vicky. In 1961, Rosamund wrote *Provincial Daughter* in the style of her mother's series. Delafield published one or more books almost every year until her death in 1943, aged 53.

□ □ □

Preface

■

E.M. Delafield is best known as the author of *The Diary of a Provincial Lady*. Delafield published one or two novels a year from 1917 to her death in 1943, of which one is the delightful *Tension*, first published in 1920 and reprinted here in the British Library Women Writers series. At turns darkly comic and desperately sad, the primary atmosphere of the novel is, well, tension!

Tension, on the surface, is a novel about gossip and insinuation focussing on shadowy events which occurred off the page. At a deeper level, it explores the roles that women occupied in society in the pre-First World War era. From those in long-established marriages to the newly engaged, from the gainfully employed spinster to the wife hidden away in a home for inebriates, *Tension* explores the limits and privileges of female life. *Tension* engages with the differences between a woman's sphere of influence and the constantly shifting power structures which were to be navigated. The key female characters are Lady Rossiter and Miss Marchrose, who at first appear to be complete opposites. As the novel progresses, we see that they were two people faced with the same central dilemma who chose different paths.

If the tension in this novel doesn't make you squirm a little, then you will certainly find plenty to amuse. The internal monologues of Lord and Lady Rossiter show the real truth of their marriage. Perhaps their only true accord comes with their dislike of the small children who constantly appear at the wrong moments with sticky hands and a lack of discipline – an excellent addition to literature's canon of unappealing children.

■ ■ ■

Tension perhaps gives us an insight into Delafield's opinion of men. Men who find themselves in sympathy with the plight of women ultimately discover the quiet life is more important. Men who believe they can break away from social norms find themselves retreating to the traditional path. Don't look to this novel for the neat ending of the romantic comedy. Reputation is what matters, and social institutions and maintaining a status quo.

Lucy Evans
Curator, Printed Heritage Collections
British Library

Tension

I

◼

"Auntie Iris has written a book!"

"A book!" echoed both auditors of the announcement, in keys varying between astonishment and dismay.

"Yes, and it's going to be published, and put into a blue cover, and sold, and Auntie Iris is going to make heaps and heaps of money!"

"What is it to be called?" said Lady Rossiter rather gloomily, fixing an apprehensive eye on the exuberant niece of the authoress.

"It's called, 'Why, Ben!' and it's a Story of the Sexes," glibly quoted that young lady, unaware of the shock inflicted by this brazen announcement, delivered at the top of her squeaky, nine-year-old voice.

"Good God!" said Sir Julian Rossiter.

His wife said, "Hush, Julian!" in a rather automatic aside and turned again to the herald of "Why, Ben!" now hopping exultantly round and round the breakfast-table.

"Did you get a letter from Aunt Iris this morning, Ruthie?"

"Daddy did, and he said it was a secret before, but now the publishers had accepted the book and everybody might know, and I said—I said—"

Ruthie consecrated the briefest possible instant to drawing a sufficiently deep breath to enable her to resume her rapid, high-pitched narrative. "I said, 'Me and Peekaboo must come and tell you and Sir Julian, because you'd be so pleased and so excited, and *so* surprised!'"

"Is your little brother here as well?" said Sir Julian, gazing distastefully through his eye-glasses at Ruthie, heated, breathless, hopping persistently on one leg, and with a general air of having escaped from the supervision of whoever might have charge of her morning toilette before that toilette

– 3 –

had received even the minimum of attention. Ruthie cast a look of artless surprise about her.

"I thought he was here. He came with me—but you know how he dawdles. He may be still in the drive."

A slow fumbling at the door-handle discredited the supposition.

"*There* he is!" shrieked Ruthie joyfully, and violently turning the handle of the door. "*Ow*! I can't open the door!"

"Of course you can't, if he is holding the handle at the other side. Let go."

"He won't be able to open it himself, he never can—and besides, his hands are all sticky, I know, because he upset the treacle at breakfast. Let go, Peekaboo!" bawled his sister through the keyhole.

"H'sh—sh. Don't shriek like that, he can hear quite well."

"But he won't let go—"

"Come away from the door, Ruthie, and don't make that noise."

Lady Rossiter herself went to the door of which the handle was being ineffectually jerked from without, and said with that peculiar distinctness of utterance characteristic of exasperation kept consciously under control:

"Is that you, Ambrose? Turn the handle towards you—no, not that way, *towards* you, I said—right round—"

"Turn it towards you, Peekaboo!" shrieked Ruthie, suddenly thrusting her head under Lady Rossiter's arm.

"Be quiet, Ruthie. There, that's right."

The door slowly opened, and a rather emaciated, seven-year-old edition in knickerbockers of the stalwart Ruthie advanced languidly into the room.

"How do you do?" he remarked, extending a treacle-glazed hand for the morning greetings entirely omitted by his excited elder sister.

"Good morning, Ambrose dear. You're paying us a very early visit."

"Auntie Iris has written a book!" announced Ambrose, more deliberately than, but quite as loudly and distinctly as, his senior. "And it's called, 'Why, Ben! A Story of the Sexes.'"

"Yes, dear, Ruthie told us," said Lady Rossiter, a rather repressive note in her voice indicating a renewed sense of outrage at the singular title selected by Ambrose's aunt for her maiden attempt at literature.

Ambrose turned pallid eyes of fury behind a large pair of spectacles upon his sister.

"You said you wouldn't tell them till I came. ... It's very, very mean of you. ... I'll tell Daddy the minute I get home. ... I ... I ..."

His objurgations became incoherent, though none the less expressive for that, and gaining steadily in volume as he sought, in vain, to overpower the torrent of self-defence instantly emitted from Ruthie's lungs of brass.

Sir Julian Rossiter laid down his paper, opened the French window, and thrust both his visitors into the drive.

"Bolt the window, Julian," said his wife hastily. "And I will tell Horber not to let them in at the front door. Much as I love children, I can't have them rushing in on us at breakfast, it's really too much."

"Do you suppose all their morning calls end like this?" remarked Sir Julian, as he watched their departing guests stagger down the drive, Ambrose's large head still shaking with his wrath, and the voice of his sister still audibly browbeating and calling him "Peekaboo."

"Why does she call her brother by that senseless and revolting nickname?"

"I don't know. I think it's a nursery relic, and dates from the days of their unfortunate mother."

"The dipsomaniac?"

Lady Rossiter said nothing. She was aware that Mrs. Easter's enforced retirement into a home for inebriates was an ancient scandal, and that Julian had only introduced a reference to it in the idle hope of trapping her into disregarding her favourite touchstone in conversation—"Is it kind, is it wise, is it true?"

Unlike his wife, but in common with many people less apt at analysing the idiosyncrasy than himself, Sir Julian habitually preferred silence to speech, unless he had anything unpleasant to say. It was one of the many differences which did not make for unity between them.

"I wonder," Sir Julian presently observed, "what publisher is undertaking the responsibility of 'Why, Ben!' How exactly like Auntie Iris to choose such a preposterous name, and to call it 'A Story of the Sexes' into the bargain! She can't be more than twenty."

"It rather made me shudder when those two poor children spoke the name so glibly. 'A Story of the Sexes'—imagine their knowing such a word at all, at their age!"

Sir Julian shrugged his shoulder. "Nothing could surprise me, from the egregious Ruthie. I suppose I shall have to congratulate Mark Easter on his half-sister's achievement this morning."

"Are you going to the college?"

"I must. There is a meeting of the directors, and I have to take the chair."

"Not a General Committee meeting?" said Lady Rossiter quickly.

"No, Edna," replied her husband, with a great finality. "*Not* a General Committee meeting."

If he did not add an ejaculatory thanksgiving aloud to the statement, his wife was none the less aware that he regarded with the extreme of disfavour her presence at the general meetings of the committee which presided over that venture known as the "Commercial and Technical College for the South-West of England." On this reflection, Lady Rossiter infused as much proprietary interest as possible into the tone of her next enquiry.

"Have we got a Lady Superintendent yet? I can't bear to think of all my girls without a woman to look after them. There are so many little things for which women need a woman."

"One of the subjects before the meeting to-day is to discuss an application for the post. Fuller thinks he has found someone."

Edna Rossiter raised her well-marked, dark eyebrows.

"Surely Mr. Fuller is hardly qualified to judge?"

"Probably not. That's why the question is to be laid before the directors," said her husband drily.

Lady Rossiter, tall and beautiful, with the maturity of a woman whom the years had left with auburn hair unfaded and opaque white skin almost unlined, moved restlessly about the room.

Sir Julian, aware instantly that she was anxious to pursue the subject, perversely remained silent behind the newspaper.

"Do you know anything about this woman? Is she a lady?"

"I have not the least idea."

"Is she from the West Country?"

"She writes from London."

"Ah, our Devonians won't take to her if she's a Cockney. I should prefer someone *de nous autres*, Julian."

"So she may be, for all we know."

"You had better tell me her name, Julian."

"Why?" enquired Sir Julian childishly, and also disconcertingly.

"*Why?*" echoed his wife, momentarily nonplussed.

She looked at him for a moment with black-fringed, amber-coloured eyes.

"Why not?" she demanded at last.

"It would convey nothing more to you than to the rest of us."

"Oh, the perversity of man!" cried Lady Rossiter playfully. "Here am I backing up the great venture heart and soul, knowing every member of the staff individually and offering prizes to every class in every subject, and even putting all my savings into the concern—and then I'm not allowed to hear what the high and mighty directors are going to talk about! Really, Julian, you men are very childish sometimes."

"She is a Miss Marchrose."

"Marchrose!"

Sir Julian, perceiving recognition in the tone of the exclamation, and recollecting his own prediction that the name would convey nothing to his wife, looked annoyed.

"It is a most uncommon name."

Julian carefully refrained from questioning.

"I told you I might know something about her! The girl who jilted poor Clarence Isbister in that abominable way was a Miss Marchrose."

"It doesn't seem probable that this girl could have any connection with the woman who jilted your cousin Clarence; she is a certificated teacher of shorthand and typewriting."

"Well, Clarence's girl was nobody at all, and she was older than he, poor boy—the Isbisters were not at all pleased about it, I remember. But they'd made up their minds to it, and it was all arranged, and then came this thunderbolt."

"If it was such an unpopular engagement, the Isbisters may owe her a debt of gratitude for throwing him over."

"Ah, it was more than that. Don't you remember, Julian? They'd been engaged six weeks, and Clarence was like a lunatic about her, and simply *made* his father and mother consent to it all, and they kept on saying the girl wasn't good enough for him, and didn't seem to care for him much. And then he had that appalling hunting smash."

"I remember," said Sir Julian, "when they thought he was going to be paralysed for the rest of his life, poor chap."

"So he was, from the waist downwards, for nearly a year, and all the doctors said that his recovery was a perfect miracle. But when he was still helpless, and nobody knew if he had to be an invalid or not, he offered to release Miss Marchrose from the engagement—and she gave him up."

"H'm," said Julian noncommittally.

"There have been women," said Lady Rossiter, with tears in her eyes, and in her voice that peculiar emotional quality which indicates that the general is merely being used to indicate the particular, "there have been women who have waited all their lives long for just such an opportunity of *giving*."

"On the whole, I am of opinion that the majority of *fiancés* would prefer not to provide the opportunity."

"Ah, Julian, it's easy enough for you to be cynical. But to me it's simply inconceivable—how she could do it. How any woman could be so utterly heartless—"

"Didn't Clarence Isbister marry somebody else last year?"

"Thank God, yes."

Lady Rossiter was always ready, in a reverent and uplifted manner, to render verbal recognition to her Maker. "Thank God, it didn't destroy his faith in women. He married a true, pure, sweet, loving girl—and one in his own class of life—just a well-bred English maiden."

"And what happened to the other one—Miss Marchrose?"

"I don't know, but she was very badly off, and had been teaching when

— 8 —

Clarence met her—of course, it was the money and position that made her accept him, one supposes."

"Only the price was too high when it included attendance on an invalid?" suggested Sir Julian, with a malicious satisfaction in thus encouraging oblivion of the "Is it kind, is it wise, is it true?" axiom.

Perhaps a similar recollection flashed rather tardily across Lady Rossiter's mind, for she replied with circumspection:

"God forbid that I should judge another! But one holds Love so infinitely sacred, that it is unbelievable that, if she had once known it, she could have profaned it so."

"I remember now; we heard about it at the time. Wasn't young Clarence very much cut up?"

"Poor boy! He took it very hard. Don't you remember?—his nurse came to me last year when I had influenza, and of course she talked—they always do—"

"So long as they find anyone to listen."

"Do you know, Julian, that after she had thrown him over, they could do nothing with him? The nurse told me herself that they thought he was going mad. He actually beat his head against the wall of the bedroom in the nursing-home."

"How sensible!"

In the face of this reverend and sympathetic comment, Lady Rossiter not unnaturally ceased the recital of her relative's unfortunate *affaire du cœur*.

"I suppose if this turns out to be the same woman, you will advise the directors to refuse her application?"

"On what grounds? We did not advertise for a Lady Superintendent of undeviating constancy and infinite capacity for self-sacrifice. If she is a woman of business and has the experience necessary, I really don't see how I can bring it up against her that she once gave the chuck to Clarence Isbister and was responsible for his beating his head against the walls of his nursing-home."

"I am only a woman, Julian," said Lady Rossiter incontrovertibly, but with a certain pathetic smile which she reserved for that particular statement, "but I somehow don't like to think that the Superintendent who is to look after the staff to whom the girls and women and boys whom I have grown to know, will turn to—that she has no higher ideal of Life than poor Clarence's Miss Marchrose."

"Most probably it is not the same person at all."

"I could remember her Christian name, if I were to think a minute. ..."

"Then please don't, Edna. I have not the slightest wish to connect her with the Clarence drama, if it should turn out to be the same woman. In fact, I had much better not know it."

"It began with an 'L,' I'm almost sure," said Lady Rossiter, unheeding.

"I hear the car," said her husband, rising hastily.

"Laura—Lilian—Lena—Lucy—Louisa. ... It was *Pauline*, Julian—I remember it now."

"I have not the least idea what the Superintendent's Christian name may be, Edna." Sir Julian went into the hall. "I shall not come back to lunch. What time do you want the car this afternoon?"

"Oh, that doesn't matter," declared Lady Rossiter brightly. "Don't think of that, dear. It's only my nature-class this afternoon, you know, and I can quite well walk down to the meeting-place. It's only at Duckpool Cove. I want the class to see some of those wonderful effects in sepia and green in the rock-pools when the tide is out."

Sir Julian made the unwonted effort of restraining a strong inclination to ask whether the class could not witness these natural phenomena unchaperoned by their president.

"I will send the car back, then. I shall walk home."

"As you like, but it really isn't necessary."

Sir Julian began to pull on his driving-gloves.

"Don't forget, Julian, to say something about 'Why, Ben!' to Mark Easter. I suppose he will be pleased. And couldn't one—without hurting his feelings, of course—say something about the children being up and about rather early? I mean to say, I'm fond of the little things, when Ruthie behaves and Ambrose doesn't whine, and they don't quarrel—but we can't have them getting into the habit of running in and out of the house at breakfast-time."

"Heaven forbid!"

"Well, try and say something, if you can."

"I'll see."

Sir Julian took his place at the steering-wheel.

He was a tall, thin man, ten years older than his wife, his dark hair already sparse upon the crown of his head, his clean-shaven hatchet face wearing an habitual look of sardonic melancholy. His dark eyes, set in a network of wrinkles, betrayed humour, but, nevertheless, they seldom smiled.

At the bottom of the winding, shady drive he turned the car out of the stone gateway and on to the high road. A hundred yards further on he stopped in front of a small slate-roofed villa standing in an enclosure of raggedly-growing laurel hedge and untidy fencing, of which half the wooden palings were tumbling down.

At the first sound of the horn hooting an announcement of arrival, the small, pretentious-looking front door burst open, and Miss and Master Easter precipitated themselves down the garden-path, vociferating greetings in unresentfully complete oblivion of their recent unceremonious ejection at the hands of their neighbour.

"Is your father ready?"

"Coming this minute," said Ruthie, and added in a sudden falsetto, designed to penetrate to an upper window of the villa, "Aren't you, Daddy?"

"I'll sound the horn to let him know you're ready," volunteered Ambrose, outstretching a pair of hands, noted with disgust by Sir Julian as displaying the identical traces of syrup proclaimed by his sister an hour ago.

"No, Peekaboo! Not you—me!"

"Neither of you," said Sir Julian succinctly.

"May I get up beside you?"

"No."

"Will you take me into Culmouth too? Oh do!"

"Certainly not. You are too dirty."

"There, Peekaboo," said Ruthie, with a sudden access of extreme virtue. "What did I tell you? I've washed, Sir Julian."

"I am very glad to hear it."

"What's that?"

"Don't touch. It's the foot-brake."

"What's a foot-brake?"

"Is it a nice foot-brake?"

"Do you like having a foot-brake?"

"Have all motor-cars got foot-brakes?"

"Does Daddy like foot-brakes?"

The extreme idiocy of the questions launched at him drew forth a stifled ejaculation from the owner of the foot-brake, but Ruthie and Ambrose received no further enlightenment on the subject of their enquiries.

"Here's Daddy!"

"Good morning, Sir Julian. Sorry to have kept you."

"Good morning."

"Go into the house, children. Sarah is looking for you."

"Oh, she wants to wash my hands," aggrievedly said the boy.

"Get under the laurels, flat, and I'll run and say that Daddy's taken you in the motor to Culmouth," suggested his sister with great readiness.

Mark Easter made no slightest attempt to cope with his offsprings' ingenious admixture of uncleanliness, deceit and disobedience.

He took his place beside Sir Julian and the car started forward.

"I'm afraid those brats of mine came up at an unearthly hour to disturb you this morning. I had no idea where they were, or I'd have fetched them back."

"They didn't stay long," said Sir Julian, with perfect truth.

"The fact is, Lady Rossiter is much too good to them. But I'll see it doesn't happen again. They were rather beyond themselves this morning."

Mark hesitated and Sir Julian waited, rather amused to hear how his simple, straightforward agent and man of business would explain the cause of his children's objectionable upliftedness.

"I daresay they told you I had a letter from my sister this morning. It seems that she's written a novel, and Messrs. Blade have agreed to publish it. Of course, she's very delighted about it, and asked me to tell the kids, and the idea somehow took hold of them. I don't see quite why it should appeal to them so much, but you know how excitable children are."

"Have you read the book?"

"Good Lord, no! I never took her scribbling seriously."

Mark took off his cap and let the wind ruffle up his brown hair and moustache. His blue eyes laughed, while his face was still screwed up into a look of perplexity.

"She's given it a very odd name. I daresay the children told you."

"Yes. They did."

"I hope it's proper, I'm sure," said Mark Easter doubtfully. "They say that girls always write the most improper books. I suppose because they don't know what they're talking about."

"I daresay it's innocent enough."

Mark repeated thoughtfully, "It seems an odd thing to call a book, 'Why, Ben!' but I don't mind saying that I wish she hadn't added that it was a story of the sexes—and the worst of it is that the children have got hold of it, and I am afraid that we shall never hear the last of it."

Sir Julian, feeling quite unable to suggest an optimistic alternative, wisely abandoned the subject.

II

◼

The College stood not far from Culmouth Cathedral, the biggest building of the many that surrounded the open grass patch of the Cathedral Green.

It was a restored Georgian house, well in keeping with its surroundings, and with a square paved court at the back shaded by immense elm-trees.

Julian Rossiter always went up the shallow stone steps that led to the big green double door with a sense of satisfaction.

The satisfaction, however, from an artistic point of view, diminished sensibly and at an ever-increasing rate as he penetrated to the inside of the dignified red and white exterior.

The large square hall was paved with uncovered stones and surrounded by doors of varnished deal, each bearing an announcement in staring white letters.

"Nearly eleven o'clock," said Mark Easter. "Do you want to look in at the classes, Sir Julian? Fuller is probably giving a lesson till eleven."

Sir Julian signed assent, and the two men turned to the stairs, also of uncarpeted stone.

On the first floor, which produced the same aspect of chilly cleanliness, a door was held open from the inside by a wooden kitchen chair, revealing the interior of Class-room No. V., which bore the white-lettered announcement, "Demonstration Room."

A monotonous female voice, raised to a high, expressionless monotone, came from beside the large blackboard facing a double row of desks and forms.

"Gay lengthened for the final syllable *ture*—li-ga-ture. *Through* the line for a third-place vowel. Is that quite clear?"

An expressionless murmur of assent came in reply.

"Once again then, please, and without putting in the vowels. Are you ready? Take the same words down again and the vowels to be indicated by the placing of the outline."

"Aperture—adventure—ligature—"

"Class-room pretty nearly full," said Mark under his breath. "There are always more students of shorthand than anything else."

"Who's giving the dictation?"

"Miss Farmer."

"It's an uneducated pronunciation. I wish we could get a better class of teacher."

"Young Cooper is pretty good. He takes French and accountancy and book-keeping."

"Cooper has two gifts to a degree which I have never seen equalled," Sir Julian said grimly. "He has a genius for extracting a personal application from everything he hears or sees, and he is firmly convinced that his every action, trivial or otherwise, is worthy of comment."

Five minutes later an opportunity presented itself for immediate verification of this pleasing summary.

Brisk, snub-nosed and sandy-haired, Cooper emerged bustling from "No. II., Book-keeping," just as Mark and Sir Julian turned away from No. V.

"Good morning, Sir Julian. Good morning. I thought you'd be in to-day."

"Is Fuller disengaged?"

"I think so—let me consult my watch." Cooper shot into view a rather bony wrist with a large watch on it. "I see by my wrist-watch that it's just on eleven. Let me pop it out of sight again. Fuller will be in his room, I fancy, but I'll go and find him at once, Sir Julian, and tell him you're here. I'm just on my way down now, to put these books away. I'll look into Fuller's room on my way past."

"Thanks," said Julian laconically.

Cooper hastened ahead of them, murmuring as he went:

"I'll just give a knock on Fuller's door, and look in to say Sir Julian's here, and then I can get rid of all these books ... down the stairs, and one hand on the books so that they don't slip from under my arm ..."

In an incredibly short space of time he had sped up the stairs again and made the rather self-evident announcement:

"Run up again to let you know Fuller's there, Sir Julian. I thought I'd let you know, so ran up again."

"Right. See you at the meeting, I suppose, Cooper?"

"Yes, Sir Julian. I think I've always attended every meeting since we first opened here. Half-past eleven, the meeting this morning; that gives me just half an hour. I leave you here, then, and turn off to the locker room. ... Dear me, a sneeze is coming; now, can I get at a handkerchief in time?"

They left him rehearsing the procedure of his sneeze in a sub-audible manner.

"That boy always reminds me of a curate," said Sir Julian unkindly.

In the ground-floor room where the Supervisor sat intrenched behind an enormous table piled with papers, the subject of the vacant post of Lady Superintendent was embarked upon.

"The girl I wrote to you about from London, Sir Julian, is practically a lady," said Fuller, in a very earnest manner, fixing a pair of black, straight-gazing eyes on his chief. "In a general way, I wouldn't have a girl who is a lady on the staff for anything you could offer me, but this one has had three years' experience in Southampton Row, and has the highest testimonials, and certificates for shorthand and typewriting and a diploma for French."

"What salary does she want?" said Mark Easter.

"She'd take the figure we decided on, because she wants to come to the west of England."

"A hundred-and-twenty and exes?"

"That's right."

"Free to come at once?"

"To-morrow, if we want her."

"That's good. She's prepared to undertake a certain amount of tuition, and supervision of the staff, of course?"

"Quite."

"Well, Sir Julian," said Mark Easter, turning to him, "shall we put it to the directors?"

Sir Julian made no immediate reply, and Fuller, nothing if not intent upon his business, laid both arms upon the paper-bestrewn table, leant well forward, and began in an earnest and expostulating tone:

"I see you're hesitating, sir. I wish you could have had a personal interview with the young lady, for I really was most favourably impressed—most favourably. As I say, a superior young woman is always an influence, if there's no nonsense about her, and Miss Marchrose certainly has none, so far as I could judge. Of course, sir, the decision rests with you, but I must say I should like to give her a trial. I believe we might do worse."

"What sort of age is she?"

"She told me she was twenty-eight," said Fuller, with a grin that revealed dazzling teeth in his swarthy face.

"I should have preferred an older woman."

"I doubt if she'll ever see thirty again, sir," said Fuller simply.

"Well, Fuller, I know you've the interests of the College very much at heart, and I'm quite willing to give her a trial on your recommendation," said Julian. "We'll put it before the directors at the meeting."

"Thank you, Sir Julian. I thought you'd probably trust my judgment," Fuller remarked, with satisfaction. "And I don't think you will regret it. She struck me as being a thorough woman of business, most capable, and as hard as nails."

At this final qualification Sir Julian looked rather glum, irresistibly reminded of the heroine of that episode which had wrought so much havoc in the household of his wife's relatives.

"However," he remarked to Mark Easter, as they went towards the committee-room at the appointed hour, "I really do trust Fuller's judgment, so far as the good of the College goes, though I haven't his own implicit belief in his absolute infallibility."

"He thinks the whole show rests on him," said Mark Easter, and added with belated justice, "And for the matter of that, I really don't know where we should get another man like him. He's a nailer for work."

"I hope his protégée will be a success. If he talks to the directors about her being practically a lady, as distinguished, I suppose, from a 'young lady in business,' he'll fetch that old snob Bellew."

"He probably won't mention it," said Mark Easter shrewdly. "He looks upon it as a disadvantage in the abstract, but he told me yesterday that he thought he could explain it if any objection were raised."

"Fuller would think he could explain it," Sir Julian rejoined drily, "if the creation of the world were in question."

The committee-room was a long, low annexe to the main body of the building, with the usual green-baize covered table placed lengthways down the middle of the room, mahogany chairs at regular intervals round it, an armchair at the head for the chairman, and on the table the usual disposition of clean blotting-paper, pencils, note-books, and a carafe of water covered with an inverted glass.

A clock ticked on the chimneypiece.

Young Cooper was the sole occupant of the room, and observed brightly, "No one has arrived yet, sir, but I see the clock gives it as two minutes to the half-hour."

"Got an agenda there, Cooper?" said Mark, and proceeded to study the typewritten slip of paper.

Sir Julian went to the chair at the head of the table.

He also looked idly at the agenda, listening the while with the rather revolted fascination with which young Cooper's peculiar style of sub-audible self-communion always inspired him.

"I must move my chair or pull down the blind—sun coming right in through the window. If I lift it—so—that oughtn't to interfere with anyone else. Just caught the edge of the carpet, though—that won't do … put the chair-leg down on it, and then we're all right."

"Now, Sir Julian, it's just striking the half-hour."

"I hear it."

"So do I," agreed Cooper agreeably, as the clock on the chimneypiece chimed loudly. "I'm just going to the window to see if Mr. Bellew's car is in sight."

Having, as usual, suited the action to the word, Cooper was shortly able to announce that the car was there, and that he would come back to the table and just see if the blotting-paper was straight.

"They'll draw on it," he said mournfully. "They always do. That's a thing I couldn't do myself, even if I weren't taking down the Minutes. I couldn't pay attention if I were drawing."

They did draw on the blotting-paper.

Sir Julian, leaning back at the head of the table, giving only half his attention to the meeting, which followed lines so habitual as to have become almost routine, watched with idle amusement the verification of Cooper's resignedly doleful prophecies.

Old Alderman Bellew, oily and apoplectic, made meaningless circles and semi-circles with a pencil grasped between the swollen knuckles of his first and second fingers, and only glanced up once or twice as a question of finance was touched upon by Fuller, Financial Secretary to the College as well as Supervisor of Classes.

Another director was yawning almost unconcealedly, until, catching the eye of the chairman, he assumed an expression of acute concern and hastily inserted a forefinger into his still open mouth as though in search of an aching tooth. This simple manœuvre was apparent to Sir Julian, and his eyes half involuntarily met Mark Easter's laughing blue ones in an instant's exchange of silent amusement.

Julian looked down again at his own share of blotting-paper, left immaculate in deference to Cooper's feelings, and his thoughts dwelt upon Mark Easter.

He thought of the good-looking, light-hearted fellow that Mark had been all his life, of his casual marriage, embarked upon out of pure good-nature, with a woman older than himself, and for no better reasons than the ones that he had once put forward, half apologetically, to Julian himself.

"She was having such a rotten time when I met her in Ireland—no one ever asked her to dance, and the other girls all seemed to be younger and prettier and having more fun. I used to take her for drives, you know, and then dance with her in the evenings; and upon my word, I was the only chap that ever took any notice of her, I do believe. And I really did want to settle down and have a home, and it somehow seemed more likely she'd take me than one of the pretty little fly-aways who could get all the fun they wanted before settling down. She was by way of being a good housekeeper, too, and fond of kids. I'm fond of kids myself," said Mark Easter wistfully.

Sir Julian wondered, not for the first time, how long that fondness had survived the shrieking, stamping, bullying era inaugurated by Ruthie, and the whining, unwashed, question-asking proclivities of her junior.

Mark Easter never spoke of his children except with a sort of apologetic tolerance, but neither was he often to be seen in their company.

He was agent to the Rossiter estate, and more often found about his work and at the College in Culmouth than in his untidy, servant-ridden, mistressless house.

Julian's thoughts turned for an unwilling moment to the recollection of the rapidly-growing gossip that had saddled Mark Easter, ten years ago, with an alternatively morphomaniacal, drug-taking, inebriate or homicidally insane partner; to his own ever-increasing, silent certainty that disaster threatened the only human being whom he cared for in the world; to Mark's haggard face and prolonged absences from home.

Then to a grey dawn, when Mark had ridden up to ask in three inarticulate words for help that Julian had given in almost unbroken silence. Mrs. Easter had gone away, and there was no more occasion for furtive surmise, for everyone knew at last that she had been steadily drinking her way into the home for inebriates that now had sheltered her for more than seven years.

And Mark, with an elasticity at which Julian had never yet ceased to marvel, had recovered his habit of easy laughter, his keen interest in his work, his old enthusiasm for the Commercial and Technical College schemes.

Sir Julian secretly admired and envied his almost childlike absorption in the College. He sent sidelong glances from time to time at Mark's keen, handsome face, at the shrewdness of the gaze which he kept upon each speaker.

Fairfax Fuller—never was there a worse misnomer, thought Julian, with a grim half-smile, as he looked at his swarthy-faced subordinate—Fairfax Fuller might have made a good speaker—say, a political agent. Kept to his facts, always sound, and with a weight of personal conviction that told. But there was nothing to look interested about, Julian reflected, as Mark Easter was looking interested.

Fuller always put forward the same arguments: for a better class of teacher, for an extension of advertisement, always with the same implication of his own indispensability as managing Supervisor.

Alderman Bellew was tedious, obviously only speaking at all so as to impress the fact of his presence on his fellow-directors, and Mark Easter said nothing, until Miss Marchrose's application for the post of Lady Superintendent was brought forward by Fuller.

The discussion of the appointment was merely formal, and Sir Julian gave it formal sanction.

"I think that concludes our business for to-day, gentlemen. Thank you all very much."

The chairman rose.

"Anything else you want me for, Fuller?" he enquired, as the meeting dispersed.

"I don't think so, thank you, sir," said Fuller, with a manifest air of dissatisfaction.

Sir Julian, knowing his Supervisor, lingered.

"Lady Rossiter has kindly asked the members of the staff out to Culmhayes on Sunday, Sir Julian."

Sir Julian looked quite as much annoyed as did Mr. Fuller.

Few things were, in the opinion either of the Supervisor or of his employer, less to be commended than Lady Rossiter's benevolent attempts at keeping in touch with the staff of the College.

Appearances, however, were discreetly maintained.

"I hope as many of them will come as care for the walk," said Sir Julian, with gloomy civility.

"I am sure they will be delighted, and it will make a nice beginning for Miss Marchrose on her first Sunday."

Sir Julian walked away even gloomier than before at the recollection that his wife's hospitality would not improbably be extended to the perpetrator of the outrage which had driven Captain Clarence Isbister to such extreme demonstrations of despair.

"Do you happen to remember—did you notice—what that woman's Christian name was?" he enquired of Mark Easter.

"The new Superintendent?"

"Yes."

"Let me see. I saw her letter to Fuller—something unusual. ... Was it Pauline?"

"I thought so," said Sir Julian.

It was characteristic both of Sir Julian's dislike to anything which came, in his opinion, under the extremely elastic heading of officiousness, and of the care with which he had impressed his dislike upon Mark Easter, that his companion did not ask him why he thus dejectedly took for granted the name bestowed at baptism upon Miss Marchrose. Mark Easter, talkative and open-hearted, was yet the only man from whom Sir Julian said that he had never received an officious enquiry or an unasked offer of assistance.

If the remark might be looked upon as a form of the highest commendation, it was one which Sir Julian had never yet shown any disposition to make in regard to his wife.

Nothing had as yet persuaded Edna Rossiter of the inadvisability of addressing personalities to a man whose surface cynicism was used to cloak extreme sensitiveness, and whose bitterness of speech was the outcome of such disillusionment of spirit as comes only to those capable of an idealism as delicate as it is reserved.

"Are you going home, Mark, or will you lunch at the club?"

"The club," said Mark decidedly, with an intonation that brought before Sir Julian's inner vision a lively picture of the probable congealed mutton, underdone potatoes, and lumpy milk-pudding of Sarah's providing, doubtless to be consumed to an accompaniment of senseless comments and enquiries from Ruthie and Ambrose on the engrossing subject of "Why, Ben! A Story of the Sexes." As the thought crossed his mind, Mark observed:

"Iris is coming down here later on. Of course, she wants to be in London for the publication of her novel, but that won't be out till the winter, she says. Poor girl! I wish people would not put it into her head that it is her duty to come and look after me and the children at intervals."

"Who does put it into her head?"

"Various old aunts. I wish people would mind their own business. Poor Iris hates the country."

"Is she still living in the flat?"

"Yes, with another girl. I believe they sleep in the boot-hole and do their own cooking, but it's all a great success, and Iris is very happy, and has the sort of Bohemian society she likes. It is a much better arrangement than her being down here with me. I'm not sure," said Mark thoughtfully, "that I approve of relations living together after they are grown-up."

Sir Julian agreed with him so cordially as to suggest that the case in point was emphatically one in which the proposed arrangement would be eminently undesirable.

"I don't know that Iris, devoted though she is to them, is the best possible person to be with the children."

"No," said Julian, with restraint, considering his private opinion to be that if anything on earth could render Mark Easter's progeny more insufferable than nature and the maternal shortcomings had already made them, it was the society of their affected, suburban, and distinctly under-bred young relative. It was a source of continual wonder to him, what sort of a person the second Mrs. Easter could have been, to have presented Mark with such a half-sister as the twenty-year-old perpetrator of "Why, Ben!"

The conclusion long ago come to by him, that Mark had been afflicted with the most intolerable set of relations ever owned by man, was destined to be furnished with yet another proof of validity at the end of the day.

As the two men came back across the fields of Sir Julian's property late in the afternoon, Mark whistling under his breath and Julian silent in the comfortable companionship of long association and mutual understanding, a sound of hoarse, ceaseless yelling that could have been produced by no other human larynx than that of Mark Easter's daughter came from the garden of the villa.

"I'm afraid that's Ruthie," said her parent, sensibly slackening his pace. "I'm certain it is."

Ruthie was bent double across the dangerously-creaking top bar of the wooden paling.

She raised a face, flushed and distorted, indeed, as much from her unnatural position as from her vocal efforts, but unstained by tears, and proclaimed aloud:

"Daddy, Peekaboo has been such a naughty boy. Sarah is putting him to bed and I'm singing so that he can hear me from the night-nursery window. He has written up in ink all over the drawing-room door, and the dining-room door, and the nursery door, 'The two best books in the world are "Why, Ben!" and the Bible.'"

III

Edna Rossiter, in common with the majority of her sex, supposed herself to be a religious woman because she had, from early girlhood, indulged nightly in five minutes spent on her knees beside her bed, her face pressed against the satin quilt, while she thought about herself.

Very soon after her marriage she formed the habit of prolonging the five minutes into ten, or even fifteen, while she consecrated a few vindictively earnest thoughts of forgiveness to her husband.

Within the last ten years, all the forbearance which she was capable of displaying being apparently without any effect upon Sir Julian, Lady Rossiter had rather disgustedly transferred her allegiance from the Almighty, *in propria persona*, to God as He is found in Nature.

Nature, primarily, meant out-of-doors generally, in warm weather, and the sound of the sea two miles off, audible from beside the boudoir fire, in the colder seasons.

Lately, however, Nature had also embraced such of humanity as had its place rather lower than that of the Rossiters in the social scale.

Edna sought for the Divine Spark in her fellow-creatures, and frequently discovered it, with renewed satisfaction to herself and to its possessor.

As she often said, smiling a little:

> "There's so much bad in the best of us,
> There's so much good in the worst of us—"

She never finished the quotation, except by the smile, because she knew it to be at all times easy to trip over its inversions and repetitions, and thus risk the transition from the sublime to the ridiculous.

One of the most recent manifestations of what Julian had once designated in his wife's hearing as the "Hunting of the Spark," was her wholesale invitation to the staff of teachers at the College to spend Sunday afternoon at Culmhayes.

A few stray and tentative young women had availed themselves of it once, showing a marked disposition towards wandering arm-in-arm round the gardens, avoiding their hostess as much as possible, and Cooper had twice walked over from Culmouth and made nervously easy conversation to Lady Rossiter, which had dwindled into a sort of alert silence when her husband came in.

"Mind you bring them all next week," had been Lady Rossiter's farewell injunction, to which Cooper had replied with great confidence and assurance.

Preparing for her guests on Sunday afternoon, therefore, Lady Rossiter gazed smilingly out of her window at a cloudless day of August. Evidently Nature was in league with her votary.

Lady Rossiter told her maid to bring the black-and-white *mousseline de soie*. No other colours suited her fairness so admirably, and she always wore the combination when embarking upon any enterprise of particular benevolence. The thick pallor of her complexion could afford to defy the sun, and she seldom wore a hat in the garden. A black-and-white-striped sunshade made quite as effective a background for her mass of auburn hair and black eyebrows and lashes.

Before going downstairs she thoughtfully slipped the rings from her long white fingers, and bade her maid substitute a small crystal cross on a velvet ribbon for her pearl necklace.

The maid had not been with her very long, and obeyed the mandate with such wooden matter-of-factness that Lady Rossiter added gently:

"One doesn't want anyone to feel the least little—difference—in any way. We have all grown to have such false ideas of values …"

"Yes, m'lady," said Mason, looking so thoroughly bewildered that Lady Rossiter resolved to read extracts from Ruskin aloud to her while her hair was being brushed at nights.

She went downstairs slowly, to find Julian reading in the hall.

"Jorrocks?" she enquired playfully, but with a meaning that she knew would not be lost upon her husband.

Ever since she had wrung from a monosyllabic Julian the admission that neither Ruskin, Pater, nor Stevenson "meant" to him that which they meant to her, Edna had assumed, by almost imperceptible degrees, that her husband's only literature consisted of Jorrocks and the volumes of the Badminton series.

Dickens she had unwillingly conceded to him, since Dickens made no appeal to her personally, but she was more apt to dwell upon his liking for the "Pickwick Papers" and "Nicholas Nickleby" than for "Great Expectations" or "David Copperfield."

At her enquiry Julian closed his book.

"Jorrocks, of course," he assented expressionlessly, putting down Huysman's "En Route," and not troubling to display the title.

"Did Mr. Fuller tell you how many of my staff meant to come this afternoon?"

"No. I don't suppose, in any case, that they would have told him."

"That's so curious to me, Julian. To work together all the week, and yet know nothing of one another's *real* life—nothing of what goes on in the free time, or the one holiday of the week."

"What generally goes on, I imagine, is that the girls have their hair waved on Saturday afternoons, stay in bed on Sunday mornings, and go out with their young men on Sunday evenings. I doubt if the procedure ever varies."

"And that with God's own blue sea less than a mile away!" ejaculated Lady Rossiter under her breath, but nevertheless quite audibly.

"Cooper generally goes for a walk on Saturday afternoon," said Sir Julian consolingly; "and Fuller, and I imagine a good many of the other fellows as well, to a football or cricket match."

"Can you wonder that we long to win them to clearer, wider ideals?" his wife enquired.

She waited for no reply, aware of old that Julian invariably professed a supreme indifference to the outlook of the College staff when outside their College walls, but trailed into the wide, cool drawing-room containing little furniture and an abundance of roses and heliotrope.

Lady Rossiter arranged the flowers herself, and did so exquisitely. She often said that flowers were literally a necessity to her—an opinion frequently held by those whose financial situation has never compelled them to regard flowers as an alternative to, let us say, butter for breakfast, in which case the relative value of the commodities in question is apt to undergo alteration.

Poised over her bowls of pink roses, Lady Rossiter was taken by surprise when her guests eventually arrived.

Sir Julian strongly suspected that had the drawing-room window given on to the drive, instead of on to the green bowling-alley, his wife would herself have met her visitors at the hospitably open hall door, thus sparing the dignity of Horber, undemocratic as only a butler can be, from the announcement which he stiffly made out of the extreme corners of his mouth.

"Miss Farmer, Miss Sandiloe, and Mr. Cooper, m'lady."

Miss Farmer, in a green linen which accorded singularly ill with a sallow complexion; Miss Sandiloe, girlish, pretty and full of giggles that threatened disaster to a tightly-fitting and transparent white muslin; and Mr. Cooper, obviously in the toils of Miss Sandiloe, came one by one into the drawing-room, where Lady Rossiter, in point of fact, had never intended them to penetrate at all.

Sir Julian, watching the entry in an angle of the hall window-seat which he trusted to be invisible from the drawing-room, could not forbear the tribute of an unwilling admiration to his wife's handling of the rather embarrassed trio.

"Ah, but how nice! Miss Farmer, of course we've met before; and Mr. Cooper "—a shake of the hand to each. "And-?" A pause, with pleasantly uplifted eyebrows, in front of Miss Sandiloe.

"Miss Sandiloe," Miss Farmer supplied, and added rather haltingly, obviously unsure of the etiquette governing the position:

"The junior teacher of shorthand, Lady Rossiter."

"I'm so glad to see you," said the lady, with an additional graciousness designed, Julian imagined, to set the youthful stranger at her ease.

The unexpectedly high-pitched note, however, upon which Miss Sandiloe off-handedly replied, "Oh, thanks!" did not indicate shyness.

Julian viewed it as an example of the law of cause and effect that his wife's next observation was made in tones that savoured less of kindly welcome and more of rather distant patronage.

"I am always anxious to get to know all the members of the College staff, and have them out here if I possibly can. I take a great interest in the College. In fact, I'm on the committee of management."

"Are you?" said Miss Sandiloe indifferently. "What topping flowers those are!"

She thrust her face into the fragrant mass which Lady Rossiter had just left.

"You must all come into the garden, when it's a little cooler."

Lady Rossiter addressed herself to Miss Farmer.

"Meanwhile it's too bad of me to keep you standing in this hot room. Come into the morning-room."

Julian fancied that Miss Farmer, heated and wearied, and with dusty patent-leather shoes that creaked as she walked, and bore a large crack across each, as though they were too tight, cast a rather wistful look at the large, beautifully-shaded room of which they had penetrated no further than the threshold.

But she obediently followed her hostess, and Miss Sandiloe, giggling slightly, tripped behind her with Cooper in tow.

From sheer curiosity, Julian went into the morning-room twenty minutes later.

His wife, looking unusually harassed, was seated near the window, Miss Farmer, Miss Sandiloe and Mr. Cooper having unconsciously placed themselves in a semi-circle in front of her, each seated upon the edge of an upright chair.

"Why," Lady Rossiter was exclaiming in her brightest voice, "one of my greatest friends is a dear little dressmaker who lives in Culmouth, and another is the quaint old man who looks after the lifeboat-house down in our Duckpool Cove."

Edna must be hard put to it, Julian reflected, to have made use of both her dear little dressmaker and her quaint old man within one sentence. Both, he knew, were frequently in requisition for the dissipation of any sense of awkwardness which she suspected might be assailing her visitors, but one was generally held in reserve to supplement the effect of the other if necessary.

"Here you are!" Edna exclaimed, almost with relief in her voice, as he entered, thereby, Julian told himself, depriving young Cooper of a remark which he would certainly have made his own.

Young Cooper, however, was not to be defeated.

"We've accepted Lady Rossiter's kind invitation, you see, Sir Julian," he observed.

"How are you, Cooper? How d'y'e do?" He shook hands with the shorthand teachers. "Were you the only people energetic enough to walk over, in this heat?"

"Why, yes. The new Lady Superintendent spoke of coming since Lady Rossiter was so kind, but she didn't turn up, so we've come without her."

"Tell me about the new Superintendent," said Edna quickly. "Miss Marchrose, isn't she?"

"Most pleasant and energetic," said Cooper rapidly. "The sort of young lady *I* call capable."

"She's got into the way of things very quickly," Miss Farmer supplemented.

"I wonder if she is connected with a Miss Marchrose whom I used to hear about, some years ago—" said Lady Rossiter thoughtfully.

"Here's Easter!" exclaimed her husband, looking from the window and feeling thankful for any interruption to Edna's possible intention of recapitulating the scandal attaching to the unfortunately uncommon name of the new Superintendent.

Young Cooper sprang up.

"Let me make rather more room. I'll move to this chair, if I may, Lady Rossiter."

Mark Easter's arrival improved matters greatly, even though he was accompanied by the preposterous Ruthie, adopting a sudden pose of extreme shyness, and concealing her face on her left shoulder, after the manner of a timid infant of two years old. The members of the staff knew Mark, had laughed at his jokes in and out of office hours, had experienced his pleasant, courteously-abrupt authority in work-time, and knew him for a fellow-worker who spared himself less than he did them.

Miss Sandiloe launched into the shrill fire of giggling repartee which was her nearest approach to naturalness. Miss Farmer's frown of strained attention relaxed, and she leant back, as though for the first time able to look at her surroundings, and Cooper ceased to fix bulging and attentive eyes upon his hostess.

Julian marvelled, not at all for the first time, at the invariable effect upon his surroundings of Mark Easter's elementary witticisms and gay, indefinable charm of manner.

He knew that his wife liked Mark, if only because he was always ready to let her talk to him in low-voiced, womanly sympathy of the otherwise unmentioned Mrs. Easter. Lady Rossiter often said that, but for her, the tragedy of Mark's life would have been left to corrode in silent bitterness.

Perhaps it was true.

Julian knew that to his wife was it frequently given to rush in where others might not only hesitate, but positively refuse, to tread, and he knew that Mark's simple gratitude for her interest in him was as genuine as it was outspoken.

He wondered, sometimes, at that very simplicity, in a man of acute sympathies and unfailing intuition such as Mark again and again proved himself to possess in almost every relation into which he entered. There were even times when he asked himself, in utter perplexity, whether Mark could himself be as sensitive as his quickness of perception for sensitiveness in others appeared to denote.

He thought that he had seldom seen Edna look more relieved than at the dissipation of the constraint amongst her tea-party, caused by Mark's entrance.

"Will you ring for tea, Mark?" she asked smilingly. She had the trick, not uncommon to a certain type of woman, of assuming a more proprietary tone and manner when speaking to a man not her husband.

Julian's restless and observant mind almost automatically registered the subconscious irritation instantly produced in the other two women.

Miss Farmer, turning to young Cooper, asked him if he would be so very kind as to reach her little bag, which contained a handkerchief.

Miss Sandiloe, more actively resentful, as well as far more self-confident in the youthful security of possessing good looks and an evident admirer in the shape of Cooper, was bolder.

"Oh, Mr. Easter, I'm awfully glad you're here. I mean, really I am. I've got some killing things to tell you, about the Coll. We've got some freaks there now, really we have."

"What have you done with the young gentleman who wanted to learn enough shorthand to get him a post in a newspaper office in six lessons?" enquired Mark, as usual full of interest.

"Oh, him! It wasn't him I was thinking of so much, really, though he certainly is a caution. I mean, really he is. But he's come off the six lessons stunt, all the same."

"Well done! Have you persuaded him to take a course?"

"I don't know what *I've* got to do with it, I'm sure," Miss Sandiloe said, with a self-conscious laugh. "But I'm taking him for private tuition now, three times a week, as well as him going to the usual classes, and he'll be in the Speed in no time."

Miss Farmer, looking more animated than when making impersonal and agonised conversation with her hostess, joined in.

"Miss Marchrose is taking the High Speed room now, Mr. Easter. She's got a beautiful pronounciation—so clear, it is."

Lady Rossiter smiled—a kind, faint smile, that, to her husband's perceptions, admirably succeeded in underlining her determination to avoid noticing Miss Farmer's slip.

"It's so wonderful of you, I think, to be so devoted to your work," she said. "That is one reason why I love the society of workers. They are always so eager about their work, and I think it is so wonderful of them."

Edna did not generally repeat herself, but the curious hostility vibrant in the air surrounding her philanthropic enterprise was making her nervous.

"I've always been keen on my job," said Cooper complacently, "but I ought to have been an engineer. I should have liked that."

"But then—why not have followed your vocation?" Edna enquired, with tilted eyebrows.

Cooper shook his head.

"It's an expensive training, Lady Rossiter. If I'd had the capital, I should have liked it, though."

"I understand," gently said Edna, with a whole world of implication in her tone, at which Cooper looked rather astonished, and Miss Sandiloe decidedly resentful.,

"Daddy!" said a sudden voice.

Everybody looked at the forgotten Ruthie, who stood on one leg beside her father's chair.

"Daddy, I'm afraid I shall forget my piece, if I don't say it soon," said Ruthie in an excessively audible aside, and with the evident determination of displaying her histrionic attainments to the assembly.

Mark laughed, with the injudicious tolerance that he was all too apt to accord to the ill-timed demonstrations of his offspring.

"Not now, Ruthie. Perhaps Lady Rossiter doesn't want you to say your piece at all."

Few suggestions could have been better founded upon fact, and Lady Rossiter made no attempt to contradict Ruthie's father.

Julian wondered if it was altogether undesignedly that Miss Sandiloe instantly exclaimed:

"Are you going to recite to us, dear?"

"Yes, I am," said Miss Easter in loud, confident tones. "I always recite when I go out to tea."

The relentless inevitability of the proposed entertainment deprived even Miss Sandiloe of further utterance for the moment.

"You will not be asked again if you give yourself such a bad character," said Mark in a rather hopeless voice.

"Oh yes, I shall. Lady Rossiter always likes me and Peekaboo to come; she said so! We can come whenever we like."

Sir Julian's regard for Mark Easter alone prevented him from disclaiming aloud any share in the unlimited hospitality so rashly proclaimed by his wife in the days of Ruthie's and Ambrose's comparatively innocuous babyhood, and so unscrupulously worked to death by them ever since.

"Is Peekaboo a pet?" asked Miss Farmer kindly.

"Not always," Ruthie replied literally. "Sometimes he's a very naughty boy. Sarah has locked him up in the boot-cupboard this afternoon, because—"

"Hush, hush," hastily said Mark, "we don't tell tales out of school."

Julian wondered grimly what story of misdoing the exhortation to fraternal charity might cover. The unforeseeable and disastrous ingenuity of Ambrose's misdeeds was only to be compared to the skill with which his partner and instigator in crime invariably managed to extricate herself at the eleventh hour from complicity and leave him the solitary victim of blame and punishment.

Tea and cakes, arriving opportunely, staved off Ruthie's recitation, and brought the relief of movement.

Lady Rossiter crumbled a very small sponge-cake behind the silver-kettle, and said in a general sort of way that she hoped everyone would make a very good tea and eat a great deal. She herself always thought of Sunday tea as one of the principal meals of the day, as it would only be followed by cold supper in the evening.

Whether cold supper was to be the portion of her guests or not, however, the piled plates of buns and the large cakes, bearing a certain superficial resemblance to preparations for a school-treat, were better patronised by Ruthie than by the members of the College staff.

"We mustn't leave it too late to be starting back," Miss Farmer said nervously. "I mean, it's quite a longish walk."

Julian gauged the measure of Edna's discouragement by her omission to insist graciously upon an expedition first round the garden.

"You must come again one Sunday," she said, not, however, making precise mention of any date. "I should like you to see my view of the sea. There is a beautiful little glimpse to be had from a corner of the garden. … You must so need a draught of blue distance after working inside four walls all the week."

"Thank you, Lady Rossiter," said Miss Farmer meekly, turning a pale brick-colour.

"Thanks," said Miss Sandiloe, her nose in the air and her voice aggressive; "but really I can get all the view I want of the sea from Culmouth. My window looks right over the bay—that's why I took the apartments I did. Are you ready, Horace?"

"Ready," said Mr. Cooper, with an alacrity that might be partly attributable to the unprecedented use of his Christian name—Miss Sandiloe's not too subtle retaliation for Lady Rossiter's frequent "Mark."

"Come along, Ruthie," said Mark Easter. "We'll walk with you part of the way if we may, Miss Farmer."

The teacher looked pleased, and they followed Miss Sandiloe and her admirer, Mark adjusting his long, easy stride to the very obvious limitations of Miss Farmer's patent-leather shoes.

Edna looked after them, wearing a rather exhausted expression.

"I am very tired, Julian. I shall go to the boudoir and enjoy the silence till it's time to dress. Nothing is so restful as complete silence, after all."

Julian honoured the assertion by making no reply to it whatever.

"I have been told," said Edna, with gentle solemnity, "that my spirit is burning itself away. I know you don't sympathise with that necessity for pouring out, Julian—this afternoon, for instance, has taken a great deal out of me—but I noticed that you gave out nothing at all—not one spark. Isn't it rather a pity? One can do so little, materially, but the things of the spirit ... Ah well, I grudge none of it."

She went upstairs, however, very slowly, and leaning heavily upon the banisters.

Julian's gaze did not follow her.

IV

"We've found a treasure," Mark Easter enthusiastically told Sir Julian. "Miss Marchrose is the best worker I've ever struck. And she'll do anything—doesn't mind what she turns her hand to. You'll have to see her, Sir Julian—dashed good-looking girl into the bargain."

Sir Julian was not insensible to the attraction of the last qualification, but he felt no security of endorsing Mark Easter's ready acclamation of a pretty face. His own taste was eclectic and the witless pink and white, the unsubtle contours that constitute the ideal feminine to the average Englishman, held no appeal for him.

He soon saw Miss Marchrose at the College, in the room adjoining Fuller's office that had been designed for the personal use of the Lady Superintendent.

She was talking to Mark Easter, standing beside him in the window, and the afternoon sun struck full upon her, revealing every little finely-drawn line of fatigue round her eyes and mouth.

Sir Julian's first sensation was of involuntary, surprised satisfaction at the slim, tall distinction of her whole bearing; the next, one of surprise at Mark Easter's verdict on her looks.

"Ten years ago, perhaps," he reflected. "Now she probably varies according to her state of health. But she'll never be called pretty."

Nevertheless, it seemed to him easy enough to trace a softer, rounder contour to the oval face, and to erase in imagination the shadows underlying black brows and hazel eyes, and the tiny, indelible marks that some past bitterness had left at either corner of the closely-curved mouth that was Miss Marchrose's most undeniably beautiful feature.

Her hair was brown, a soft dead-leaf colour that held no gleams of light and framed her square forehead loosely. Julian, looking at her, received the impression that her face held possibilities full of colour and animation, and yet was more often only faintly coloured, and shadowed with weariness.

"Charming at eighteen—and probably not admired, except by an occasional connoisseur—and now absolutely dependent for looks on the state of her vitality," he summarised her to himself.

But he ceased to entertain any doubts as to the vitality of Miss Marchrose when he heard her speak.

At the first sound of her voice he recognised that therein lay the charm which had made Mark Easter declare her to be good-looking. The soft beauty of a woman's speaking voice such as that of Miss Marchrose might well prove responsible for greater delusions.

The contrast between the extraordinarily musical inflexions of her tones and their rather curt, business-like utterances almost amused Julian.

He remembered Fuller's complacent recommendation, "Hard as nails, I should think," and surmised that Miss Marchrose had addressed him with the same abrupt, impersonal manner.

Unlike the majority of women, she seldom smiled. When she did so—and presently Julian noticed that Mark Easter could elicit that quick, soft change of expression more often than anyone else—it altered the character of her face very much, and made her look much younger, and rather appealing.

Her powers of organisation were admirable and, as Mark had said, she was ready to concentrate her whole energies upon her work, indifferent, apparently, to the after-office hours which constituted the whole reality of life for those who only lived through the day's business in order to attain their freedom at the end of it.

"I hope you have found comfortable accommodation in Culmouth," Sir Julian said to her.

"Yes, thank you."

Miss Marchrose appeared so little expectant of any further interest in her welfare that Julian almost wondered whether her definition of officiousness might not prove to coincide with his own.

A month after her arrival, however, Mark Easter told the Rossiters that Miss Marchrose was lodging at a farm outside Culmouth, nearly half an hour's walk from the College.

"It wouldn't be far for her to come over here, if you thought of asking her, Lady Rossiter," said Mark. "I am afraid she must be rather lonely, for she knows no one down here."

"I wonder why she came here," Edna remarked.

"For love of the country, I think," Mark answered, with sufficient assurance in the assertion to make Julian wonder if he had received a confidence.

"I want to know this Miss Marchrose," said Lady Rossiter with decision. "I think I must go to the College to-morrow—I have been quite a long time without seeing any of my friends there. Dear Mr. Fuller! I love Mr. Fuller—he and I have such long talks over the welfare of the staff."

"I shall be in there all day to-morrow. Won't you look in and let Miss Marchrose give you a cup of tea?" said Mark.

"Of course I will. They love dispensing a little hospitality, don't they, and I'm always *most* ceremonious about returning their calls here. Not that Miss Marchrose has come over yet with the others."

Mark looked a little perplexed, and Julian, unexpectedly even to himself, said rather curtly:

"You won't be able to ask her to make one of your Sunday Band of Hope expeditions, Edna."

"No?" said his wife, still smiling. "I know there are wheels within wheels, and one reason, I think, why they trust me is that I respect all the little prejudices and etiquettes that mean so much to them. Give Miss Marchrose due warning, Mark, will you, that I shall call at tea-time to-morrow and see if she is not too busy to let me have some tea. I want to get into touch with all of them, you know."

Julian, in rather grim anticipation of the process as regarded Miss Marchrose, announced his intention next day of accompanying his wife to the College.

"My dear, I am not often honoured, but shall we not rather overwhelm the young woman?"

"I don't think she is easily overwhelmed."

Edna laughed musically—that is to say, Sir Julian felt convinced that she herself so designated the low, controlled sound of amusement that she so seldom enough judged it *à propos* to emit.

But her voice was very serious the next instant, and had even dropped a semitone, as she made enquiry:

"Julian, can you tell me yet whether she is really connected with poor Clarence's tragedy?"

"No, certainly not—I haven't tried to find out."

"I wonder why, when you knew that the whole question touched me very nearly. Nothing has much sacredness to you, Julian, has it?"

"I see nothing sacred in the amorous extravagances of your cousin Clarence, certainly."

"And you care very little whether the woman who is charged with the welfare of all those young men and women—sharers, after all, of our common humanity—can give them true, pure-hearted love and service and fellowship," mused Edna. "And yet to me those ideals which you dismiss so lightly seem the most important things in all the world. You see, Julian, love seems to me to matter more than anything in the whole world."

"In the case of a Lady Superintendent for the College, a knowledge of shorthand is more important," said Julian indifferently.

He had long since fallen into the habit of uttering the cheap jeers that had once inadequately served to protect him from blatant references that now had almost lost effect.

"God forbid that I should condemn anyone—who am I, to judge of another?—but I can't pretend to you, Julian, that it won't become a question of conscience with me, if I find that a position of such responsibility towards my boys and girls is held by a woman who could throw a man over heartlessly, break her given pledge, just at the moment when he was more in need of her than ever before."

"If she was heartless, he may have been well rid of her, as I said before."

"At what a cost! His first faith shattered, poor boy. You remember what that nurse told me about him."

"I remember perfectly, but I should think both Clarence Isbister and the girl he married would very much rather have it forgotten."

"I don't forget easily, Julian."

"Then in kindness to Clarence, I should advise you to keep your recollections to yourself. I doubt if he would thank you or anyone else for reminding the world that he ever saw fit to beat a tattoo with his head on the walls of his nursing-home for the sake of a young woman whom he afterwards forgot all about."

"We can never tell that. Certain wounds do not heal, although they may be hidden from sight."

"Then I'm sorry for Mrs. Clarence."

"I wonder if Miss Marchrose knows that he has married," said Edna, rather viciously.

"I wish you would not take it for granted that this is the same woman," said Julian irritably.

Edna laid two fingers upon his sleeve in a manner designed to emphasise her words.

"I shall take nothing for granted. But you see, Julian, I can't take life quite as you do—quite as callously, as cynically. There is a big responsibility for those of us who see a little—ah, such a very little way it is—further into the heart of things. We can only hope, and give, and spend ourselves—and judge no man."

Julian, who disliked being touched, moved his arm out of reach, and replied to these humanitarian sentiments unsympathetically.

"Your remarks have not the slightest bearing upon the case, Edna."

He thought to himself bitterly, not for the first time, that a stronger man would reject the weapons of obvious, meaningless satire, but nervous irritability again and again drove him to seek an outlet in words that he despised.

In silence, he entered the College with Edna, and let her proceed to the Supervisor's room, aware that he had purposely timed their arrival for an hour when Fairfax Fuller would be engaged in one of the class-rooms. Few things discomposed Mr. Fuller more than a feminine intrusion which could not be accounted for by a question of business.

"He will be disappointed," seriously said Edna, turning away from the empty room. "But we shall have other talks. I don't despair yet of getting Fuller to Culmhayes, for all his misogyny." It was a principle with Lady Rossiter, her husband knew, never to allow their differences to degenerate into an offended silence when they were alone.

He sometimes thought that he could have borne it all better had she been a woman to make scenes, and to oppose him with tears or temper, instead of with that considered, brightly-unconscious, eternal loving-kindness.

They found Miss Marchrose in her own room, at work on the typewriter. She wore a long blue pinafore, and Julian noticed with an odd satisfaction that this was one of the days when her variable face showed colour and unmistakable beauty.

"Good afternoon," said Julian. "I hope we are not too early. My wife— Miss Marchrose."

Lady Rossiter, shaking hands, revealed her rather large white teeth in a smile, but Miss Marchrose, after her fashion, remained calmly serious.

"Won't you sit down?"

Lady Rossiter glanced slowly round the room.

It was a large, light office, the window thrown open and looking on to the square paved court at the back of the house; the furniture scanty and of the most utilitarian description.

Miss Marchrose's writing-table was orderly, although papers were stacked upon it in wicker trays. A telephone with a glass mouthpiece stood at one corner and an electric reading-lamp at the other.

The typewriter had a very small table to itself, and a high chair with a small cushion placed in front of it. Except for three or four chairs and a strip of carpet, there was no other furniture in the room.

"I've not seen this room furnished before," Edna Rossiter observed. "You've hardly had time for the finishing touches yet, though, have you?"

Her tone was that of assertion, not of enquiry, but Miss Marchrose replied as though to a question.

"I'm afraid there isn't anything more to come. Mr. Fuller has kindly let me have everything I want."

"Even to a glass mouthpiece for the telephone?" enquired Edna smoothly.

A similar adornment distinguished her own telephone in the boudoir at Culmhayes, and Julian knew that his wife frequently drew attention to it by apologies for her own fastidiousness.

"That was brought by Mr. Easter. I used to dislike the old one so much, and he found it out, and very kindly gave me that."

"I shall talk to Mr. Easter about infringing my patent," laughed Edna. She turned to her husband.

"Mark must have seen the glass one in my boudoir, of course."

Julian was perfectly aware of the instinct which had prompted his wife to make use, in addressing herself to him, of Mark Easter's first name.

He smiled rather grimly.

"I think you must have some flowers in here," Edna said to Miss Marchrose. "It does make all the difference, doesn't it, when one is chained to a desk all day?"

"But I'm not chained to a desk," said Miss Marchrose tranquilly. "I take two or three classes, and I'm very often in Mr. Fuller's room. Besides, I don't like flowers in an office, do you?"

"Ah well," said Edna, in a voice the measured graciousness of which contrasted with the Superintendent's matter-of-fact utterance, "flowers mean rather a lot to me. I'm not happy unless I have a great many all round me.... But I know many people simply look on flowers as flowers, of course. Tell me, do you care for out-of-doors?"

Miss Marchrose looked unintelligent.

"Because I have some little nature-classes, as we call them, for looking into the heart of our West Country rather more closely. One week I take my little band down to the sea, another time up to the woods, sometimes just to study the wonderful colour in a Devonshire lane. I can't help thinking you might find a great deal to admire round Duckpool Farm. Isn't that where you're staying?"

"Yes. I hope you're going to let me give you some tea, Lady Rossiter."

"Presently, but you mustn't let us put you out. Don't alter anything—I love taking things just as I find them.... But tell me why you went to the farm; I thought it rather wonderful of you to strike out such a new line, instead of going to rooms in Church Street or St. Mary-Welcome's, as they all do."

"There are no rooms vacant in Church Street, I believe," said Miss Marchrose, very curtly indeed.

Julian felt convinced that she wished the implication made that had rooms been available she would have selected them, and equally certain that the implication would have been untrue.

"Is Easter here to-day?" he enquired abruptly.

"Yes; I'll let him know you've come. He generally has tea in here, and so does Mr. Fuller."

She went to the telephone.

"You mustn't let us interrupt your work if there's anything you want to finish before tea," Edna told her. "I know what it means to all of you to get through by six o'clock sharp, especially in these late summer evenings when it's already getting dark early. It must be too cruel to be robbed of even a few moments of fresh air and liberty."

Julian remembered Mark's eulogies.

"What time do you leave the College, I wonder?" he asked her, smiling slightly.

"It depends on the work. There's been a good deal of correspondence lately and I've stayed late to finish it up. If I may, there is just something I want to finish here."

She laid her hand on the typewriter.

"Please do."

Without further apology, Miss Marchrose sat down to her machine and completed the sheet upon which she had been engaged. As she drew it off the roller, Mark Easter came in.

She looked up with a sort of pleasure in her glance, and handed him a thin pile of foolscap sheets.

"Five copies," she said.

Mark glanced at the papers.

"I'm so grateful!" he exclaimed. "That's exactly what I wanted. Do you know what that is, Sir Julian?"

"What?"

"Estate business," laughed Mark. "Miss Marchrose is good enough to help me through with some of it, as she *only* works ten hours a day here."

"You ought to be ashamed of yourself for letting her do it."

"Well," said Miss Marchrose gaily, "he boils my kettle for me."

Mark had placed the big kettle on the gas-ring and cleared the table of the heavy typewriter.

He was in his usual excellent spirits, and made indifferent jokes at which Miss Marchrose laughed with an absence of constraint such as Julian had not seen in her before. It was evident that Mark's gift for making friends had not failed him, any more than his magical capacity for diffusing contentment throughout his surroundings.

Contentment, however, stopped short at Lady Rossiter, as it was always apt to do when the focus of general attention was diverted to an object which she considered unworthy.

"Isn't Mr. Fuller coming in to tea?" She quietly interrupted Mark's exchange of chaffing allusions with Miss Marchrose.

"He generally comes. I'll go and dig him out," Mark volunteered.

"Your presence has frightened him away, Edna," said her husband, not without malice. "Fuller is a shy bird."

Edna smiled serenely.

"Poor Mr. Fuller, he and I are great friends."

It might be doubted whether Lady Rossiter found cause for thankfulness in the presence of her great friend when he eventually joined the tea-party, his face black with scowls at the interruption to his work and suffused with shyness at her complacent greeting.

Miss Marchrose poured out tea and talked to Julian, who sat next her, and Mark, to whom self-consciousness was unknown, handed plates of bread-and-butter and cut up a small plum-cake and endeavoured to win smiles from the recalcitrant Fuller. Edna, her voice modulated to careful sweetness, manufactured kindly conversation.

But Mr. Fuller, his elbows very much squared and his bullet head thrust well forward, devoted his energies to the rapid demolition of his meal, and replied monosyllabically to Mark's kindly derision and Lady

Rossiter's benevolences alike. His shyness, however, appeared to place him under a mysterious compulsion to recite aloud, in an inward voice, any scrap of printed matter upon which his eye chanced to fall, regardless of relevance. This necessity, though common enough in any assembly of not too congenial strangers, did not add to continuity of discourse.

As thus, when Lady Rossiter moved a pot of plum jam towards him, saying that she was so sorry that the injunction to make *no* difference had not been attended to, Mr. Fuller was constrained to reply in a very severe way, No; he never ate jam—Three gold medals at the Paris and Vienna Exhibitions—but it was there every day, he believed.

"It is there, because *I* like it," said Miss Marchrose. "They never had anything but bread-and-butter till I came."

Edna's ever-ready eyebrows went up, but she still addressed herself exclusively to Fairfax Fuller.

"Plum jam is quite my favourite. I never really care for the expensive varieties, or think them a *bit* better than the others."

"Inspection invited at the manufactories." Fuller pursued his way, almost turning the jam-pot upside down in an apparently agonised search for further literature.

"Jam on bread-and-butter is quite a luxury. Julian and I never get it at home," Lady Rossiter persevered.

"London, Edinburgh, *and* at Sharplington in Essex," said Fuller, without looking at her.

"Have you ever been over one of those big factories? It would be rather interesting," Mark said, in a charitable endeavour to introduce some element of continuity into the conversation. Lady Rossiter at once seconded the attempt.

"I've always so wished to have an opportunity of that sort. I should like to know just how the poor factory hands live, and what the conditions of work really are in those great places."

"I don't suppose that Sharplington in Essex is on the same scale as London or Edinburgh," Mark suggested.

At which interesting initial stage of an interchange of views, Mr. Fuller suddenly disconcerted everybody by looking straight across the table at the almanack which hung upon the wall, and declaring with a sort of suppressed violence:

"Five thousand souls gained last year alone—The Church Mission Society."

Edna's pale skin absolutely flushed and she set her lips. Mark hastily bent down to pick up an imaginary handkerchief, and Miss Marchrose laughed.

"That's settled it," thought Julian. "Edna will never forgive her that laugh."

He saw no reason to reverse the judgment while his wife took her cool, kindly farewell of the Lady Superintendent.

"You must come out to Culmhayes one day. Of course, I know Saturday afternoons and Sundays are your only free times, so I never issue workday invitations. But I'm always so glad to see any of you, and you can just rest and do anything you please, and not feel obliged to make conversation."

Julian watched the recipient of these attentions rather curiously.

She withdrew her hand from Lady Rossiter's kind, enveloping clasp and put it into the pocket of her pinafore very deliberately.

"On Saturdays I'm going to the estate office with you, I hope. Didn't we arrange that?" she asked Mark Easter.

"If you have nothing better to do, I should be most grateful. Everything is in confusion there, since my clerk had to leave on account of sudden illness."

"I shall like it very much," said Miss Marchrose, with a very charming smile, and still addressing herself exclusively to Mark. "And I've nothing better to do at all, thank you."

Julian, while inwardly applauding her, wondered whether she had herself been entirely aware of the full efficiency of that oblique retaliation.

On the whole, he thought that she had.

V

As Julian pursued his acquaintance with Miss Marchrose—and he was by no means minded to let it drop—he came more and more to the conclusion that she had been quite as conscious as himself of the mutual antagonism which Edna and she had roused in one another on the rather disastrous occasion of their meeting.

She neither came over to Culmhayes nor showed any disposition to join Lady Rossiter's cherished nature-classes, the final sessions of which were drawing near with the approach of the colder weather.

Julian saw her at the College, where she worked hard and successfully, and once or twice at his own estate office, where she frequently replaced Mark Easter's absent clerk.

"I don't know that we ought to let you spend so much time here, though it is quite invaluable to the business," he once said to her.

To which Miss Marchrose returned very candidly that it was always the greatest possible pleasure to her to do anything for Mr. Easter.

Julian quite believed it.

The friendship established between her and Mark was founded on excellent good comradeship, a mutual respect for one another's power of work, and the very admirable sense of humour possessed by each.

Julian, watching the frank gaiety of her manner as she came to accept him in the light of Mark's friend instead of merely as a director of the College, found himself wondering from time to time if Miss Marchrose, sharp-tongued and quick-witted, apt at satire even at her gentlest, could by any possibility ever have been the heroine where Captain Clarence Isbister, youthful, sporting and essentially British, had once been the hero. His wife appeared inclined to let the question rest, and Julian had no desire to remind her of it; but for the satisfaction of his own curiosity, he told himself, he would have liked to establish the proof or otherwise of Fuller's verdict to which he was only half inclined to subscribe—"hard as nails."

It was Edna, however, who returned to the charge of Miss Marchrose's identity.

"I might have known it," her husband reflected.

He heard with his accustomed phlegm of manner, that Edna, conducting the nature-class through a certain small wood just off the Rossiter estate, in order to introduce it to a sunset effect visible through the beech-trees, had met with an interruption before anyone had had time to do more than ejaculate a preliminary "Wonderful!"

"They are apt to be a shade blatant, poor dears! and talk about the sun looking like a ball of fire in the sky and that sort of thing."

"You could scarcely ask for a more accurate description, after all," murmured Julian.

"But what one's there for, of course, is to get them to see a little deeper, a little more into the heart of Nature's beauty and wonderful, wonderful tenderness. I wanted to show them the glint of red on the stems of those trees, and the miracle of *hush* that comes over the world just as the sun goes down. ..."

Lady Rossiter paused, absorbed in the regretful retrospect of the showman whose curtain has accidentally come down with a run in the midst of his star performer's best turn.

"Well, what happened? Did the sun refuse to go down after all?" was Julian's rather ribald interruption to her thoughts.

"The sun was in the most exquisite blaze of red and gold, and one could only hold one's breath in awe at the most wonderful pageant the world can show, when that Marchrose woman from Culmouth College came crashing through the undergrowth, ringing a bicycle bell, and with her back—actually, *her back*—to that sunset!"

"What did you do?" asked Julian, with considerable interest.

Lady Rossiter made the strangely contradictory statement that her sex, when describing the character of a crisis, so frequently appears compelled to proffer.

"I didn't say one word, Julian. I felt that I simply couldn't have spoken. I couldn't help holding up my hand and saying very quietly indeed: 'Ah, hush! Can't you feel that it *hurts*, somehow, to disturb such a moment as this?' It was such hideous profanity, Julian!"

"Did you tell her so?"

"I could never say anything that would deliberately hurt another," Lady Rossiter made grave reply. "But I laid my hand on that terrible bicycle, and the girl had to keep still for a minute or two."

"Was she angry?"

"I hope I sent out some calming, loving thoughts, for the whole evening was terribly jarred, one could feel it. Poor foolish, defiant creature! I could see her hands shaking, as she tried to take her machine from me. I couldn't let her go like that, of course, and I tried to say a little something, very quietly, about the glory of God's own evening light all round us. But she kept her back to the sunset all the time.

"And, Julian, to my dismay and astonishment, she was not alone. Mark was with her."

"Why shouldn't he be?"

"Have you forgotten my poor Clarence so soon?" reproachfully enquired Lady Rossiter, whose cousinly affection for her poor Clarence appeared to increase by leaps and bounds in proportion to the growth of her disesteem for Miss Marchrose.

"Clarence has nothing to do with it. The circumstances are entirely dissimilar."

"We can't tell that in the case of a woman whom I *must*, much as I dislike uttering any shadow of condemnation, call utterly heartless. Shall I ever forget what that hospital nurse told me of poor Clarence's state of mind after that heartless betrayal—"

"In any circumstances, Edna, Mark isn't in the least likely to knock his head against the walls of the cottage, and if he does, they will very probably fall about his ears. I wish he would attend to his own house, before doing up the tenants'! Those children have nearly broken down the whole of the garden palings. But go on—did you achieve any *rapprochement* between Mark and the sunset, or was he also ringing bicycle-bells and turning his back on it?"

"Mark made some foolish explanation about seeing the girl back to Duckpool Farm, but they were evidently walking, and pushing the bicycle between them."

"I don't see how they could do anything else, if there was only one bicycle," said Julian, idly desirous of making more obvious a want of sympathy that was already perfectly well *en evidence*.

"You may not understand it, Julian, but Mark is very dear to me. To you he may be merely a good fellow, and an excellent estate agent, but to me he has been something more ever since that ghastly tragedy of his wife. I gave him all the help that a woman could give, then, and I can't ever forget it. I can't let Mark break his heart a second time. Not that she's attractive, or even pretty," said Edna, distinctly divided between her determination to exploit Mark Easter's peril and her reluctance to allow to Miss Marchrose any of the usual advantages attributed to a charmer of men. ...

"I know no one less likely than Mark Easter to make a fool of himself in that particular way," said Julian emphatically.

"It's not Mark that I'm afraid of," inconsistently said Lady Rossiter. "A friendship with a good, true woman is often a man's best safeguard."

Julian wondered whether it would be worth while to simulate a belief that the good, true woman in question was Miss Marchrose, but Edna left him no time to adopt this amiable pose.

"I am going to find out once and for all whether that girl—I suppose she calls herself a girl—is really poor Clarence's evil genius or not. Personally, I believe she is."

Julian left it at that, not desirous of sparing his wife the trouble of her proposed investigation by telling her Miss Marchrose's identity without more ado.

Making his own observations, he thought Mark in no danger of falling a victim to the *beaux yeux* which, if their smile was chiefly kept for answering his, were far more often bent upon a typewriter or an

– 50 –

account-book than diverted towards him. Fuller continued to extol the Lady Superintendent, and Sir Julian went oftener to the College than usual, not concealing from himself that he found the enigma of her personality of interest.

She continued gaily impersonal towards him until one evening in October, when he overtook her at the door of the College, and on an impulse born of unacknowledged, overwhelming loneliness, suddenly asked her if she would care to drive down to the shore with him and go on to the farm afterwards.

He had long ago decided that Miss Marchrose, although her manner was often abrupt, was devoid of shyness as of conventional politeness. If his suggestion displeased her, she would undoubtedly decline it.

But she exclaimed with undisguised pleasure, and took her place in the car beside him.

Julian was more than usually dissatisfied with life, and made no attempt at conversation. It struck upon him with relief that Miss Marchrose was equally silent, and presently he glanced at her.

She was leaning back, her hair blown from her temples by the soft, salt-laden breeze, and she looked neither young nor pretty in the waning light, but exceedingly weary.

"Do you like your work?" Julian enquired with extreme abruptness, and a sudden, genuine desire for information.

"At the College? Very much indeed."

Her tone was guarded, he felt.

"I mean the whole thing. What made you take up this sort of thing? Tell me about it."

He almost heard her hesitate before she answered with careful lightness:

"Oh, I had to do something, and I should dislike teaching children— and do it very badly. I trained as a shorthand-typist, and am really qualified for a secretary. I rather like doing shorthand."

The acuteness of his disappointment actually surprised Sir Julian. He realised that he had made the most tentative of efforts to get into touch with one whom he had vaguely thought of as a kindred spirit, and that he had been lightly and unmistakably rebuffed. He kept silence, making a pretence of absorption in his driving.

Unexpectedly, Miss Marchrose made a sort of inarticulate sound of interrogation.

"Sir Julian?"

He turned his head.

"I'm sorry," she said gently. "You really wanted to know, didn't you?"

"Yes."

"After I'd said that, I—I thought you were disappointed."

"You are very quick to detect an atmosphere."

"I'm sorry," she said again. "Sometimes I don't realise when the platitudes that one keeps as stock answers to enquiries are unnecessary."

"Thank you," said Julian.

"I took up work because I was tired of living at home. A good many girls are like that. However, in our case there was very little money, and it was just as well that I should do something. I thought I should like secretarial work; it all sounded interesting, and I had always cared for books and writing. I didn't know in the least what it was going to be like. I'd never even been to school. The six months at the training institute wasn't bad; it was all quite new, and I liked learning the things, and doing well in the shorthand tests. At the end of the course, the training institute undertook to find one a post—and they got me a job with a firm in London. It was supposed to be a very good one—short hours and decent pay. My mother—my father was dead—was upset at the thought of my staying on in London alone, but I wrote and said that I'd been able to manage perfectly while I was at the institute—one lived 'in' there, as a matter of fact—and that anyway I'd made up my mind to do it, and to make a success of it. After all, I was twenty-two—and she could give me a small allowance, and I thought that with that and my salary it wouldn't be very difficult."

"I should imagine that by yourself, in London, at twenty-two, it might, on the contrary, be very difficult indeed," said Julian significantly.

"Not in the way you mean," Miss Marchrose remarked candidly. "From what one reads in novels, girls who work have to be on their guard from morning till night against—undesirable attentions. It was the one thing I thought I should have to beware of. ... And all I can say is, that unless one asks for trouble of that sort, it simply doesn't happen to the average woman."

Julian thought of his own inward verdict on a beauty that had probably been very much too subtle and unvivid for universal recognition, and said nothing.

"I was five years working in London," Miss Marchrose told him simply, "and I have never in my life been spoken to or followed in the street. And no one has ever tried to make love to me."

Julian noted with a flash of appreciation that she did not add, "against my will."

"All the difficulties and all the miseries were quite different. Things I'd never thought of, or realised at all ..."

"Tell me about them."

"I was ashamed of minding it so much—but the difference between being a girl living at home, however poor, and a girl going out every day to earn her own living. There were such a lot of things I didn't know. For instance, I had to be told, at that first office I went to, about calling the manager 'sir' when I spoke to him, and his son was 'Mr. Percy' to the clerks and typists, always.

"And then I'd never lived in London, and at first I used to go to Slater's Restaurant for lunch, and think how economical I was, and all the time the other typists were laughing at me and thinking I was giving myself airs because, of course, I ought to have gone to Lyons or an A.B.C. or bought sandwiches and eaten them in the office. And another thing I hadn't realised beforehand was the deadly monotony of it—day after day, sitting in the clatter of all those machines, and typing as hard as one could go. Nothing to look forward to, except Saturday afternoon and Sunday, and then I was dead tired, and I hated my rooms, because they were cheap and ugly and uncomfortable. They weren't really, you know—I had a bedroom and a sitting-room, that first year, and a fire whenever I wanted it—most people have a bed-sitting-room and go to bed when they want to keep warm—but I'd come straight from my home."

She paused.

"How long did you stand it?"

"Eight months. And then I knew I'd been a fool, and I thought that if my mother would forgive me and let me come home, I'd try again. She had a small business and I could have helped her—she always wanted me to. But of course my pride didn't like giving in, and after I'd once made up my mind that I *was* going back, it seemed easier to bear it all, and so I kept on putting off writing the letter, thinking I'd at least have done a year of it before collapsing. And then my mother died, quite suddenly, and so I never went home at all, except just to settle everything up—it wasn't even our own house. And there was not much more money than before, so when I'd sold the business, which was luckily quite easy, I took another post."

"Was that the only alternative?" asked Julian, his voice as matter-of-fact as hers had been throughout.

"There was an aunt, but she had two daughters of her own, and they seemed to think it extremely providential that I *could* do something for myself. They are very kind, and I generally spend my holidays with them. They live near London."

"You don't like London," Julian affirmed, guided by something in her tone.

"No, not much. However, the aunt's husband got me the offer of a post as shorthand teacher at that big place in Southampton Row, and I went there, and it was a success. I got a lot of private tuition work, and they raised my salary every year, and I actually saved money. That's why I'm here now."

Julian remembered Mark Easter: "She comes here for love of the country, I think."

"But I've never liked any work better than this," said Miss Marchrose warmly, "and I wanted to be in the country. In some ways, I'm happier here than I've been anywhere in my life."

"I'm glad. Only I'm afraid perhaps it's lonely, if you don't know anyone here. Do they make you comfortable at the farm?"

"Very, and I've always wanted to live on a farm."

Julian stopped the car as they came in sight of the shelving declivity of fine, powdery sand, lying in uneven hillocks, with tufts of stiff grasses amongst the boulders.

A broken line of white, flecking the darkness, showed the receding tide.

"Would you like to go down to the edge of the sea?" Julian asked her.

"I'd like to very much."

She did not ask whether he meant to accompany her, but after a moment moved away, and Julian remained in the car, feeling the sting of the salt on his lips and listening to the faint sound of the water on the grey expanse of gleaming sand.

No one knew how many nights in the year he came to the edge of Culmouth sands and paid silent, involuntary tribute there.

He came nearer to making a confidence than perhaps ever before when Miss Marchrose came back again, and took her place beside him.

"I always wanted to go to sea," said Sir Julian Rossiter slowly. "It wasn't practicable because I was the only son, and my father wouldn't hear of it, on account of the place. But that was what I wanted."

"Yes, I see," said Miss Marchrose.

And something underlying the note of beauty which he had before admired in her voice carried to Sir Julian the conviction that she did see.

He drove her to the gate of the farm, and they talked a little, with comfortable inconsequence, on the way.

When she got out of the car, Miss Marchrose thanked him cordially, and her movements, as she crossed the yard and went up the stone steps to the house door, were no longer eloquent of weariness.

Julian drove back to Culmhayes through the dark lanes.

It was characteristic of him that he should observe, as he took his place opposite to his wife at the end of the dinner-table that evening:

"I took Miss Marchrose back in the car this evening. She came out of the College just as I was going past."

He was quite aware, without looking at her, of the exact angle to which Edna's eyebrows raised themselves.

"I thought she stayed at the College working till all hours, and then had to be escorted home by unfortunate Mark?"

"Apparently the procedure is not invariable."

Edna waited until the servants were out of the room, and then spoke again.

"Julian—about that girl—I couldn't leave it at that, you know. God knows how much I dislike any form of interference, but then it's for Mark Easter—I can never feel that Mark hasn't a very real claim on me."

"In the name of fortune, Edna, what are you talking about?"

"You mean," said Edna, fixing him with a coldly thoughtful eye, and perfectly aware that he meant nothing of the sort, "You mean that, with my ideals, *all* humanity has a claim on me. I do hold that it is so, and, as you know, I am always ready to give what I can, though it may not be silver or gold. I was rather struck by a curious little incident this morning, Julian, which illustrates my meaning. I think I must tell you."

Edna placed her white arms upon the table and leant a little forward, her handsome face full of the absorption that is the expression common to most faces, handsome or otherwise, of which the owner is talking freely about him or herself.

"For the last week or two I have been having a poor woman out from Culmouth in here to do some sewing, because Miss Brown is ill. I went in to talk to her for a minute or two, the first day she came. I hate them to feel as though they weren't of the same flesh and blood as oneself—and I was struck by the sort of hard dreariness in her face, as though she had never known the meaning of love or gladness. I asked no questions, of course, but just laid my hand on her shoulder and said quietly, 'I don't know if you've ever read Browning—perhaps not—but there is a line of his that I want you to think about while you're mending those curtains: "God's in His Heaven—all's right with the world!"' And then I left her.

"Well, she didn't make very much response, poor thing, but every time I saw her when she came here I've just, in my own thoughts, thrown a little Cloak of Love round her. It seemed to me all that I could do. And this morning—after all these weeks, when one just went quietly on without any, visible sign of success—this morning, Julian, when I came into the sewing-room—she looked up and smiled."

Julian looked as though this consummation struck him as being in the nature of an anti-climax.

"Day after day, I'd thrown my little Cloak of Love round her—and she'd come to feel the warmth of it at last. It has made me very happy, Julian. You will smile at me, very likely, but the winning of that poor little seamstress to a brighter, truer outlook seems to me—well, just extraordinarily worth while."

There was silence, while Lady Rossiter's softened expression denoted that she was devoting her reflections to the recent conquest. But presently she went back to her original ground of departure.

"About Mark, though—I care for him too much to see him take any risks. And I find—would to God I hadn't!—that my original instinct was correct."

Lady Rossiter waited, but her husband showed no disposition to ask for elucidation, and she was obliged to go on unquestioned.

"It was this very girl—Pauline Marchrose—who threw over Clarence Isbister because of his accident."

For once, Sir Julian displayed astonishment in the right place.

"Good Lord!" he said, in a startled voice. "I'd forgotten all about that business."

There was a long pause. Then Julian remarked slowly:

"Yes—I should rather like to hear the rights of that story. Perhaps, after all, Clarence Isbister wasn't quite such an ass as I always thought him."

VI

"How's the 'Tale of Two Sexes,' or whatever it's called, getting on?" flippantly enquired Sir Julian of his agent.

"Coming out any day now," said Mark, with a grin, "and the gifted authoress is coming to stay with us next month. Will you and Lady Rossiter come and dine one night? I'm afraid you'll get a very poor dinner, but you know what to expect of Sarah. I should like to make it rather more amusing for Iris, if you can face it."

"Delighted," said Sir Julian untruthfully.

The proposed entertainment was one which he had sampled before, and for which he had conceived a profound distaste.

An element of novelty was introduced, however, at the eleventh hour, when the evening of the dinner-party arrived. Mark greeted Sir Julian and Lady Rossiter on the threshold.

"A creature called Douglas Garrett has turned up, by what he and Iris call a coincidence. Of course, I had to ask the chap to dinner, and he's gone to the 'King's Head' to get his things."

"The more the merrier," said Julian rather gloomily.

"I've got Miss Marchrose to come, so we shall be even numbers," said Mark cheerfully.

"Good."

"You should have let me know," murmured Edna gently. "She may perhaps want keeping in countenance a little, as regards evening dress. I could so easily have put on a high gown."

Regrets on the score of Edna's modest and extremely becoming *décolletage*, half shrouded in tulle, proved unnecessary.

Miss Iris Easter was in full dinner-dress, of a rose colour that enhanced her extreme fairness and prettiness.

Small as was Julian's admiration for her personality, he was always struck afresh at the sight of her, at the size of her enormous eyes—as nearly violet as any eyes outside the pages of a novel—her crinkled, fluffy hair, her general delicacy of form and feature. Even the misguided instinct which had led her to outline a charming upper lip with sealing-wax red could not detract from her porcelain prettiness.

She was the possessor of a high, youthful, lisping voice that always reminded Julian of the adjective "fluted," and a pronunciation that is best indicated by the fact that she always pronounced her own name as though it were spelt "heiress."

At the sight of Lady Rossiter she cried:

"Eoh! *heow* blessed to see you again, dear Lady Rahsittur!" and almost similarly greeted Sir Julian, with her head very much on one side.

Lady Rossiter said "My dear!" in a tone which simultaneously conveyed protest at Miss Easter's excessive effusion and the unspoken admission that any lesser enthusiasm would never have met the case, and Julian laughed a little, simply because Iris was so pretty and her monstrous affectation had not yet had time to produce its usual effect upon his temper.

"Where's your young man?" Mark asked her, with a laugh. "He ought to be back by this time."

"Douglas?" said Iris, in a careless and interrogatory way, as though the enquiry might refer to any number of attendant swains. "Oh, he'll be here directly. I can hear the dear kiddies, Mark."

So could everyone else, as Ruthie and Ambrose whined, argued, and stampeded their way downstairs.

The usual violent onslaught on the door-handle ensued, but after it had been wrenched from Ambrose by Ruthie's superior height and strength of muscle, they effected a decorous entry into the drawing-room hand-in-hand.

"Oh, you sweet pets!" was the misguided exclamation of their Auntie Iris. Julian wondered if it were provoked by the unwonted starchy white-ness of Ruthie's skirts, which had a look of having been outgrown by her some months previously, or by the long, pale sausage of hair that had been forced into an unwilling curl on the extreme top of her brother's head.

"Say how do you do," Mark admonished them, with a rather puzzled look as he took in the cleanly aspect for once presented by his progeny.

"How fast Ruthie is growing!" said Lady Rossiter, in a slightly disparaging tone. Mark gazed regretfully at the legs of his daughter and muttered under his moustache:

"They want someone to see to their clothes. Sarah does her best, but servants can't be expected—"

Lady Rossiter turned upon him a deepened gaze expressive of compassion, comprehension, and much else that was destined to remain unappreciated, as further sounds of arrival took Mark to the door.

"That was a cab, surely," said Lady Rossiter. "I suppose it's Miss Marchrose. That seems rather an expensive item for her."

"How dear of you, Lady Rossiter! I do believe you always think of every little thing."

On this extravagant assertion of Miss Easter's, her brother returned to the drawing-room with his two remaining guests.

Mr. Douglas Garrett was a tall, saturnine youth, whose conversation principally consisted in emphasising the gulf separating the rest of humanity from himself and some persons unspecified, but amalgamated under the monosyllable "we."

"We poor motor-cyclists can't hope to be as punctual as the rest of the world," he observed to Lady Rossiter, to whom he was presented by Iris as "My great friend, Mr. Garrett, dear Lady Rossiter, but everyone calls him Douglas."

"You will hardly need to be told that I have Scotch blood in me, after that," gravely said Mr. Garrett. "We Kelts are faithful to the traditional old names of the Clan."

"Oh," said Iris, her head more on one side than ever. "Isn't there some poem about, 'Douglas, Douglas, tender and true'?"

Mr. Garrett inclined his head towards her in acknowledgment and murmured something about "we lovers of the dear old bard" which nobody seemed quite to catch.

The room, not over large, now appeared to be rather uncomfortably crowded, and pervaded, moreover, by a growing consciousness that something must be happening to the dinner.

Lady Rossiter said to Mark, "I always love a *little* house, especially in winter. They are so much warmer," at the same time holding a newspaper between herself and the fire, the size of which was out of all proportion to the room and to the number of its occupants.

"I know you love kiddies," Auntie Iris remarked in a general sort of way to Miss Marchrose, Julian, and Mr. Garrett. "These little people are too quaint for words, aren't you, children?"

The rather embarrassing enquiry appeared to present no difficulty to Ruthie, who made it the ground of a sudden onslaught upon Mr. Garrett.

"Are you married?" she enquired with loudness and assurance of the astonished young man.

"Certainly not," said Mr. Garrett, with emphasis. Ruthie immediately took an uninvited seat upon his knee.

"Come here, Ambrose dear," said Auntie Iris hastily, "and talk to us."

"Eh?" said Ambrose, looking enquiringly at her through his spectacles.

It needed no intuition to recognise either the intonation or the vocabulary of Sarah in the pleasing monosyllable shot forth by Master Easter.

"What have you been doing to-day?" rather rashly pursued Auntie Iris. "Eh?"

"Don't say 'eh,' like that, darling. I can't imagine what's come over the child."

"That's Peekaboo's new bad habit," his sister gleefully proclaimed. "He says 'eh' to everything now."

Ambrose looked venomously at her, but said nothing.

"Do you know what we Scotch lads and lasses used to be taught in our nursery days?" Mr. Garrett enquired.

"Eh?"

"We used to be taught," Mr. Garrett said, with great distinctness and an air of originality, "Birds in their little nests agree."

"That's what Sarah says."

Mr. Garrett looked rather depressed at this unenthusiastic reception of his scholastic axiom.

There ensued a pause, during which Julian could hear his host and Lady Rossiter pursuing a conversation in which the last thing had long been said.

He turned to Miss Marchrose, and ill-adapted as were her twenty-eight years, her tired eyes and her rather worn mauve foulard to bear comparison with the radiant Iris, Julian found it pleasant to look at her and to listen to her charming voice.

The satisfaction, however, was not afforded to him for long. "Auntie Iris! Shall I say my piece?" Ruthie asked in her accustomedly penetrating accents.

Everybody looked doubtful.

"Hark!" exclaimed Julian, quite involuntarily. "Isn't that—?"

Sarah, looking heated, announced dinner.

"Oh, what a pity!" said Ruthie. "But I daresay me and Ambrose will be still here when you come out from dinner. So I can say it then."

With this altruistic reassurance still ringing in the air, to an accompaniment of stubbornly reiterated "ehs" from Ambrose, the dining-room was reached.

"I see that your novel is being very well advertised," Sir Julian began conversation with his hostess. "We have it on order, but it has not yet arrived. I hope that means that the sales are going well."

"Don't hope that," said Mr. Garrett in a deep voice across the table.

"Why not?" said Mark, after giving Sir Julian due time for the enquiry which nothing would have induced him to make.

"'Why, Ben!' is not to be lightly put before the multitude. Iris has shown extraordinary courage in attacking a problem which could only present itself to thinking minds. The very title tells one that—a Story of the Sexes. By the by, Iris, we realists of the new school are inclined to wish that you had made *that* the name of the book outright."

"No, no," said Mark, and added courageously, "Besides, I like 'Why, Ben!' It's so original."

"Is your book a novel?" Miss Marchrose enquired of Iris.

Mr. Garrett took the reply upon himself. "An extraordinarily powerful study of man's primitive needs," he explained.

"Iris—Miss Easter—has gone straight down to the very bed-rock of the soil. We present-day pagans are gradually winning our way back to Mother Nature, don't you think?"

Julian involuntarily glanced at his wife at this perverted example of her own theories.

"Perhaps," said Edna very sweetly, "Mother Nature is herself leading us home. One has only to look round one after all. Personally, I have a tiny, tiny little nature-class which means a great deal to me. And I make everyone join who has one little spark of the Divine Fire, whoever it may be. But then I'm afraid I'm a socialist—a rank, rank democrat."

The announcement provided ample opportunity for the more strenuous form of egotism known as General Conversation.

"Oh, Lady Rossiter!" piped Iris; "but I always say that if the socialists divided everything up and made everyone equal to-day, things would all go back to the old way to-morrow!"

"I must admit that we thinkers are all in favour of democracy as a rule," said Mr. Douglas Garrett, obviously resentful at having to agree with anyone present; "but take the Keltic element alone—perhaps I shall make my point best by putting my own case to you. ..."

His sombre gaze was fixed upon Miss Marchrose, who brazenly ignored the whole of the last half of his sentence, and said pleasantly that she knew nothing about politics and had always been brought up to believe the whole subject quite unfit for feminine ears.

"This from an emancipated lady who has taken up a business career!" said Edna, with a hint of mockery. "I quite imagined you an advocate of woman's rights, Miss Marchrose."

"The cry of Woman's Rights, my dear Edna, was a catchword which had passed out of the language while Miss Marchrose was still in the nursery," said Sir Julian suavely; "consequently it probably conveys nothing to her generation, whatever it may do to ours."

Julian was quite conscious of the anything but doubtful taste of this chivalrous rebuke, and felt rather grateful to Iris for breaking in with the artless and time-honoured statement that *she* always had all the rights she wanted, and men always seemed ready to give up their seats in omnibuses or railway carriages so as to offer them to *her*. She also added that she could not think why this was.

Sir Julian gave her the required explanation of the phenomenon, while Mark turned with a certain aspect of relief to his neighbour, Miss Marchrose, and Mr. Douglas Garrett and Lady Rossiter looked disapprovingly at one another and both began to talk at once with immense firmness and determination.

Julian never knew by what means his wife accomplished her end, but at a later stage of dinner, when Mark and Miss Marchrose had been laughing at one another's jokes for some time, Edna's voice suddenly fell audible on the other side of the table addressing herself to Mr. Garrett: "… but Clarence Isbister is the only son, and a particularly nice boy."

Julian would not look at Miss Marchrose, but Edna's voice had been so distinct that both Mark and she stopped speaking. It was Iris, however, with the praiseworthy instinct of her kind for following up any clue, however remote, that might eventually lead to an only son, who asked:

"Are those the Shropshire Isbisters?"

"A branch of the same family. But I was telling Mr.—er—"

Edna made a slight and insultingly-meant pretence at having forgotten Mr. Garrett's name. Nobody supplied it, unless an exception be made of Iris, who murmured that everyone called him Douglas.

"—About some dear cousins of mine, Isbisters—people who live in Queen's Gate Gardens most of the year."

Lady Rossiter paused, looking straight at Miss Marchrose, who said nothing at all, and looked calmly back at her.

There was complete silence for an instant. Before it had assumed significance Mark Easter broke it with cheerful trivialities.

Julian wondered whether Miss Marchrose was conscious of challenge.

Her face was inscrutable, but he felt by no means sure that she had not very accurately interpreted Edna's unspoken warning that Mark Easter, if necessary, should yet be told how Clarence Isbister had fared at the hands of his betrothed.

When the not-too-successful dinner had come to an end, and Mark had returned to the drawing-room with the reluctant Julian and a now eloquent Garrett, whose discourse on the convivial proclivities of "we-fellows-about-town" had met with the smallest possible amount of attention from either of his seniors, success seemed within more measurable distance of the evening's entertainment.

Julian was not, indeed, pleased to find the son and daughter of the house sprawlingly occupying the hearthrug, to the exclusion of everyone else from sight or heat of the fire, but he perceived that Ruthie and Ambrose, objectionable in themselves, had at least served to obviate possible mutual friction between the remaining occupants of the room.

Lady Rossiter was maintaining with persevering sweetness a kindly catechism as to the tastes and habits of Master Ambrose Easter, who responded with his newly-acquired monosyllable, reiterated upon a loud, enquiring, unintelligent note. Iris was picturesquely turning over a heap of music just where the lamplight fell on her bright, soft hair, and Miss Marchrose, leaning back in an armchair, hearkened with an unsympathetic expression to Ruthie's noisy and highly-emphasised rendering of an objectionable poem blatantly entitled "I am Grandpa's Little Sweetheart."

"Children, I thought you were in bed long ago," said Mark, eyeing them in a rather dejected fashion.

"Sarah can't put us to bed yet, she's got to wash up," said Ambrose, in a practical way.

"Listen, Daddy!" cried Ruthie:

> "So *I'm* the little girlie who always has to *go*
> And stand each happy Christmas beneath the mistle*toe*,
> And Grandpa comes up softly—"

"Ruthie! Stop that."

"But Daddy, it's my piece!"

Mark sank into a chair with a sort of groan.

"The Rector's daughter gives them lessons, and she will teach them these things," he confided to Miss Marchrose, who responded almost more sympathetically than was courteous.

"We've just come to the end."

Accordingly, when Ruthie's final assertion of her hypothetical grandparent's infatuation had died away, and Lady Rossiter had said coldly, "Very nice, Ruthie dear," and Mr. Garrett had muttered something about we votaries of the Muse to Iris, and everybody else had maintained an unenthusiastic silence, Mark Easter bribed, commanded and cajoled his children into immediate disappearance from the drawing-room.

"Auntie Iris will come and tuck you up, darlings," exclaimed Miss Easter winningly, waiting until they might safely be assumed to be well out of hearing, and merely with the evident intention of captivating Mr. Douglas Garrett.

He immediately joined her as she stood, still fluttering music-leaves.

"Won't you sing?" he enquired tenderly.

But Iris was in the case of the majority of those of her sex known to sing. She had studied for some time, reported ecstatic opinions of her voice, its power and its quality, possessed a large quantity of music, and had never been heard to utter a note.

"The Signora won't hear of my trying my voice yet," said Iris, in the accustomed formula of these carefully sheltered nightingales. "She thinks it may take eight or ten years to develop it, and then I might even think of Grand Opera. It seems too quaint, doesn't it?"

This last tribute to modesty appearing to require no reply, Mr. Garrett turned to Miss Marchrose.

"I fancy from your speaking voice that you can sing," he said kindly. "We musicians are not over-critical, as I'm sure Iris will tell you, and I'm sure it would be delightful to hear you."

Miss Marchrose looked at her host.

"Do," he said.

He and Julian listened to her, while Iris and Mr. Garrett retired to a distant sofa and conversed in undertones, and Lady Rossiter put on one of her kindest expressions.

Miss Marchrose had chosen the only old-fashioned volume from amongst Iris's extremely modern selection, and she sang "Annie Laurie" and "Jock o' Hazeldean." Her voice had the indescribable quality of pathos that is sometimes heard in Irish voices, and was fairly well trained, though it was quite evident that no cherishing Signora had ever had the charge of it. It was not a beautiful voice, but every note within its small compass was exceedingly sweet.

"Thanks—thanks so much," said Mr. Garrett from his sofa. "We Kelts have a very soft corner for the Songs of Hame. Won't you try 'Loch Lomond'?"

But Miss Marchrose said no, and that she was afraid that she had quite forgotten that part of her audience was Scotch, or she would never have attempted Scotch songs, thus making an end of the pretty illusion that her selection had been out of compliment to Mr. Garrett and his nationality.

"Isn't your voice sufficiently trained to be of a little use to you?" Lady Rossiter asked the singer. "Private engagements are really not so very difficult to get, and I'm sure you'd like adding to the music of the world better than that eternal shorthand."

"I am better qualified to add to the music of the world on a typewriter than on a piano," said Miss Marchrose.

"Go on singing," Julian told her.

This time she sang popular musical comedy songs, rather amusingly, and with the slightest of accompaniments.

Mark roared with laughter, Lady Rossiter substituted a tolerant look for the one of kindness, and Iris and Mr. Garrett exchanged a slight shudder.

"Well done!" said Sir Julian, when she stopped. "But sing 'Annie Laurie' once more."

He listened with peculiar satisfaction while she did as he had asked her.

The dinner-party was broken up by Lady Rossiter, who said to Miss Marchrose as she bade her good night:

"We mustn't keep your cab waiting; that 'King's Head' fly charges abominably as it is. Besides, I don't forget that you have to be at work at nine to-morrow morning. Good night."

She drew on her fur coat, preparatory to walking with Julian the few hundred yards to their own gates.

As they turned away, Mark Easter handed Miss Marchrose into her cab, and they heard him say, "Good night, Annie Laurie."

VII

After that evening, Mark often called Miss Marchrose 'Annie Laurie.'

Julian frequently wondered what the result might be if he ever did so in the presence of Lady Rossiter.

Lady Rossiter, however, was much engaged with the valedictory meetings at which the members of the nature-class bade nature farewell until the return of warmer weather, and had no immediate leisure to bestow upon the growing friendship between Mark and Miss Marchrose.

Julian made his own observations, and was more than ever convinced that Mark Easter was in no danger from a repetition of the fate which had overtaken Captain Clarence Isbister. That episode, moreover, remained to him utterly incomprehensible. He surmised that the clue to it might be found in that contradiction between the half-mocking, half-defiant directness of Miss Marchrose's eyes and the curiously unconscious pathos of her mouth.

At the villa, Iris Easter for the time being remained installed, reaping an astonishing harvest of press-cuttings, variously indicating surprise, disgust and admiration at the startling character of 'Why, Ben!'

Mr. Douglas Garrett remained in Culmouth and interpreted the press-cuttings to her in his character of "one of we poor literary hacks."

In the first week of December there took place at the College one of the general committee meetings so abhorred of Sir Julian.

"There are a great, great many things," said Edna thoughtfully, "that I want to speak about at the meeting. I have been so little to the College lately, but it is not often out of my thoughts."

"Bellew is taking the chair," Sir Julian observed, less irrelevantly than might have been supposed.

He was aware, and knew that Edna was aware, that no check or limit would be placed by Alderman Bellew on the College problems that Lady Rossiter might choose to regard as coming within the scope of her influence.

He wondered for the hundredth time whether it would not have been possible to decline the complimentary offer of a position on the general committee of management which had been made to Lady Rossiter as wife of the leading director, and which he knew that she cherished the more from being the only representative of her sex at the meetings.

"By the by," he said suddenly, "the position of Lady Superintendent carries, *ipso facto*, a place on the general committee. You will have another lady to keep you in countenance, Edna."

"What, poor Miss Marchrose?"

"Miss Marchrose," Julian assented, tacitly refusing the epithet.

Lady Rossiter was silent for a moment and then said quietly, "I'm so glad that I can spare the time to come in to-day. She could never have faced all those men by herself, poor thing, and they would probably have disliked it as much as she would, or more. An unmarried woman is always at a disadvantage."

Julian left undisputed this cardinal article of faith characteristic of the wedded Englishwoman.

In the hall of the College they found Cooper, who said in a congratulatory way, "Sir Julian, *and* Lady Rossiter! You've come for the general meeting. Let me take your coat, Lady Rossiter, and put it here— just lay it across the chair-back. We're going to have a good meeting, I think—no absentees. Will you wait in Mr. Fuller's room, Sir Julian? I'll open the door."

Mr. Fairfax Fuller greeted his chief with an air of relief that turned into a look of smouldering resentment as Lady Rossiter shook hands with him, which she always did, as she said, on principle, either disregarding or not observing the Supervisor's strong tendency to entrench himself behind a writing-table and thrust both hands into his pockets.

She did not, however, shake hands with Miss Marchrose, but nodded to her in a very kindly way and said "Good morning" in a pleasant undertone.

Old Alderman Bellew was talking in the window to Mark Easter.

"How are things going, Mr. Fuller?" Edna enquired with grave interest.

"Going right enough," muttered Fuller, looking at his watch.

"Oh, I'm glad. You know I care so much. What are you putting before the committee to-day?"

Fuller turned his back upon her.

"Miss Marchrose, give Lady Rossiter an agenda."

"Yes, yes," Edna cried, barely glancing at it, "but I don't mean just the headings. For instance, 'Proposed Saturday afternoon classes.' Is there really any chance of it? You know the whole question is very, very near my heart, Mr. Fuller."

"It's for discussion to-day," said Mr. Fuller, bending over his writing-table and intently studying the cover of Pitman's Shorthand Dictionary.

"Oh yes, but then there's so much that doesn't always come up at the big meetings. *Le dessous des cartes*. In fact," Edna tactfully amended, "the other side of the cards."

"Pocket Shorthand Dictionary, Centenary Edition," was Fuller's explosive reply, as he traced the words on the book before him with a square, tobacco-stained forefinger.

Julian was vividly reminded of the highly unsuccessful tea-party given in her office by Miss Marchrose. He refrained from glancing at her, feeling intimately convinced that the same thought was in her mind at the moment.

"Shall we make a move, Fuller? It's just time."

Fairfax Fuller, with extreme and obvious thankfulness, hastily rose to comply with the suggestion.

Lady Rossiter's traditional seat was at the right-hand side of the chairman. She placed herself there and glanced round. Miss Marchrose entered just behind Sir Julian. She looked not at all shy, but merely rather doubtful.

Edna half-rose, with benevolent shielding in every line of her admirably-hung coat and skirt, but Mark Easter was before her.

"Here, Miss Marchrose, if you will," he said quietly, and making way for her at the table as he spoke. She gave him a quick glance of acknowledgment and took the place that he indicated, between young Cooper and himself at the end of the long table furthest from the chair. Julian was seated at the bottom of the table, facing the Alderman.

"Well, ladies and gentlemen," said the chairman, "I'm happy to tell you that our Commercial and Technical College is doing well, doing very well. I know how much you all have this enterprise at heart, and, indeed, I may say that to the youth of this country, it is an enterprise which cannot—which can, rather, or—er—I should say can*not* be of anything but inestimable advantage."

The Alderman's opening gambit was new to nobody. Cooper put his pencil behind his ear until such time as the minutes of the conference should claim it from inaction, and only began to fidget when old Bellew made allusion to the increased attendance in the evening classes for French, "so ably presided over by Mr. Cooper."

"The financial statement submitted to the directors by our good friend Mr. Fuller there, is a highly satisfactory one, and the recent audit was conducted to the complete—er—satisfac—to the complete—that is—to the—er—general—"

The Alderman paused again, struggled, was defeated, and ended defiantly, "To the general satisfaction."

"I will ask Mr. Fuller to read to the meeting those figures which will best serve to put the position clearly before the meeting."

Fairfax Fuller, standing at attention, his voice impassive, and his face full of triumph, recited a rapid litany, in which the words "two thousand eight hundred and eleven "predominated.

"Bravo," murmured Mark Easter, thus encouraging the members of the meeting to a general rustle of applause at this indication that something, evidently numbering two thousand eight hundred and eleven parts, had been gained, or saved, or judiciously made use of, for their benefit.

"That, if I may say so, gentlemen," Mr. Fuller impressively remarked, "is a very remarkable result. When I came here as Supervisor, three years ago, matters were not in this state. Far from it. Mr. Mark Easter here can tell you that, so can Sir Julian Rossiter. The College, if I may say so, has pulled itself together since then. I don't wish to claim any credit for myself."

("Liar!" mentally ejaculated Julian.) "But the figures at the end of each year have shown a very marked improvement. I hope next year we may do better still. I may say, that I hope so confidently."

Fuller sat down again, pulling up the legs of his trousers at the knees, and sufficiently intent upon the operation to miss the smile of congratulation that Lady Rossiter was holding in waiting for him.

The old chairman, breathing heavily, leant across the table and addressed Sir Julian Rossiter.

"Now, Sir Julian, you're a younger man than I am, and I'm going to ask you to raise the one or two points we have here on the agenda. I think we want the opinion of the meeting on one or two matters, eh?"

Julian spoke rapidly, and as concisely as possible. Cooper's pencil flew across the pages of his note-book.

"The question has been raised of keeping the College open on Saturday afternoons. There is plenty of evidence that, if we did so, we should get quite a number of town pupils. The early closing of the shops would bring us various shop employees, who are only too anxious to give an hour or two of their spare time to learning. That, I believe, applies especially to the shorthand and typewriting classes. The other subjects, of course, have always been in less demand. The number of students is easily covered by the evening classes on Tuesdays and Fridays for such subjects as accountancy, for instance, or French. The question is, therefore, whether it would not be worth while to arrange for a later closing on Saturdays, so as to hold a weekly class for beginners in shorthand and typing."

Sir Julian paused and Fairfax Fuller said eagerly:

"I could engage for our having five pupils, straight off the reel, sir. I actually hold that number of applications."

"Excellent," said the Alderman, from the head of the table.

"Ah!" breathed Lady Rossiter. "One would be so glad and proud, I feel that too, very strongly—to help lay the foundation of knowledge—of that efficiency which is to build up the forces of our Empire. After all, it is the class we are trying to reach that is the very backbone of the country."

The irrelevant diatribes to which Lady Rossiter was almost invariably moved by a General Committee meeting contributed in no small measure to her husband's distaste for them.

He looked straight in front of him and addressed the chairman.

"The whole question, of course, hinges on the staff available. Miss Marchrose and Mr. Fuller are of opinion that it could be arranged, but before approaching any of the teachers, it was thought desirable to get the committee's opinion."

"The question being," ponderously repeated the old Alderman, looking round the table, "the question being, whether or not the College is to open on Saturday afternoons for a special shorthand and typing course."

"I have here a scheme," began Fuller eagerly, but Lady Rossiter's clear voice interrupted him.

"Mr. Chairman, I am only a woman, amongst all you men, but I want you to let me speak."

Edna leant forward in her favourite attitude, her arms folded upon the table, her furs flung back.

"Delighted, Lady Rossiter, delighted to hear your views," growled the Alderman.

Julian, looking down his nose, saw Fuller thrust his bull-neck forward and jab viciously at the blotting-paper in front of him with a blunt pencil.

Mark Easter was pulling at his moustache, leaning well back in his chair, and Miss Marchrose was gazing at Lady Rossiter. Her dark brows were drawn together in a slight frown, that might have indicated puzzledom or disapproval alike.

"It seems to me," said Edna, in the time-honoured opening phrase of the amateur, "it seems to me, that we perhaps none of us quite realise what it would mean to ask any of the staff to give up that precious Saturday. I always feel that it must mean so much to them. We, who can wander out into God's beautiful sunshine at will, can hardly grasp what it must be like to be imprisoned between four walls all the week, without free time, without access to the fresh air, the movement of the world outside. Oh," cried Edna, in a very impassioned manner indeed, "I think if one only puts oneself into the place of those girl and women prisoners toiling for their bread and butter all the week, it will become impossible to take away the poor little Saturday half-holiday which is all they have! There is no one, I can confidently say, who has our great national cause more at heart than I have, who would do more to bring the light of education into the drab lives of those poor shop creatures, but it seems to me that, as members of the committee, we must give our first thought, our first consideration, to our own—our very own workers. I, personally, have always felt the staff at the College to be my very own."

Julian dared not glance at the representatives of Lady Rossiter's very own, so vividly did his imagination set before him the infuriated lowering of Fuller's dark brow, and the probable line of satire round Miss Marchrose's curving lips.

He had frequently before heard Lady Rossiter moved to a very similar eloquence, but neither custom nor a resolute avoidance of any eye in the room could prevent him from wincing inwardly while her voice rang out.

"It almost seems to me, that we forget sometimes—oh, I'm not speaking personally, Heaven knows, I'm weak enough myself—but sometimes I think we forget that it's flesh and blood like our own that we're dealing with. These men and women who work for a living are human beings like ourselves!"

An electric silence followed the announcement.

Edna's head was moved slightly backwards, in the manner of one who has flung down the gauntlet fearlessly. Her eyes travelled slowly round the table.

Suddenly she uttered an impulsive "Ah!"

Julian, taken unawares, glanced up quickly. His wife's eager, ardent gaze had fallen upon Miss Marchrose, motionless in her place.

"My dear!" she exclaimed half under her breath, but entirely audibly, "I forgot you—I forgot you were here. Have I hurt you?"

"Good God!" broke from Fairfax Fuller, and almost at the same instant Mark Easter, with ingenious clumsiness, sent an empty chair to the floor.

Sir Julian set his teeth and stood up.

"I am afraid that we have strayed from the subject under discussion. May I suggest that Mr. Fuller should outline the scheme?"

"Certainly, Sir Julian, by all means—by all means," said the chairman, looking harassed.

Fuller's scheme anticipated the humanitarian doubts raised by Lady Rossiter. The Saturday class should be open from two o'clock to four, and Saturday duty taken weekly in rotation by each one of the three shorthand teachers belonging to the College. The classes of the week should be so rearranged as to enable those members of the staff who had been at work on Saturday afternoon to return to the College at midday only on Monday morning.

"Excellent," said Mark Easter.

"The Lady Superintendent, who will herself kindly undertake one Saturday class in three, is of opinion that the proposition is entirely practicable and would meet with every response from the teachers concerned."

He turned enquiringly to Miss Marchrose.

"Yes, certainly," she said briefly.

"Then if Miss Marchrose will speak to the two lady teachers, Miss Farmer and Miss Sandiloe—"

Mark paused.

"Unless anyone else wishes to raise any further point in that connection," said the chairman, "I may take it that we are all agreed?"

Sir Julian, half against his will, received the odd impression that everyone was suffering from a strange sensation as of being shattered, so that scarcely any discussion of the point at issue ensued, and the remaining business of the day was disposed of between Mark Easter and Alderman Bellew with unwonted rapidity.

Fairfax Fuller spoke no word, and as soon as the meeting ended left the room with no slightest pretence at the civility of a valediction.

"Poor old Fuller!" said Mark to Julian, with his tolerant laugh.

"My sympathies are with Mr. Fuller," declared Edna lightly. "He is a misogynist, poor dear. I know he thinks that women at a meeting are a mistake; he was looking at poor Miss Marchrose with such an expression of contempt and fury! However, he carried his point as to the Saturday classes, and his scheme certainly appealed to one. All the same, I'm glad I had the courage to utter my little testimony before you all."

Julian refrained from looking at Mark Easter.

"I am thinking of resigning from the committee," he remarked gloomily. "Like Mr. Fuller, I am a misogynist."

VIII

After this gratifying announcement from her husband, it may be supposed the more readily that Lady Rossiter, on the day following the General Committee meeting, should elect to discover various small items of business requiring her presence in London.

She left Culmhayes on Friday evening, and the following morning saw Julian at Mark Easter's front door.

"Come out after wild duck, Mark?"

"Rather."

"The keeper tells me there are any amount out Salt Marsh way. Could we raise another gun?"

"There's that fellow Garrett."

"Well, bring him along, if he cares to come. Start from here at two o'clock?"

"That'll do. I have to be at the office this morning."

"Good Lord, Mark, you live at that office, I believe, when you aren't at the College. What does your sister say to you?"

"She has other fish to fry," said Mark drily.

Julian admitted the truth in the implication when he presently encountered Miss Easter loitering along the lane. Her golden head was uncovered, and she wore a curious cockney medley of black fur, silk *décolletée* blouse, tweed skirt, silk stockings, and high-heeled shoes of thin suède.

She said, "Oh, Sir Julian!" with great enthusiasm, and insisted upon tripping along the hard, frozen lane beside him as far as his own gate.

Sir Julian, who thought her pretty, if absurd, was always able to endure her society with equanimity for a short while, and made amiable enquiry after "Why, Ben!"

"Oh, isn't it too, too wonderful?" said Iris, in slightly awe-stricken tones. "The little tiny seed I tried to sow bearing such wonderful fruit and shedding light in so many dark places!"

"Very wonderful," Julian agreed, mentally applying the epithet to the phenomenon of any seed possessing the peculiar property of shedding light in dark places.

"It's perfectly dear of you to say so," warmly responded the authoress.

"Douglas Garrett, you know, my great friend, he knows the most fearful amount about books, and he says that 'Why, Ben!' has simply gone straight back to earth."

"Sounds rather like a fox."

"I always think there's something so pure and strong and passionate about the soil. That's why I gave Ben a rural setting. The peasantry are so primitive. I'll tell you a secret. I'm really down here to study the setting for my next book."

"Are you writing another one now?"

"Oh no," said Iris, in rather shocked accents. "I'm simply absorbing local colour in at every pore."

"You'd better come out on Salt Marsh this afternoon and see the wild duck. I've asked Mark to bring Mr. Garrett and we're going to have a shot at them."

Julian did not make the suggestion without first calculating the chances to be in favour of Miss Easter's declining the proposed arrangement. Nor did she fail to reply with the typical suburbanism:

"I can't bear seeing things killed, and I hate the noise of guns going off. Besides, it's so cold. But we'll come and meet you at tea-time."

"We?"

"Oh, I'm going to take that girl that Mark likes so much for a walk. He says she never has anyone to talk to."

"Miss Marchrose?"

"Yes, I think she's a perfect dear, and quite awfully pretty."

Julian mentally applauded her.

"It will be delightful if you'll come and meet us," he said cordially. "You must come in and make tea for us at Culmhayes, if you will. We ought to be at the cross-roads, just this side of Salt Marsh, soon after four. It will depend on the light. I doubt if we shall be able to go on much after half-past three."

Julian's prognostication was verified, but before the three men had reached the cross-roads they encountered Iris and Miss Marchrose, silhouetted against the leaden sky of a rapidly-advancing winter twilight.

"You've come a long way!" exclaimed Julian, with an involuntary thought for the silk stockings and suède shoes which he felt convinced that Iris was still wearing.

"It wasn't too far for you?" asked Mark of Miss Marchrose, with friendly solicitude.

She only shook her head in reply, but Julian, with the odd intuition of a man with whom the observation of humanity has always been of prevailing interest, knew that she was inwardly responsive with all the quick gratitude of femininity for a man's rarely-expressed consideration for her physical limitations.

Iris said in a rather enfeebled voice:

"Oh, Douglas, have you been cruel and brutal and shot all those poor dear birds? How many did you kill?"

Mr. Garrett made pretence of not having heard the enquiry, for reasons which Julian was at no pains to guess, having watched his guest's display of incompetence with some dismay throughout the afternoon.

"I want you to notice the strange, strong atmospheric smell of decay in these lanes, Iris," said Mr. Garrett, taking control of the conversation in a high-handed manner that precluded further idle enquiries on the day's sport.

"The whole place is redolent of winter and the dying year. We realists must take in deep draughts of atmosphere."

To which Iris rather inadequately responded by a high, squeaking enquiry as to Douglas's dreadful, dreadful gun and the possibility of its going off unexpectedly and killing her.

Miss Marchrose fell into step between Mark and Julian, her hands thrust boyishly into the pockets of her coat.

"Iris is afraid of getting more atmosphere than she bargained for," said

Mark, with a laugh. "A shooting accident would make first-rate copy, I suppose."

"I wonder," said Julian. "The interest attaching to violent action always appears to me to be rather a fictitious one."

"So it is," Miss Marchrose answered quickly. "Surely in real life the majority of dramas are almost devoid of violent action, nowadays. I mean that a crisis, off the stage, is not necessarily brought about by a duel, or a murder, or an elopement."

"The world is more subtle than it used to be," Julian assented. "What you call a crisis, after all is mostly an affair of the emotions. It is generally led up to by an atmospheric tension and culminates in some ultra violence of emotion, whether of anger or sorrow or resolution."

Miss Marchrose glanced up quickly at the last words, and although it was too dark for him to see her expression, Sir Julian again felt with certainty that some inexplicable telepathy had conveyed to him her thought.

"She is remembering Clarence Isbister," he told himself in a flash.

She spoke quietly enough.

"Yes, I know what you mean by that atmospheric tension—a sort of awful, unspoken sense of disaster and yet nothing happening. Only everything is happening, inside, and everyone knows it without being able to define it."

"Give me a good honest earthquake," said Mark Easter.

"I'm with you, Mark," Julian agreed.

"A tangible misfortune is nothing, compared to those perfectly indefinable indications of disturbance on what I suppose we may call the mental plane."

"A thing you can't lay hold of," said Mark, translating into his own phraseology.

"Those are much the worst," Miss Marchrose repeated, with conviction. "Sometimes I wonder if, years and years hence, when things are very much more advanced, those weapons, belonging to what Sir Julian called the mental plane, will come to be the only ones used."

"It would simplify war."

"I wonder," said Julian. "Atmosphere is a powerful weapon."

There was a silence as they trudged on steadily.

"On the whole," was Sir Julian's summing-up, "the big calamities such as battle, murder, and sudden death, are no longer essential to constitute crisis. The same reactions in humanity's present stage of development are produced without any visible action or events. Our consciousness has shifted to a more complex level."

"A sign of the evolution of the race?"

"Well, yes. It implies a greater responsiveness to the invisible event."

"Certainly," said Miss Marchrose, "it is easier to cope with the obvious, symbolised, let us say, by telegrams, or your good honest earthquake."

Mark Easter laughed.

"Telegrams and earthquakes meet with more sympathy, and certainly with more assistance, from one's neighbours, than any amount of atmospheric pressure," said he.

Miss Marchrose laughed too, but the conviction remained with Julian that she had inwardly recalled a connection between their discussion and that story, whatever the rights of it might be, that linked her name to that of Captain Clarence Isbister.

As they neared Culmhayes, traversing deeply sunken lanes and an occasional windswept field, Iris and Mr. Garrett fell further and further behind.

It was obvious that the creator of "Why, Ben!" preferred her reversions to the soil in the figurative sense of the words.

Occasional encouragement from her escort floated disjointedly, and rather with an effect of breathlessness, upon the cold air.

"… Should like to show you our own Highland peat bogs … our native heath … us Kelts …"

It was evident that fatigue was playing havoc with the purity of Mr. Garrett's English.

"Iris isn't used to walking," Mark observed rather apologetically, "and you've come a long way."

"I hope she isn't too tired. It was my doing, I love getting out to Salt Marsh."

"I know you do," said Mark gently. "I wish you could get away from Culmouth more often."

Mark was always interested.

Therein, Julian reflected, lay the half of his charm.

"Did Iris come for you to the College this afternoon?"

"No, I called for her on my way out, but she's been up to the College quite often, and wants to learn typewriting. I should like to teach her myself if Mr. Fuller will let me."

"Fuller will let you arrange anything that you like, and think best, only you've got enough to do already. I don't know how you get through it all."

Miss Marchrose uttered neither the meaningless protestations nor the pseudo-heroic acceptances habitually reserved for such intimations of indispensability. She said, "I enjoy it thoroughly, you know. Miss Easter brought your children to the College to-day, which created a diversion."

Mark uttered a rather incoherent sound, not inexpressive of dismay.

"Dare I ask how my children comported themselves?"

"They were quite good."

"Poor things!" said Mark, with a half-laugh. "They are not often quite good. The Rector's daughter is only with them for an hour or two in the mornings, and she complains that Ruthie is very noisy and intractable, and then Sarah has them more or less for the rest of the day; but she has no proper control over them, and the boy is always in disgrace. I don't quite know what he does."

The vastness of the field of conjecture thus opened up apparently held Miss Marchrose silent.

"Iris is very kind to them, but she spoils Ruthie, on the whole. And really, you know," said Mark apologetically, "I think Ruthie is the more in need of being sat upon of the pair."

Miss Marchrose laughed, but she made no endearing pretence of a tender-heartedness roused to rebellion at the idea of the requisite discipline.

Sir Julian reflected that, however thoroughly she might be aware of the peculiar circumstances governing Mark's domestic arrangements, she had at all events no intention of making capital out of them by a display of sentimental interest in Mark's singularly unattractive progeny.

Edna's Cassandra-like prophecies of the danger threatening Mark Easter's peace of mind recurred to him, and he felt vaguely uneasy. The two beside him were talking with a complete ease that denoted at least a very secure sense of sympathy, although Julian's perceptions could detect no undercurrent of deeper emotion.

At Culmhayes, the light streaming from the open door revealed Miss Marchrose with a fresh, vivid colour that became her infinitely, and eyes full of gaiety and animation.

Julian ordered tea and was conscious of a perfectly distinct relief at the absence of Edna's habitual kind, pervasive welcome. He was aware that, had his wife been present, the tea-party would not have prolonged itself as it did over the fire in the library; still less would Iris's small, piping soprano have largely monopolised the conversation with anecdotal gush relative to the inspiration, production, and reception of "Why, Ben!"

And yet Julian, in despite of his almost unlimited disesteem for the masterpiece in question, listened to its creator's artless self-advertisement altogether contentedly, idly watching, as he did so, the firelight play on the rather saturnine face of Mr. Douglas Garrett, punctuating with portentous movements of the head and assenting monosyllables the discourse of his prettily idiotic disciple in the realms of realism. Watching also the almost motionless gaze which Mark Easter's blue eyes kept turned towards the shadow in which stood the great armchair, beside which he had drawn his own.

Miss Marchrose was leaning back, almost invisible in the flickering firelight that supplemented the distant electricity over the deserted tea equipage. Sir Julian could hardly see her, but from time to time he heard her speak, and thought again that her voice, with vibrations and intonations full of harmony, was sufficiently arresting to constitute a charm superior to that of physical beauty.

Iris, fluffy and brilliant both at once, actually failed to rouse in him that irritated scorn for her absurdity which almost invariably overpowered his pleasure in her extreme prettiness. Even her literary pretensions sounded less outrageous than usual in that assembly of which the peace and friendly well-being seemed to Julian's acute sensitiveness to be almost tangible entities. He did not seek to define to himself the most unwonted kindliness with which Iris Easter actually caused him to regard her when she suddenly spoke in praise of Miss Marchrose's singing, and said that she would like to hear her again.

"'Maxwelton's braes are bonny,'" Mark hummed under his breath.

"I'll sing it for you again, some day," said Miss Marchrose. And although she spoke quite lazily, without turning her head, in that moment Sir Julian realised that his latent compassion for the possible victim of a misplaced attraction was not destined to be called forth by his friend, by light-hearted, easy-going Mark Easter, but by Miss Marchrose, whom Fairfax Fuller had called "as hard as nails."

It was seven o'clock before they left Culmhayes.

"Mark, we shall be late for dinner," said his sister. "Not that it matters very much, since Douglas is coming to dinner, and he'll be just as late as we are. We're not dressing."

Mr. Garrett raised himself rather reluctantly out of his armchair.

"Oh," said Iris, on a sudden piercing note of inspiration, to Miss Marchrose, "do come too. I'm sure you'll be too late for anything at that awful farm place, and we should so like to have you. Then you could sing 'Annie Laurie' for Mark."

Miss Marchrose declined the invitation in spite of the one-sided angle of solicitation to which Iris inclined her golden head, but Julian thought that she seemed pleased at the younger girl's very evident cordiality.

He listened next moment with a surprise half-shadowed by a vague unformulated suspicion, as Iris suddenly urged upon her brother the necessity for his escorting Miss Marchrose to her lodgings.

Extravagant solicitude for the welfare of a member of her own sex was no habitual foible of Miss Easter's, and for a moment Julian wondered whether she thought herself to be doing her brother a service.

Miss Marchrose, however, very decidedly declined all companionship on her short walk, and Mark showed no disposition to force the point.

Sir Julian said nothing at all, but went with the guests to the gates of the drive.

"Ta-ta!" said Miss Easter in preposterous valediction, raising herself on tiptoes, and clinging in an engaging manner to Mr. Garrett's elbow.

"Good night," said Miss Marchrose generally, and turned upon her way.

Sir Julian accompanied her to the farm without evoking any protestation but a laughing one, and she told him how much she had enjoyed the afternoon.

"I'm glad," said Sir Julian.

Walking back alone to Culmhayes, he wondered whether he had spoken the truth.

His gladness, at all events, was considerably modified by the recollection of that odd flash of illumination which had come to him.

"It is no business of mine," Julian told himself, shrugging his shoulders with a timely recollection of his favourite bugbear, officiousness. And all through the solitary evening, and his exceeding appreciation of such solitude, he thought about the business which was none of his.

IX

Perhaps the closest bond of union between Julian Rossiter and his wife now consisted in the common dismay which invaded them when Ruthie and Ambrose Easter thought fit to inflict themselves, uninvited, upon the Culmhayes establishment.

On the morning after Edna's return from London, she was writing in the morning-room, when a respectfully resentful servant informed her that Miss Ruthie and Master Ambrose were at the front door, declaring an urgent necessity for seeing Lady Rossiter.

"Tell them I am busy writing," said Edna hastily, certainly not pausing for the application of her favourite, "Is it kind, is it wise, is it true?" since it was neither the first nor the last, and eventually turned out to be far from compliant with even the second regulation, since the visitors, accepting Horber's rebuff with deceptive quiet, immediately made their way round to the window of the morning-room, where they startled Lady Rossiter considerably by suddenly appearing, with flattened noses and glaring eyeballs, against the pane.

She made imperious signs at them with an ivory penholder, without avail. Unable to contemplate the prospect of pursuing her morning avocations under the mouthing pantomime by which Ruthie sought to convey her desire for immediate admission, Lady Rossiter flung open the window, shivering at the rush of the raw morning cold.

"Good morning, children," she said forbearingly.

All Lady Rossiter's Christianity was required to induce her to accept as even faintly probable the ultimate evolution of a Divine Spark from the personality of Ruthie. But she always felt bound to act upon such an assumption, if only because Sir Julian so firmly and completely rejected it.

"I thought Horber told you I was busy, Ruthie. I can't see either of you now, you must run home again."

"Auntie Iris is here, too," said Ruthie triumphantly.

Lady Rossiter did not relegate the value of Auntie Iris's society to the abysmal depths of contempt to which Sir Julian had long since uncharitably consigned it, partly because her principles never allowed her any point of view other than one consciously superior to that of her husband's, and partly because Auntie Iris had always been prone to seek her advice with a certain gushing deference that was not without its appeal. Nevertheless, she received with a very apparent absence of elation the announcement of her young neighbour's proximity.

"Where is Auntie Iris?"

"She is with Sir Julian. He met us all in the drive."

"Did he tell you to come up to the house and find me?"

"Oh no, we came all of ourselves. We've got such a piece of news."

Lady Rossiter was reminded of an earlier occasion, when the heralds of Auntie Iris had thrust themselves unbidden into her presence.

"Has 'Why, Ben!' gone into a second edition?"

She had not reckoned with the proneness of a new interest to oust an old one from youthful minds.

Ambrose and Ruthie both looked at her with the lacklustre gaze and hanging under-jaw of utter unresponsiveness.

"I can't keep the window open any longer, it's too cold. Run back to Auntie Iris, now."

"But we haven't told you the news."

"Quick, then."

"You must guess first," said Ruthie loudly and inexorably.

Ambrose thrust his large pale face forward and unexpectedly snatched the dallying announcement from the lips of his sister, perhaps from a well-grounded fear that it must otherwise be uttered from without an abruptly-closed window.

"Auntie Iris is going to marry Mr. Garrett!"

Lady Rossiter was left no time in which to utter possible congratulations, as the momentary advantage reft from his senior by Ambrose was dearly paid for by him in the gale of buffetings to which she instantly subjected him.

"Ruthie! Let go of your little brother this moment! How dare you?"

Slap!

Scream!

Bang! Slap!

"*Ruth!* I am ashamed of you."

Lady Rossiter clung to the curtain with one strong white hand and endeavoured to reach and to separate these makers of a hideous brawl with the other, but was placed at a disadvantage by the extreme probability of overbalancing herself and contributing an anti-climax to the situation.

"I'll pay you out, Peekaboo, I will," bellowed Ruthie viciously, and abundantly making good the threat as she uttered it.

Nor did she cease belabouring her victim until he had torn himself from her grasp and fled back to the security of the avenue as fast as his short legs could cover the ground.

Edna raised her person from its attitude of perilous incline.

A more unprecedented opportunity for preaching the great rule of love, with the text, as it were, under her own window, had never yet come to rouse that passion for propaganda which is so vital a characteristic of those who know least of human nature.

It may definitely be assumed that Edna, gravely compelling the representative of a younger generation into the morning-room, and confronting her with earnest tenderness, was more bent upon delivering herself of beautiful truths than upon ascertaining their applicability or otherwise to the individuality of her exceedingly unpromising convert.

"Ruthie, Ruthie, do you know that cruelty and violence are the very worst sins that anyone can commit? To hurt somebody else is to hurt one's own soul. … You are sinning against the greatest law in the whole world when you behave as you did just now—the Law of Love."

Ruthie was silent, and Lady Rossiter, with a fleeting thought of what an admirable mother she would have made, drew the child gently to her.

"Don't you know that we all contribute, by everything we do and say, to the good and bad in the world? When you are angry, you send out black, ugly thoughts that help to destroy all the good and beautiful harmony that God has put into this lovely world."

Ruthie cast an enquiring glance out of the window at the bleak, grey sky, perfectly bare borders and rather uncompromising Scotch firs which were alone visible at the moment of this lovely world.

"When you have gentle, loving, beautiful thoughts," said Lady Rossiter eloquently, "they send out little wordless messages into the air and go to join the great Divine chorus of Love that is going on everywhere without stopping. You know we are all giving out something all the time?"

Ruthie for the first time looked faintly interested.

"Am I giving?"

"Yes, dear, that's what I'm trying to tell you about. That's why little Ruthie must—"

"Is Daddy?"

"Certainly."

"Is Peekaboo?"

"Yes," said Lady Rossiter, beginning to wonder if a *catalogue raisonné* of the Easter family and its connections was to be unrolled before her.

"Even Ambrose is not too little to—"

"Do you give?"

"I try to do so, Ruthie, certainly."

"Does Sir Julian give?"

Lady Rossiter not impossibly struggled for a moment with an unhallowed impulse before answering.

"I hope so. But will you try to remember what I've been telling you, Ruthie? It is not our business to think about whether other people give out in the right way or not—never, never judge others," said Edna parenthetically. "But I do want you to remember about Love. That it is the biggest thing in all the world and that nothing is quite so bad and ugly as to be angry, or unkind, or unloving. Love is what matters most, always."

Miss Easter, *more suo*, contrived to combine a sort of perverted relevance with indecent vulgarity in her bored reply.

"Mr. Garrett kissed Auntie Iris this morning. Me and Peekaboo were hiding in the cowhouse and we saw. Auntie Iris said it was love."

Lady Rossiter received in silence this singular application of the Divine Law which she had promulgated so often and so indiscriminately that she had long ago come to look upon it as her own production.

"What have the children been doing?" said Mark's voice at the window. "Lady Rossiter, I'm afraid they've been worrying you dreadfully. I'm ashamed of them."

"Come in, Mark," said Edna, not without relief. "I hope, after what I've been saying to her, that Ruthie is going to make it up with Ambrose at once."

Mark lifted his daughter out of the window and despatched her in immediate search of her injured junior.

He leant against the low sill of the open window as Lady Rossiter came towards it.

She had long ago formed the habit, which she would not have admitted as being exceedingly agreeable to her, of taking it as her right to advise and question Mark Easter on all personal matters connected with his wifeless household. She belonged, indeed, to the class of those women who have a perfectly genuine love of approaching any admittedly *scabreux* topics which intimately and painfully touch the life of another—a form of prurience sometimes decorated with such titles as "the tender touch of a good, pure woman."

"Poor little Ruthie! I've tried to talk to her a little bit. It's motherhood that's lacking in their lives, Mark."

It might reasonably be supposed that such motherhood as the unfortunate victim to alcohol who had partnered Mark's few, unhappy years of matrimony had afforded to his children was as well out of their way, but Mark made no such unsympathetic rejoinder. He gazed at Lady Rossiter with the straight, candid look that had never held anything but honest gratitude and admiration for Sir Julian's beautiful wife.

"They are getting older," he said disconsolately, "and they do not seem to improve."

Mark paused, as though weighing this extremely lenient description of his objectionable family.

"Ambrose can go to school in a year or so," said Lady Rossiter hopefully.

"I suppose so, but the worst of it is that he really is delicate. Now, Ruthie is as strong as a horse, but then I never did like the idea of sending a little girl to school."

"I can't see any alternative," Edna said decidedly. "She will have to be properly educated, and a governess, in the circumstances, is out of the question."

"I suppose so," doubtfully answered Mark.

"It's very unlikely one could get a good daily one, down here, and a resident one—you're a young man still, Mark, and people would talk," said Edna, seizing instinctively on the aspect of the question that it would afford her the most enjoyment to discuss. Had Mark been less than extraordinarily single-minded, it would also have afforded him the maximum of discomfort in listening to her.

"You see, the circumstances are altogether exceptional, and make things very hard for you, I'm afraid. You are a married man still, and there are always dangers. Well, you know as well as I do that there are things one can't put into words," said Edna, with no intention of being taken *au pied de la lettre*.

"And Mark, there's another thing. Ruthie is old enough to begin asking questions about her poor mother. What are you going to do about telling her?"

"I don't know," Mark said simply. "I've never thought about it."

Lady Rossiter gave a sort of musical groan.

"For all one knows, servants and people may have told her already, and it should have been so tenderly, so delicately done!"

"No, no," said Mark. "Sarah is a good creature, though she's rough; she has always been loyalty itself."

"I'm sure she has; but after all, Mark, it is a thing which everybody round here knows. Ruthie may hear something any day. If ever she does, remember that you can always send her straight to me. Although it hurts so to dwell on those sad, ugly things, I would always put all that aside if I could help you or yours, Mark."

Edna eyed the recipient of these anticipated sacrifices with a long, compassionate look. If a deep, secret gratification held its place in that thoughtful gaze, Mark Easter was not likely to be any more aware of it than was Edna herself.

"Tell me," she exclaimed, as though struck by a sudden thought, "I'm right in thinking that everybody does know? There's no mystery, no conspiracy of silence about it all?"

"Not that I know of," said Mark, frankly astonished. "You know, you couldn't expect people to come up and ask me how I like it, or anything of that sort, could you?"

Edna's gravity did not for an instant relax at the rueful extravagance of the suggestion.

"I don't know if I ought to say this, Mark—but I think I must. One can't let one's friends risk shipwreck just for lack of a little moral courage."

It might well have been supposed that any shipwreck destined to Mark Easter had long since passed into the realm of accomplished fact, but it was evident that Edna had in view other and more pressing possibilities of disaster.

"You've thought of the trouble, the wretchedness that might be entailed on others, and the self-reproach to yourself, if there was any want of openness about the whole miserable question?"

"But I don't think there is any want of openness," said Mark blankly.

"Mark, forgive me. You don't resent my speaking about it all? You know I do it only because I'm so dreadfully sorry, and couldn't bear that there should be anything further …"

"You are everything that is kind," said Mark steadily, "and you and Sir Julian are the best friends I have in the world."

Edna could have dispensed with the inclusion of her husband's name.

It served, in fact, to stem her tide of warning, the more especially as she felt more or less convinced that Mark was not making the intended application of her words.

She gave smilingly graceful congratulations to the newly-betrothed Iris, the more strongly tinged with motherliness from her consciousness of recent success with Ruthie, and even endured a prolonged wringing of her hand from Mr. Garrett, who had followed his new lodestar to Culmhayes.

But that evening, after a silence more fraught with thoughtfulness even than usual, and in consequence even more studiously ignored than usual by Sir Julian, she said to him abruptly:

"Have you any idea whether Clarence Isbister's jilt knows the true facts of the case about Mark?"

Few things could be more designedly insulting than Lady Rossiter's practice of invariably alluding to Miss Marchrose in her capacity of a wrecker of hearts. Julian, however, replied imperturbably:

"Do you mean the dipsomaniac?"

Lady Rossiter liked the term no better than her husband liked that of "jilt," as applied to Miss Marchrose, and as she would not be guilty of making use of it, she merely inclined her head gravely.

"Because, Julian, if that woman knows into what she is drifting, then it will be a case of Clarence over again, and I am going to save my poor Mark from her. And if she *doesn't* know, I am going to tell her, whatever it costs me to speak about it, that Mark is a married man."

X

Edna had no immediate opportunity of putting her altruistic designs into execution. Miss Marchrose was not easily available, and Mark Easter was reported to be less frequently at the College in consequence of the business devolving upon him in connection with Iris's approaching marriage.

"I don't know why Iris is in such a hurry, but they are going to be married at the beginning of the new year," Lady Rossiter told her husband. "Mr. Garrett is going to stay on down here."

"What an ass!"

Lady Rossiter always looked a little pained at a flippant or unkind reference to anyone. She did so now, and replied gently:

"He is very young and first love is a very beautiful thing. He naturally wants to stay where Iris is."

To which Sir Julian responded, with an even greater intensity of conviction in his voice than before:

"*What* an ass!"

The chief manifestations indulged in by first love, as personified by Miss Easter and Mr. Garrett, were perhaps not altogether unaccountable for Sir Julian's lack of enthusiasm.

To their habitual attitude of mutual admiration they now added an apparently inexhaustible stock of recondite jests and allusions utterly unintelligible to anybody but themselves.

When Lady Rossiter made civil enquiry of Mr. Garrett as to the length of time he could afford to remain away from his journalistic work in London, he scarcely troubled to answer her, but directed a meaning look towards Iris and said darkly:

"Ah, what would the old man say to *that*? It tallies quite oddly with that letter we were speaking of, doesn't it?"

"Yes, indeed," said Iris obligingly. "You know what I said about telepathy, too, Douglas."

"What?" Lady Rossiter not unnaturally wanted to know.

Iris's reply was unsatisfactory rather than informative.

"Oh, just something foolish Douglas and I had been discussing. He's *too* silly sometimes, you know."

"You forget our old friend McTavish," retorted Douglas, with an air of dry repartee that would have been more effective had anyone, with the presumable exception of Iris, been in possession of any clue as to the identity of McTavish.

An appreciative laugh from Miss Easter rippled lightly through the rather embarrassed silence.

"Oh, poor McTavish! You're always flourishing that creature at me!"

"Who or what is McTavish?" said Mark, in a tone which voiced the inexplicable but growing feeling of umbrage which was invading the minds of the assembly in regard to the unknown.

Douglas and Iris exchanged mirthful looks that seemed charged with meaning.

"Oh, McTavish! He's a friend of Douglas—a sort of friend. I suppose you would call him a friend, Douglas?"

"Well, hardly *my* friend, perhaps."

"Well, perhaps hardly!"

Iris fell into transports of laughter.

"A friend of a friend of yours!" she gasped.

At this sudden introduction of a brand-new element into their exchange of witticisms, Mr. Garrett's expression of rather satirical humour relaxed also into unrestrained laughter.

"We Scotch lads are accused of having no sense of fun," he ejaculated, in accents broken with mirth, "but, my certie, a real pawky bit of Scotch humour like that makes a perfect child of me!"

It was not often that Mr. Garrett relapsed into dialect, and his auditors were left to conclude that extreme wit and point must have characterised the reference which had left them so entirely cold.

"Half the time I don't know what they're driving at," Mark disconsolately told Lady Rossiter, but he added that Iris seemed to be very happy and that Garrett was fortunately not dependent upon his profession. That this was vaguely literary was all that could be gathered by those not in Mr. Garrett's confidence, but he now assumed a more than proprietary tone in discussing "Why, Ben! A Story of the Sexes."

"I can't help thinking, Iris, that your next novel will certainly bear an impress of greater maturity," Mr. Garrett academically observed, "when you have entered upon the second phase of a woman's deeper experience."

Iris looked as though she were undecided whether to blush or to look extremely modern and detached.

She finally produced a rather unconvincingly coy flutter of the eyelids, which committed her to nothing.

The second phase of a woman's deeper experience was to be entered upon in the beginning of January, and Iris spent a great deal of her time in going backwards and forwards between London and Devonshire. She had developed an enthusiasm for Miss Marchrose, and refused to give up her course of typewriting lessons at the College, where her presence produced the slight stirring of interest always provoked by a bride-elect.

Even Lady Rossiter, although her opinion of Miss Easter's conquest was far from being an exalted one, displayed a certain deference to the interesting situation by driving her into Culmouth and talking all the way, in a very candid and enlightening manner, of the sacrifices entailed by matrimony.

At the College, Lady Rossiter, as though struck by a sudden thought, said that she would come upstairs with Iris and seek the Lady Superintendent.

"A very little gratifies them, and I always like to keep in close touch with the staff. I must arrange for one of my little Sunday tea-parties next week, and you must come and help me entertain them all, Iris."

The social status, *ipso facto*, conferred upon the wearer of an engagement- or a wedding-ring, by whomsoever bestowed, is curiously typical of the point of view of certain feminine minds. It might be doubted whether Miss Iris Easter, unattached, would have been considered in any way competent to help the *chatelaine* of Culmhayes in her entertainments.

Iris, however, was never lacking in responsiveness.

"I shall adore that, dear Lady Rossiter. I think Miss Marchrose is simply too sweet for words, you know, and Mark admires her awfully."

Lady Rossiter was only too well aware of it, but the observation served to strengthen the decision that she had already taken.

"This is my last lesson," Iris said sentimentally, as they went up the stone stairs. "I shall be able to help Douglas, of course, so much more, now that I can really type. Oh, Mr. Cooper, good morning!"

The young man returned cheerful greetings. "You'll find Miss Marchrose in the High Speed, if you're looking for her. I'm on my way downstairs."

"I have not been in to any of the classrooms for a long while," Lady Rossiter said graciously. "What is happening in the High Speed?"

"A test, I believe, Lady Rossiter. Perhaps you would care to come in and have a look. A stimulus," said Cooper, with great gallantry, "is always desirable. I will escort you if I may. I'm afraid I always go upstairs two steps at a time. Sometimes three."

The High Speed room was fairly well occupied. Half a dozen young girls, between the ages of fifteen and twenty, a couple of middle-aged women, a precocious-looking little boy with eyes that seemed ready to pop out of his head, and several half-grown youths, sat at the wooden desks. Miss Marchrose stood at the top of the room, book in hand, and turned as Cooper opened the door.

It was an understood thing that the wife of the principal director had the right of entry throughout the College precincts, and Miss Marchrose, whatever her feelings, had no alternative but to direct the disposal of chairs next to her own rostrum.

"You mustn't be nervous," Lady Rossiter said to her smilingly, in an undertone that might have answered its purpose better but for the absolute silence pervading the room. "I've heard these tests given before, and I always think it's nervous work for the reader. I know I should be in terror myself of coming across quite unpronounceable words. But you probably know the book. What is it?"

Miss Marchrose showed her the text-book in silence, and Lady Rossiter, though she smiled and nodded at it, did no more than glance at the covers.

"This is the speed test," Miss Marchrose announced clearly. "Are you ready?"

Nobody answered, but the tension in the room was obvious, and the little boy in front squared his shoulders, bending his head forward until it almost touched his note-book, and grasping a short pencil in a stubby hand of which each fingernail was quite neatly and symmetrically outlined in black.

"In the United Kingdom there are over 500 railway companies, the lines of which … are worked or leased by about forty of the principal companies. … It was in the first half of the nineteenth century that the majority of the great undertakings received parliamentary sanction. …"

Miss Marchrose's voice was quite level and her enunciation distinct. She varied neither her intonation nor the rate at which she read from the printed page before her, already carefully subdivided into phrases.

Most of the shorthand-writers seemed able to take down the test—a shade behind the reader, however, so that their pencils were never altogether off the paper. The youths in the back of the room displayed greater facility, sometimes able to pause with the end of a sentence and relax an aching right hand. Only the little boy dashed down his dots and outlines as the words left Miss Marchrose's lips, and sat with pencil impudently poised in the air during the regulated pause separating each phrase. Both the elder women in the class, who might have been of the less superior type of hotel-clerk or assistant manageress, came to early grief.

One of them laid her pencil down outright after the first five-and-twenty words, shaking her head, and looking resentfully at the aggressively proficient child in front of her; and the other one, though scribbling frantically, her pencil almost piercing the paper, with a painfully flushed face and a hand that shook from strain, was quite evidently unable to keep up with the dictation, and was, moreover, scribbling down a large proportion of the words in almost illegible longhand.

Iris Easter watched the class with very evident interest and amusement, and smiled at the precocious little boy until she had extorted from him in return a significantly triumphant grin.

Lady Rossiter also looked at the class with that gravely observant gaze that, more often than not, denotes complete absorption in something quite else, and thought about Miss Marchrose.

She also glanced at her once or twice, as she stood facing the room, very erect, with her eyes on the book, and with no trace of shyness or nervousness in her bearing.

Edna, whose very decided beauty was of the type that seldom or never varies, could on this occasion look at Miss Marchrose with complete satisfaction, and even ask herself whether that woman could possibly be a day under thirty-five. Neither the strong sunlight of a frosty January morning nor the contrast with Iris Easter showed her to advantage.

Her voice stopped.

There was a general, inarticulate sound of relief throughout the room.

"When you have transcribed the test into longhand," said Miss Marchrose serenely, "please give your papers in at the desk, Classroom I, and for the benefit of those who have not done a speed test before I may add that the students must not assist one another in the transcriptions."

The class gathered up note-books and pencils and left the room, with much scraping of benches and shuffling of feet.

"Oh, Miss Marchrose, I do think you're clever," was the remark made by Iris, rather unnecessarily, to Lady Rossiter's way of thinking.

"Will they all pass that awful test?"

"Oh no; 'getting it back,' as they call it, is the part they seem to find most difficult. Some of the less intelligent ones seem to have absolutely no sense of the meaning of words. If the shorthand outline isn't clear, they guess at the word and put in almost anything, whether it makes sense or not. Of course, that's where the majority of stenographers do fail."

"But if they make those little scrabbles clearly enough, then it's all right?" said Miss Easter.

"Yes, that's where the younger ones score. The children nearly always learn much faster than the older ones and make the outlines more clearly, and then they can transcribe easily enough, whether they understand the meaning of what they've taken down or not."

"Oh, that awful little boy with the eyes!"

"He'll pass," said Miss Marchrose, laughing. "He's a dreadful child."

"Iris, dear," said Lady Rossiter softly, "when do you have your lesson?"

Thus obliquely recalled to the immediate duties of her state of life, Miss Marchrose conducted her pupil to a small classroom where the Remington machine awaited her, and in front of which Iris took her seat with obvious and immense satisfaction in the flashing of her engagement-ring as her small hands moved backward and forward on the keyboard,

"If you don't have to stay with her while she's practising, I should like to have a look at your own office," said Lady Rossiter very sweetly. "I so often wonder if you don't find it cold in this weather."

"It is very cold indeed, but as I keep the window wide open, that's my own fault," Miss Marchrose answered brusquely.

But she led the way into her room and prepared to shut the window, which was, as she had said, wide open.

"Oh, but don't! There can never be too much of God's own fresh air to please me," Lady Rossiter exclaimed, at the same time fastening the high collar of her fur coat. "Besides, I know you get so little out-of-doors you must want all the sunshine possible. Tell me, do you like your work here?"

"Yes."

"That's rather wonderful of you. Mr. Easter, our agent, you know, and also my very dear friend, tells me that you work so well and conscientiously. I am sure you like working for Mr. Easter: everyone does."

"Yes."

"I'm so very, very glad about dear little Iris and this engagement. Quite suited to each other in every sort of way. After all, deep can only call to deep in very exceptional cases, and they are both so young and happy. Besides, it will be a great weight off her brother's mind."

Miss Marchrose did not even return her former unbrilliant monosyllable, and Lady Rossiter was obliged to persevere.

"There had been so much sadness already, there—of course, he never talks of it, except to me sometimes—but one has to tread, oh so lightly and delicately! It is all past now, as far as such things can be past when there are constant grievous reminders, but he and I went through it all side by side at the time—shoulder to shoulder."

Edna paused, and looked rather resentfully at her unresponsive auditor. Evidently the warning of which she stood in such need was to be delivered without any assistance from herself.

She looked full at the Lady Superintendent, who gazed back at her with calm hostility in her eyes.

"You know that Mark Easter is a married man?" Lady Rossiter said slowly and very distinctly, as though determined, which indeed she was, that the fact should be made clear beyond the possibility of misunderstanding. "His wife, unfortunate woman—God forbid that I should condemn her!—is in a home for inebriates. But she is still alive, and may live for years."

Silence ensued, and Lady Rossiter considerately averted her eyes. She wondered for a moment whether she should lay her hand upon the other's shoulder with a silent pressure of sympathy, but decided that to do so would be a tacit assumption of facts better unrecognised.

Then, for she was of acute perceptions, she became subtly aware that disturbance was in the air.

Miss Marchrose had whitened, quite perceptibly, and then Lady Rossiter received the odd impression that some weapon of vengeance had been seized upon by her, suspended for an instant, and tacitly rejected as unworthy.

The impression was instantly intensified when Miss Marchrose spoke at last, although she merely said, "I have to speak to Mr. Fuller. Forgive me if I use the telephone for one moment."

Hastily and unwisely, Edna tested her own sudden suspicion.

"Did you know Mark Easter's story already?"

Miss Marchrose looked down as though from an infinite height, her mobile face purposely supercilious.

"Oh yes," said she, her voice full of deliberate scorn.

Edna did not ask from whence the information had emanated, since she was suddenly aware, with all the certainty of intuition, that Miss Marchrose had undoubtedly derived her knowledge of Mark Easter's affairs direct from himself.

XI

As Lady Rossiter proceeded on her way downstairs, leaving Iris to the completion of her lesson, she was waylaid by young Cooper.

"I've been waiting for you, in the hope that you would spare me one moment, Lady Rossiter. There was a little matter about which the staff wanted me to consult you."

Such a reference appealed to Edna at any time, and came as balm to the present state of her spirit, at the moment so seriously discomposed that she had been obliged to repeat to herself more than once, as she went downstairs:

> "Still lovingly to bear a fool,
> Nor speak till wrath has time to cool,
> And thus live out my golden rule."

"I always have time for the business of the College, as you know," she responded graciously. "What is it?"

"Why, the staff thought—the idea, as a matter of fact, originated with me, and they have all taken it up quite enthusiastically—we thought that we should very much like, in view of our long connection with Mr. Mark Easter, to make a little presentation to Miss Iris Easter, in honour of her wedding. Just a small affair, you know—subscribed for by the staff of the College."

"But how charming of you all! Only—no one must be put to serious expense. I am sure Miss Easter would be dreadfully distressed if *that* happened."

Cooper looked rather offended.

"Certainly not, Lady Rossiter. I think you may rely upon my judgment not to make excessive demands. But, of course, if you think anyone else had better collect the money, I shall resign the job into other hands with the very greatest pleasure."

Edna hastily uttered the necessary disclaimers.

"It was suggested," said Cooper, still with reserve in his voice, "that you would be so very kind as to assist at the presentation, which might perhaps be made the occasion for some small gathering such as we had last year at Christmas. I find that the members of the staff are quite anxious for it."

Lady Rossiter remembered, without much enthusiasm, a New Year party at which the staff of the Commercial and Technical College had entertained their directors, pupils and acquaintances, in a large classroom decorated with bunting for the occasion.

"That is a most excellent idea," she said slowly, partly because it sounded sympathetic and partly in order to gain time. "But perhaps Miss Easter might feel rather shy in the presence of so many people who would be strange to her. What about a little informal tea-party? But, of course, all that can be settled later. What are you thinking of giving her?"

"Nothing has been actually decided upon, though *I* should suggest some little thing in silver. The ladies always like silver. I remember selecting a wedding-present for a lady friend," said Cooper, looking slightly sentimental, "that proved highly acceptable. A silver serviette-ring it was, with her initials—her *new* initials—engraved upon it."

"I'm sure it was delightful, and Miss Easter is certain to like anything that you all choose."

"We all know her, and she's been here quite a lot lately, and of course Mr. Mark Easter does a great deal for the staff, and we're all very fond of him," added Cooper, with a sudden outburst of naturalness.

Edna, in common with quite a number of other people, always underwent, more or less unconsciously, a slight stirring of resentment at any spontaneous tribute to someone else's popularity.

It was perhaps this which moved her to a rather thin and repressive smile.

"It will gratify Mr. Easter very much indeed, I know. And after all, it's the thought that is of real value—not the offering. Do tell the staff how very much I hope they will let me hear any further ideas."

"Thanks very much, Lady Rossiter," said Cooper, rather stiffly.

Edna, dissatisfied, reflected for a moment.

"Couldn't you all come out to Culmhayes and talk it over with me?" she enquired, as by an inspiration. "We might form a little committee, and go into ways and means, and perhaps I could find out some trifle that would please Miss Easter, and let you know. How would that be?"

"It's very kind of you. I myself always prefer to have these things on a business footing," said Cooper, looking cheered. "I am essentially a business man."

"Then what about Sunday afternoon? Perhaps you and Miss Farmer—and what about Mr. Fuller?"

If young Cooper could have answered all too certainly, "what about Fuller" he refrained from any such disastrous candour. But he gave his grateful pledge of coming to Culmhayes on the following Sunday with as many of the staff as were considered necessary to form a small committee. Cooper was insistent upon the necessity for such.

"You notice that I like things done in order?" said he.

"Yes, indeed," murmured Edna. "Here is Miss Easter coming downstairs, so I suppose the lesson is over, and we must be going. Good-bye, Mr. Cooper—I shan't forget."

"Let me see you down. Hark!" said Cooper, with an expression of animated interest.

Iris and Lady Rossiter both paused.

"Did you hear my knee-joint crack just now? That was my knee. I put it out at football, months ago, and since then it cracks, like that."

And with this addition to the sum total of their general information, Edna and Miss Easter drove away from the College.

"Poor young man!" said Lady Rossiter leniently.

"Oh, the dear College! I wish my lessons hadn't come to an end, but of course I shan't have time now. Miss Marchrose is going to come and stay with us, later on—when—"

"When you're married?"

Iris put her head on one side.

"It is nice and generous of you to have taken a fancy to poor Miss Marchrose," said Lady Rossiter, who seldom divested the Lady Superintendent of the adjective. "But after all, there are one or two things to be considered. Your husband may not take a very great fancy to her."

Edna's warning would have tallied much more with her very real distrust of the proposed scheme had she omitted the word "not "in the last sentence.

Iris, however, answered confidently, "Oh, but Douglas will always like my friends, and I shall always like his. We have every single thing in common, you know."

Leaving Iris to her delusion, that wreathed her pretty, silly little face in dreamy smiles, Lady Rossiter leant back and indulged in reflections of her own. She was more tired than was usual with her, and her habitual serenity of mind was invaded by a certain discontent of which she did not seek to analyse the cause.

She looked at the hoar-frost, sparkling on the hedges, and at the chill blue of the sky, and perfunctorily told herself, as often before, "God's in His Heaven—all's right with the world"; recalled, in a vague and disjointed manner, fragments of R. L. Stevenson that she had often thought to be peculiarly applicable to herself, and remembered that two of her particular friends were a humble little dressmaker and a quaint old seafarer; she humorously adjured herself to "tink ob de blessings, children, tink ob de blessings." But all was of no avail. She felt saddened, inexplicably depressed.

For many years Edna Rossiter had believed that her strong suit, so to speak, was Love. She "gave out."

As a young girl, she had perhaps fancied, as young girls are prone to fancy, that only as the heroine of a *grande passion* could she fulfil herself. Her first love had disappointed her. A cheerful, beauty-loving young architect, he had failed to return adequate replies to the letters, pulsating with quotations from Laurence Hope, in which Edna had poured forth her soul during a temporary absence.

She began to doubt, to read the verses of Arthur Symons, and to think that only by suffering could she find herself. Even the breaking-off of her engagement, however, failed immediately to terminate the quest successfully.

"I have tried not to be bitter," was the keynote of Edna's twenties.

By the time she had reached the stage of quoting:

> "How many loved your moments of glad grace
>> And loved your beauty with love false or true,
>> But one man loved the pilgrim soul in you,
>> And loved the sorrows in your changing face—"

—lines which the majority of women read with such a singular sense of applicability to their own needs—Edna had met Sir Julian Rossiter.

She was a great deal more beautiful at nine-and-twenty than at nineteen, and she had, moreover, learnt to smile. Tragedy, in which she really excelled, had proved strangely unprovocative of interest in anyone but herself, and she had therefore been obliged to cultivate the large, grave serenity that forgets itself in the thought of others.

It was not this, however, which had caused Sir Julian to ask her to marry him.

Edna disliked the memory of the scene that had led to his proposal, although time and her own industry had draped the situation with much that it had lacked at the moment. She had met him on board ship, and her mother, a slightly vulgar woman who had always rather disliked the only one of her daughters whom she had not married off in early girlhood, had speedily discovered that the owner of Culmhayes was in need of a wife. Edna, who had so long and so vainly visualised herself as the ideal Héloise to an as yet unfound Abelard, had had time to become heartily sick of such barren dreams, and was by now prepared to relinquish them in favour of mere emancipation from spinsterhood and a restricted life.

For three of the endless days of a sea-voyage Sir Julian had appeared to be attracted by her, and on the fourth he had devoted himself to a blue-eyed widow, travelling second-class. The voyage was nearly over before the first-class passengers saw him again in their midst. Edna could remember still the evening before Dover was reached, when her mother, exasperated, had uttered the short, sudden gibe that had put into words the humiliating truth never before spoken between them.

She remembered still the despairing resentment that had seized upon her, at her realisation that such taunts, once uttered, may speedily become common, between people in constant proximity and without mutual respect.

Her rare tears had shaken her, and it was Sir Julian who had found her, crying in a solitary corner of the deck. Edna could remember—though never in her life did she willingly recall—that anger and misery together had made her give him, in reply to his urgent enquiry, something that very nearly approached to the raw, crude truth. And that night she had said to herself:

"Thank Heaven, I shall never see him again!"

The next morning he had asked her to marry him, making no protestations of passion such as she had once thought herself fated to evoke, but suggesting a mutual companionship, likely to prove of solace to both, and to release her from a situation which had become intolerable to her.

Julian's candour had humiliated her bitterly, for her one moment of envisaging the truth in all its bitterness had passed from her.

But she had accepted him.

She would not have believed it, had she been told that the evening of that self-betrayal, of which she thrust the memory away thenceforward, had witnessed the truest, most intimate relationship in which she and her husband were destined ever to stand towards one another.

The prosperous chatelaine of Culmhayes had had many years in which to forget the mortifications and disappointments of her pre-marriage days. She ruled an admirable household admirably, she "gave out," she discovered Nature, and she opposed a perpetual exhalation of large-hearted tolerance to the small shafts of rather indifferent satire that more and more formed the basis of Sir Julian's conjugal intercourse.

Edna indulged in no bitterness of resentment against her husband, except on the rare occasions when she, always unwillingly, remembered that chivalry and not love had prompted his offer of marriage to her. His frequent captiousness, his small verbal incivilities, his absence of any sympathy with her ideals, even his systematic reticence as to his personal thoughts and feelings, roused nothing in her beyond an appreciation of the opportunity that they provided for breadths of sunny-hearted charity. She was not an unhappy woman, and never made the mistake of calling herself one. Even the absence of children she regretted more for their own sakes than for hers, since she believed that her maternal instinct had become diverted into more universal and more spacious channels than could have been the case had it been exercised solely upon sons or daughters of her own.

That Sir Julian was "difficult "she never disguised from herself. He had, in fact, become rather more "difficult" year by year, and Edna had long since given up her early attempts to probe into his point of view. She came to the conclusion that Julian was inarticulate because he was unenlightened, that he liked "Jorrocks," and that he was permanently discontented because he had not enough to do and refused to envisage the deeper issues of life.

She reflected complacently sometimes that they had never had a quarrel—and remained unaware that the fact admirably measured the extent of their estrangement.

Lady Rossiter sighed at the end of her retrospect.

"Don't you like Miss Marchrose?" enquired Iris quite suddenly.

"But I wasn't thinking about her! What makes you ask?"

"I don't know," said Iris vaguely. "I've sometimes thought you didn't like her awfully much."

Lady Rossiter reflected before making any reply. She held the theory that the expression of an opinion should always be a well-considered matter, and was apt to say that words were like thistledown and might blow to unsuspected distances and in unforeseen directions.

There was, however, nothing of the airy quality of thistledown in her deliberately given answer.

"Miss Marchrose does not strike me as attractive," she said carefully, "but a young woman earning her own living is hardly to be judged by the rules that we should apply to one of *nous autres*. I never care to say that I dislike anyone—it seems to me so trivial, so short-sighted, to dislike the little that one can know of any fellow-creature. The Divine Spark is always lurking somewhere—although I admit that sometimes, in the less advanced, it is difficult really to hold fast to that belief."

"Oh, but you always do! *No one* is like you," said Miss Easter, in all good faith. "I don't believe I've ever heard you say an unkind word of anybody."

Lady Rossiter smiled.

"The great thing," she observed gently, "is never to say anything, unless one can say something kind. And it is very strange, Iris dear, how one can nearly always find something that is nice and yet true, to say of everyone."

"*You* can, I'm sure."

Iris was always complaisant, besides being young and happy and therefore disposed to be uncritical, and she had long entertained a simple and quite unreasoning admiration for Lady Rossiter.

Her enthusiasm for Miss Marchrose was a recent impulse only, and did not prevent her from a further endeavour to obtain light upon Lady Rossiter's views.

"She's quite too nice to me, always, and I do think she must have been pretty. In fact, she is now, in a sort of way."

"Quite," agreed Lady Rossiter serenely.

"Sometimes I wonder if she has foreign blood in her."

"Why?"

"I'm not sure," said Miss Easter impressively, "that I should quite, absolutely, always trust her."

Lady Rossiter's common sense did not altogether admit of her accepting so remarkable a reason for assuming untrustworthiness, but she was entirely in accord with the result of Miss Easter's logic, however defective the means by which that result was obtained.

"It's curious that you should say that," she remarked slowly. "Instinct is a strange thing, Iris."

"Yes, isn't it? They always say a woman's instinct is never wrong," glibly returned Miss Easter. "But I don't mean anything unkind about Miss Marchrose, truly I don't; there's only one thing I don't like about her."

Lady Rossiter made a sound expressive of enquiry.

"I never can bear people who try to be sarcastic," murmured Iris, voicing unaware the fundamental distrust which governs the whole of the British middle-classes.

"Satire is a very cheap, unworthy weapon," said Lady Rossiter, not without inward reminiscences of Sir Julian as she spoke. "But to be quite fair, I don't think I've ever heard poor Miss Marchrose try to be satirical or anything of that sort. She's generally rather tongue-tied and awkward when I'm there. You see, Iris, I'm afraid she knows that I have heard a good deal about her, one way and another."

Lady Rossiter hesitated, remembered Mark, and decided to go on.

"I am afraid there is not much doubt that Miss Marchrose once did a very, very heartless action, and I am afraid that heartlessness and meanness are only too terribly apt to go together. There is something about the hard lines of her mouth—but after all, how can I cast the first stone? I had rather let the facts speak for themselves."

Followed the narrative of Captain Isbister, his engagement to a girl not of his own class, his accident, his offer to release the girl, and her prompt acceptance of it, culminating in the unbridled display of anguish witnessed in the nursing home by Captain Isbister's attendant, which climax was received by Iris far otherwise than it had once been received by Sir Julian Rossiter.

"Oh, oh, poor dear thing! How too terrible! I am sure Douglas would go on exactly like that if I ever threw him over. But of course I never could. It's the most dreadful thing I ever heard of—how anyone could be so heartless!"

"How indeed!" sadly ejaculated Lady Rossiter. "And you know, Iris, by some miracle of science, he actually did recover, and can walk as well as you or I. So if she had been steadfast, they would have been married by this time, and she would have been in a very different position now."

"It's like a book," said Iris, awe-stricken. "But she couldn't have cared for him really."

"Indeed, no! I thank God from the bottom of my heart that poor Clarence found out in time what a mistake he had made. He was younger than she, poor boy, and it was all thoroughly unsuitable. He has found his ideal since then."

Iris looked a shade disappointed.

"Ah, my dear, you are thinking that nothing is like first love—and in a way it's true. But there's another kind of love, too, that comes later, when one has outgrown the personal part of it all—the divine selfishness that is so sweet and natural and inevitable in youth. And that is the love, the great universal tenderness, that comes to one later on, and that seeks a widening circle, and a bigger outlet, in order to spend itself on others. But you know nothing about that yet, childie dear. How should you, indeed?"

Very few people like to be told that there is anything in the gamut of the emotions of which they know nothing, and Iris looked with rather an unresponsive eye at her dear Lady Rossiter.

"After all," said that lady, rendering her usual smiling acknowledgment to the Deity, "after all, there are many compensations for growing old, in God's world."

The aphorism admitted not at all of contradiction, and hardly of agreement, and Iris accordingly relapsed into silence.

"I will let you know about my little tea-party for the staff," was Lady Rossiter's last remark. "They will like to see your bright face and pretty frock, dear. Their lives are very drab."

The bright face and pretty frock of Iris Easter, however, were not allowed to shed illumination upon the drab lives of Lady Rossiter's guests on Sunday until the wedding-present question had been inadequately discussed.

Mr. Cooper was mounted upon verbal stilts, and adorned his discourse with many tags of commercial phraseology; Miss Farmer would only say that she was sure Miss Easter would be pleased whatever they settled; and Miss Sandiloe giggled and looked meaningly at Mr. Cooper. Needless to say, Mr. Fairfax Fuller put in no appearance.

Edna was by turns kindly, practical, helpful and sympathetic, but still no decision could be reached.

"What is the amount subscribed?"

"Just over two pounds, so far, but there are a few more responses to come in."

"It isn't the *amount*, Lady Rossiter, is it?" wearily enquired Miss Farmer.

"Certainly not. The thought is everything."

It almost appeared as though the thought was indeed to be everything.

"Have you decided what you wish to give?"

The three members of the staff exchanged glances.

"So many people thought of a pair of silver vases."

"Or a little travelling-clock, Lady Rossiter."

"A good many voted for a small paper-knife, as being individual, like," said Cooper.

"Charming," warmly said Lady Rossiter, appearing to address all her three *vis-à-vis* at once.

The discussion continued at a similar rate of progress for the remainder of the afternoon.

Edna began to feel considerably taxed at the inordinate extent to which she was required to "give out," in her own favourite phrase. There were limits to the life-giving forces that could be radiated for the benefit of three discursive and unbusinesslike fellow-creatures on a cold afternoon in winter. True to her principles, she reflected, with a humourousness that remained strictly tender, that she must definitely take the responsibility for which they all appeared so inadequate on to her own shoulders.

She prepared to intimate her decision by a leading question.

"And about the actual presentation? Perhaps it would prevent little jealousies, little follies of that sort—after all, human nature is human nature—if it were presented by someone not quite of the College personnel? Of course, in the name of you all, by someone who would be able to make a little speech. Oh, nothing formal, of course, only a few words, but one wants those to be the *right* words! I don't know if—"

She paused.

"It was proposed," said Cooper—"and I may add carried unanimously—that the presentation and a few words of good wishes from us all—"

"—Being a good speaker," interpolated Miss Sandiloe.

"—And in an official position, so to speak—and a friend of Miss Easter's," said Miss Farmer, also in parentheses.

Cooper shot a repressive glance left and right. "I am just telling Lady Rossiter. The obvious person, of course, Lady Rossiter, has been approached. Miss Marchrose has kindly agreed to make the presentation on behalf of the staff."

XII

It was left to Sir Julian, as not infrequently happened, to look upon the varied assortment of flotsam and jetsam thrown up by the tide of Lady Rossiter's eloquence.

Whilst Edna sat indoors, rather limply endeavouring to maintain a high level of sympathetic brightness round the exhausted subject of Miss Easter's projected wedding-present, Julian, having ascertained the presence of his three guests indoors, hastily walked out of the house.

He sought his habitual refuge—the long, deserted stretch of shore skirted by a pebbly ridge, locally known as the sea-wall.

There he found Miss Marchrose.

If Julian had counted upon finding the foam-flecked, windy spot in its usual state of solitude, he gave no sign of being disconcerted.

They exchanged greetings and prepared to walk the mile length of the sea-wall together. In spite of the strength of the salt wind blowing full against them, the blue knitted cap that she wore needed no restraining hand, and she was restfully free from fluttering ends and tags of garments.

With great abruptness she began to speak as they walked.

"I knew that you were related to the Isbisters, of course. If you remember, Lady Rossiter said something about them that night that we had dinner together, and I thought at the time—"

She broke off, and Julian, conscious of extreme curiosity as to the reason why she had suddenly introduced so admittedly *scabreux* a topic, enquired after a moment:

"What did you think at the time?"

"I thought Lady Rossiter wished me to understand that she knew of the relationship in which I once stood to Captain Isbister."

For the life of him, Julian could think of no rejoinder.

"I know that things of that kind always *are* known, and the people I've been thrown with, sooner or later, always turned out to have heard the story. Or if they hadn't," said Miss Marchrose in a voice of calm despair, "someone took the trouble to tell them."

"Officiousness is the crying sin of the age," Julian observed sententiously.

"It seems to me a purely individual matter. It can't concern anyone else—not even the people who employ me."

"Certainly not."

"Did you know? But of course you did."

"I knew that Clarence Isbister had been engaged to someone of your name, and that the engagement had been broken off after his accident."

"*I* broke it off," she said defiantly.

"So one heard."

"Everyone has heard that," said Miss Marchrose. "Everyone has heard that when he was told that he must be an invalid and helpless for the rest of his life he offered to release me from the engagement—and I said yes. And that he was very much upset about it, just at the time."

Julian stifled a fleeting recollection of the well-worn legend accompanying the story of Captain Isbister's betrayal.

"Of course, it is inevitable that his relations should have heard about it, I suppose," Miss Marchrose said.

Julian felt inclined to reply, "Clarence Isbister is an ass, and not worth worrying about," and then decided that *that* would not do, and awaited her next words in silence. He perceived that some unusual emotion had strung her to the pitch of excitement at which self-contained people become reckless, and emotional ones untruthful. Having already formed the conclusion that Miss Marchrose belonged to the former class, he listened with the greater interest.

Her next words gave him a clue to the vexation that vibrated in her tones.

"I was angry, I'm afraid, this morning, when Miss Easter actually began about it."

"Extremely impertinent of her. I hope you told her so."

"She is very good-natured," said Miss Marchrose remorsefully. "She has always gone out of her way to be nice to me, and when I began to be angry with her she only said, 'Oh, I'm so dreadfully sorry; I should never tell a soul except Douglas, you know, so you needn't mind my knowing about it.'"

At her faint mimicry of Iris's affected little pipe they both laughed.

"As a matter of fact, poor little thing, she only wanted me to contradict the version that she had heard. She said she couldn't and wouldn't believe it, and was sure that her—her informant had been mistaken."

Sir Julian wondered grimly whether Miss Marchrose was as little at a loss as himself to identify the informant in question. Her next words rather relieved him.

"She may very well have heard it from the girl she lives with. Curiously enough, she was once governess to Lady Mary Isbister's little girl, and it is quite probable that she heard something about it there. I don't know. There seem to be no end to the coincidences that accumulate round unpleasant things. It happened more than three years ago, and he's married now, and perfectly happy—why can't it be allowed to rest?"

"No one has any right to attempt to force your confidence."

"Miss Easter didn't do that, exactly. I think she thought I should be only too ready to explain away the story as it stood, and throw some light which would show that I hadn't just thrown over a man who cared for me on the grounds of his being condemned to the life of a paralytic invalid."

"I should find it very difficult to believe that you did that," said Sir Julian gently.

There was a pause.

"The facts of the story, in the main, are perfectly correct. I told Miss Easter so."

They had reached the end of the sea-wall, and as they turned mechanically back upon their footsteps, Sir Julian for a moment found himself facing her.

The look in her eyes was doubtful, defiant, beseeching, all at once. Something in it evoked from him a very sincere and simple desire to reassure her.

"Won't you tell me about it, if you care to? I'm quite sure that, whatever the facts may be, there is another aspect to them than the obvious one."

He heard a little gasp that unmistakably denoted relief.

"Thank you very much. It's so much easier now you've said that—and I *want* to tell you about it. You'll understand, perhaps."

"Don't hurry," said Julian, more with reference to a certain breathlessness in her speech than to the increased speed at which she was walking beside him.

However, she slackened her pace and presently began to speak quietly.

"I don't suppose you know exactly what it's like for a girl with no home of her own—the difficulty of having any friends, or seeing anyone except just the people one's working with—not that there was ever anyone I wanted to see particularly, the men I associated with were all of Mr. Cooper's type, as nice and as polite as could be, always—but I had nothing in common with them except the day's work. There were a few friends of my father's—he was an architect—but after his death they rather dropped away from us. They were the sort of people who turned up their noses at the dressmaking business. My mother took it up, after he died, because it was the only thing she could do to make money, and she hoped it would mean that I need never go out and work for myself when I grew up. I'm glad," said Miss Marchrose vehemently, "I'm glad and thankful that she never lived to see the muddle I made of everything."

Sir Julian remained silent, aware that she was talking to herself as much as to him.

"After she died I got the job in Southampton Row. I lived in a hostel for women workers. It was all right in a way, but deadly lonely. And I wasn't used to the sort of girls who live at those places, and I thought myself too good for them—and of course they saw it. They used to play cards in the evening, or some of them played the piano, and sometimes they made up parties to go to the pit at the theatre—but after I'd been disagreeable once or twice, naturally they didn't ask me any more. And I never sat in the public sitting-room downstairs, but always went up to my own bedroom. And I read a book at meals. You don't know how people who do that are *hated*. So they ought to be, I suppose, but in those days I thought it was quite worth while to make them all indignant, and find myself left in peace. But all the time I was more and more lonely, and I used to sit and think in the evenings, wondering how I could bear it if all my life was going to be like that—just working on and on and then becoming like one of the older women at that hostel—there were *dozens* of them—pinched and discontented, always worrying over expense, and why there weren't two helpings of pudding at dinner, with nothing to do, nothing to remember, nothing to look forward to—knowing themselves utterly and absolutely unnecessary in the world. And they'd got used to it—that was the ghastly part of it—and yet they couldn't always have been like that. Once they must have passed through awful phases of rebellion and despair, like me, and hoping against hope that something glorious and brilliant would turn up—the sort of things that only happen in books—and then gradually they'd got resigned—and hopeless, and indifferent—the worst of all. And I felt that all that, year after year, would be coming nearer and nearer to me—"

"It couldn't," muttered Julian. "Marriage, for instance—"

"Of course, everyone said that. My mother said it—she kept on talking about 'When you marry, Pauline,' as though it was something almost inevitable. My aunt said it, when I spent my holidays at her house. At first I used to say it myself—thinking, like fools of girls always do, that love meant happiness and that it was bound to come."

The bitterness in her tone shocked him, but he said nothing.

"As I'm telling you these things that I've never told anyone, I'd better tell you the whole truth," said Miss Marchrose, her voice coldly dispassionate all at once. "I am not in the least attractive. No one, except Clarence Isbister, has ever wanted to marry me. Some girls—sometimes quite pretty ones—are like that. They don't know what it means to be wanted by anyone."

"Stop that," said Julian. "I can't stand it. No man has any right to hear this sort of thing. Besides, it's nonsense. You were never in a position to know any men of your own sort."

"I used to tell myself that. But it wasn't altogether true. There were always plenty of people at my aunt's house—she lived in Hampstead—and both my cousins went to a school of art, and had any number of friends, and they were always nice to me, and took me to all their parties when I was with them. That's how I met Clarence Isbister—at the Chelsea Arts Ball. He'd come with a party of people, and one of them knew my cousin Dolly, and she introduced him to me, and he brought Mr. Isbister and said he wanted to know me. He was only a boy—twenty-one, I think."

"Quite old enough to know his own mind."

"Was he? To my dying day," said Miss Marchrose very simply, "I shall never understand why he fell in love with me. I danced very badly, but he didn't seem to mind, and asked me to sit out with him instead. We talked, but I don't think we had anything much in common. I told him I was a teacher of shorthand, having my holiday. He kept beside me the whole evening and asked to be introduced to Dolly and if he might come and see us in Hampstead. Of course she said yes. I always remember Dolly when we got back, after the ball, and how she said, 'Pauline, that man's fallen in love with you. And, mark my words, *he's the sort who'd ask one to marry him.*'

"And she was quite right. Dolly was always right about men, though the sort of men she knew weren't the same sort as Clarence.

"Well, you know, I was engaged to him. I was twenty-five, and I'd been dreading the future, and it seemed, in a way, the most unexpected chance of escaping everything I was most afraid of. But I don't know if you'll ever believe it if I tell you how much I hesitated."

"I shall believe anything you tell me. Why did you hesitate?"

"Because he was twenty-one, and an ass," replied Miss Marchrose, with the most unexpected candour. "And I didn't even like him much; he irritated me nearly unbearably sometimes. It was very ungrateful of me, but it seemed to me that he loved me without rhyme or reason—he knew nothing whatever about me. And I told him that I didn't care for him. But I think, partly, the fuss his people made helped to make him want it all the more, just to show them that he *would* take his own way. They'd always made a baby of him at home, I gathered, and he had suddenly begun to resent it."

"Yes," said Julian thoughtfully, "that tallies with the little I remember of the Isbisters, when I met them several years ago. Did you ever stay there?"

"No. His father and mother were much too angry about it, but he had money of his own and they couldn't stop it. We were more or less engaged when he had his accident. He'd been at home, and he'd been hoping that his mother was coming round a little, and that perhaps he could take me to see her in London. He was very fond of his mother; but poor Clarence! he was like a little boy—talking of the 'lark' it would be to steal a march on them all, and get married at a Registrar's Office one morning."

"Would you have done that?"

"I thought I would—I was back at work by then, and in the hostel again. He used to come and take me for walks and drives and out to dinner—and often and often I was miserable and felt that I was taking everything from him, and giving him nothing at all. And besides—"

"What?"

"I suppose no one gives up romantic ideals, if they've had them, without a struggle," said Miss Marchrose, speaking very fast.

"Believe me," said Julian gently, "it is worth while to remain faithful to one's romantic ideals. People will tell you that to relinquish them means progress—but don't believe them. One is the poorer all the rest of one's life for having let them go."

"No one else has ever said that to me. I said it to myself sometimes—but most of the time I honestly thought that I should be a fool to chuck away what Clarence offered me. And when he had his accident, in the country, I knew nothing about it for a week after it had happened—naturally, no one thought of letting me know. I imagined all sorts of things—that he'd chucked me, you know. And I was angry and furious and disappointed—in spite of everything. But my aunt read about the accident in some paper or other, and wrote to me. And afterwards Clarence's mother wrote."

"She didn't ask you, then, to give him up?"

"She didn't say anything about my being engaged to him at all. But when he was better, still in the nursing-home, he wrote himself, and told me that most likely he would be half-paralysed for the rest of his life. They really thought he would be, then, you know. And he asked me if I thought I could bear it. That was when I first began to realise my own inadequacy. You see, all the time I'd been thinking of *him*, and how young

– 122 –

he was—how unlike what I'd sometimes fancied. But when he wrote like that, I knew that I couldn't even write the only sort of letter that would have been any good. I was worse than useless. I wrote the sort of answer that really meant nothing at all—though I put all the sort of affectionate expressions that he liked, and anything and everything I could think of—but I didn't answer one word about our engagement. I couldn't. I wrote to him every day, and all the while I was trying to gain time, to think it all out.

"You've no idea how difficult it is sometimes just to get time and a place for thinking. There was my work all day, and then I used to fancy I'd have the evening—but it was so cold in my room, and I found that I was only thinking about *that* all the time, and how I could keep my hands warm. And in bed—one always imagines one can do all one's thinking in bed. But one can't! Things look quite different in the night, somehow much more important—I can't explain; and then all the shorthand outlines one had been making all day on the blackboard seemed to come into the darkness. I'm making it all sound muddled, I know—but that's what it was. Just a muddle, and all the relative values of things seeming to turn upside down." She paused.

"I understand," said Julian.

"In the end, Clarence wrote again, and said he must release me from the engagement; he couldn't ask me to marry a man who would most likely never be able to walk again. And I thought, and thought—till I was nearly frantic. You see, in a way, it would be the impulse of every woman to feel that she was all the more bound in honour to stick to a man *because* of that—of course, I'm not speaking about those people who love one another, that's different. But it kept coming over me like a wave—how unthinkable it would be to refuse to marry a man after all, after one had promised, just when he'd had that appalling knock from Fate and everything that made his life worth living had been taken away. As though one could never do enough to make up for it all. ... But in the end it was that which decided me. You see, I knew that I could never make up—and not only that, but that I might make it far, far worse for him. It seemed to me that only a very great love could have been adequate.

And I not only didn't love him, but I knew myself—I'm not patient, I'm not an unselfish woman. Heaven only knows what I should be, married to an invalid, to an unfortunate boy who cared for me, and who would be utterly dependent on me for all the things that matter most. And I could have given him nothing—I should have been worse than useless to him. There was nothing real between us—only just his infatuation—and I *knew* that couldn't last. I believed then, when I thought of him as a cripple, that if I'd married Clarence, he would have come to hate me. Before he was hurt, I'd meant to risk it and to try and be a good wife to him, though even then I knew I was cheating—taking all he could give me, and bringing so little. But afterwards, it seemed to me that it would be a worse cheating to try and meet a tremendous demand like that with just nothing at all. So I wrote and tried to explain it to him, and tell him why I wouldn't say I'd marry him in spite of it all."

For the last time, they reached the end of the sea-wall and turned, once more facing the blustering wind. In the rapidly gathering twilight Julian could only see that her face was very pale.

"Well," she said, with a very small, rather tired laugh, "he didn't become a cripple for life, and he married somebody else, who was suitable. And I sometimes wonder whether I was a fool."

"I don't think you wonder really," said Sir Julian steadily. "You know as well as I do that you had been led into a false position, and that you had the courage to act up to your own inmost convictions, instead of making bad worse by yielding to the impulse of a generous self-sacrifice that is bound to spell disaster unless there is the capability of sustained effort to back it. Lacking that capability, as you were aware of lacking it, you were brave enough to set obvious sentiment at defiance."

"Oh!" cried Miss Marchrose, in an odd voice between laughter and sadness, "I have never before heard the case for the defence stated like that! Thank you, Sir Julian."

They climbed the sandy declivity, tufted with hillocks and boulders almost invisible in the increasing dusk, and reached the narrow and stony road at the top.

"We are not far from the farm," said Julian. "You must be tired."

"No, I like going down to the sea. I'm glad I met you. I was so angry at the beginning of the afternoon—after I'd seen poor little Miss Easter."

"I'm not at all surprised."

"Do you think," said Miss Marchrose, somewhat more than doubtfully, "that she is a discreet person?"

Sir Julian so emphatically thought the contrary that for the moment words almost failed him.

"Let us hope," he said at last, rather grimly, "that decency may induce her to hold her tongue on a subject of which she knows nothing whatsoever."

It struck him as he spoke that the foundation of the hope was but a frail one, and he wondered whether Miss Marchrose was thinking of Mark Easter as the recipient of his sister's newly-acquired piece of information.

If so, she gave no further sign of it, and he took her to the door of the farmhouse almost in silence.

Julian's thoughts that evening were occupied almost exclusively with Miss Marchrose. The complete frankness with which she had spoken that afternoon had put before him an extraordinarily new aspect of the self-contained, competent Lady Superintendent of the College. It appeared to him that he very well could imagine for himself all that she had hinted at, rather than described.

The architect father, the excellent, probably middle-class mother, who had set up a dressmaking business so that her child might live at home, and the youthful spirit of pride and intolerance that had resented the very existence of any such endeavour to shield her. Even the semi-Bohemian, semi-suburban home of the aunt and cousins at Hampstead came very clearly before his mind's eye. He felt convinced that the aunt was an elder sister of the paternal Marchrose, and that she and "Dolly "had brought much common sense to bear upon the Clarence equation and that they must have talked the matter over and over, with a great effect of giving frank and disinterested advice.

And the girl who was tired of her work, who thought herself too good for the inhabitants of her hostel dwelling, whom "no one had ever wanted to marry"—it was not altogether wonderful, Julian thought, that she should have stifled her foolish, schoolgirl dreams of romance and accepted all that the infatuated boy of "the sort who asks one to marry him" had been ready to offer her.

Her acceptance of him was much less remarkable than her subsequent rejection.

It never occurred to Julian for an instant to question that she had taken her decisive step from any reason but the one she had given: that of knowing herself unequal to meet the supreme demand suddenly made upon her. Julian remembered the words that he had twice heard applied to that refusal of hers.

"Of course she didn't really care for him."

The literal truth, Julian reflected. And it was her resolute facing of that truth, in defiance of sentiment as of condemnation from others, that, to Julian's way of thinking, had redeemed the wrong that she had done to Clarence Isbister no less than to her own inner vision.

"For when all's said and done," said Julian to himself, "what is she but an incurable romanticist, unable to put up with the second best in that which, rightly or wrongly, she rates highest in life? But what one sees ahead for her—that's another matter."

Sir Julian, pessimist and idealist both at once, shrugged his shoulders and dismissed the speculation. But it had brought him to the thought of Mark Easter.

He thought that Mark, ten years ago, would have loved her, and that he would have made her happy. Julian, who had very completely missed happiness himself, still held that in the knowledge of it lay the secret of fulfilment. Mark had known it, knew it still. It lived, fundamental, in himself. But Miss Marchrose should have known it as a gift from without, a sudden revelation, even if enduring in its entirety for a little while only. Julian wondered whether she were destined still to know it, through the man whom he believed should teach her, through Mark Easter, and if so, at what cost?

He summed it up with his usual, "It's no business of mine. But I believe she'd think it worth while, at any price—and by Heaven, she's right!"

Perhaps incurable romanticism was not attributable to Miss Marchrose only.

XIII

■

When Lady Rossiter indulged, in the presence of her husband, in a space of silent reverie, it was always her intention to meet with interruption and enquiry that should lead to a mutually beneficial discussion upon the subject of her thoughts. In spite of the many disappointments inflicted upon her by Sir Julian in this respect, it was also her custom to return good for evil by never allowing him more than ten consecutive minutes of reflectiveness without some sympathetic reminder that he was not alone.

Accordingly, when he had smoked two cigarettes after dinner in complete silence, gazing the while, with obvious preoccupation, into the fire, Lady Rossiter lifted up her voice and spoke.

"I saw the first little, wee, wonderful sign of spring this afternoon. A patch of snowdrops, just outside the gates."

"Did you?"

"Such brave little white sentinels! I always love the French name— *perce-neige*," said Lady Rossiter, who, like many another cultured soul, generally saw more beauty and expressiveness in the vocabulary of languages other than her own.

"I am afraid there was no *neige* for them to *perçer* on this occasion," observed Sir Julian, with very languid interest in the horticultural vagaries of these harbingers of spring.

"There very well might be, by to-morrow. I thought it bitterly cold. Were you out this afternoon?"

"I was. I heard Cooper being extremely eloquent and long-winded in the distance, and I thought that everything pointed to my taking a long walk."

"They came to consult me about a presentation—a wedding-present for Iris."

"I hope you told them they had much better let it alone."

"Julian, how could I? Poor things, it is rather touching of them—a sum which would seem little enough to ourselves, must mean a great deal to them—perhaps a question of actual bread and butter."

"Then why encourage them to throw it away?"

"I told them that of course it was the thought that she would value. But they'd set their hearts on having some sort of little ceremony—you know how they love anything of that kind—with speeches and an excuse for a gathering."

"Where do they want to gather? Fuller will never allow them to desecrate the College. You remember how sulky he was when they got up that party there, this time last year."

Edna uttered her usual lenient "Poor Mr. Fuller! He is heart and soul devoted to the College. But I think perhaps if I talked to him, it might be possible to soften his hard heart. He really only needs a little management, and I've practically undertaken to go and see him about it. Why shouldn't the poor things have a little pleasure in their lives? I sometimes think there's very little gaiety in the world, Julian."

"I hope you may add to it by paying Fuller a visit, but I do not feel particularly sanguine."

"I don't think I shall have much trouble with him, somehow," said Edna, with a little laugh. "Only the whole thing will need rather tactful handling, as it may be a shade difficult for Iris, if she's not expecting it. She'll have to say a few words, unless Mark says them for her."

"Of course, the whole thing is really a tribute to Mark," said Julian. "He's extraordinarily popular—as well he may be."

"Yes, they practically admitted that they hoped it would please him. But after all, Julian, 'all the world loves a lover.'"

"Does it?" said Sir Julian expressively. "Did all this conversation take place at tea this afternoon, may I ask, in the presence of the smirking Iris herself?"

Lady Rossiter looked pained at the extreme unkindness of the adjective selected by her husband.

"Iris didn't come in till later, though, as a matter of fact, her arrival interrupted us when there were several points still unsettled. One thing, though, rather vexed me."

"What was that?" asked Sir Julian, rather wearily, aware that he would be told whether he enquired or whether he did not, and for once choosing the less unamiable course.

"There was some idea," Lady Rossiter understated the case, "of getting the actual presentation itself made by the most unsuitable person they could very well have selected—that unfortunate courtesan *manquée*, the superintendent woman."

If Lady Rossiter wished to see the effect of her pleasant epithet upon her husband, she was doomed to disappointment. The complete silence in which he received it impelled her to continue.

"It is a very disagreeable word to apply to any woman, but I fail to see what else one can call her. We know that she entangled one, very young, man, with money and position, and then threw him over in a peculiarly heartless manner, and that she is now taking every advantage of poor Mark's miserable situation to try and involve him in an affair that can only mean scandal and misery, however it ends."

"I fail to see how the reckless career which you impute to Miss Marchrose, Edna, can possibly affect the quality of the silver salt-cellars, or whatever it is, that she is to present to Iris."

"Ah, Julian—a young girl, pure, innocent unsullied! How could one see it, without a sense of profanation? Call it fanciful if you like, but there is something in me that could never bear to allow *that*."

"No, I don't think I should call it fanciful, Edna," said her husband slowly.

"You think me prejudiced!" exclaimed Edna. "But *indeed*, Mark is very dear to me, and for his sake—and for womanhood's sake—I can't bear that the—the delicate bloom should be brushed from any token connected with his sister's wedding."

"Then you had better arrange to have a bonfire of the remaining copies of 'Why, Ben! A Story of the Sexes,'" imperturbably replied her husband.

Julian had for so long been in the habit of protecting himself against those peculiar shafts that are only launched by really and professedly good women, with indifferent satire, that the small, cheap fleer came almost automatically to his lips. It certainly interfered not at all with his intimate realisation that Lady Rossiter could hardly have chosen a worse moment for an endeavour to enlist his sympathies on her side in the indirect contest that she had elected to wage against Miss Marchrose.

"I would sooner make the presentation myself, absurd though it would be, than feel that *she* was making it."

"It would, however, as you say, be absurd," replied Sir Julian coldly. "Of course, it must be made by a representative of the College staff. Fairfax Fuller is the proper person."

"The misogynist!"

Sir Julian wondered, not for the first time, why his wife clung so persistently to the libel attached by her to Mr. Fuller, and came to his habitual conclusion, that she had found it necessary to her self-respect to deduce a wholesale hatred of the female sex from the Supervisor's taciturn reception of her own advances.

"I will talk to Mr. Fuller, Julian, and see what can be arranged. I thought of going in one afternoon next week. There is not too much time for arranging details now. The wedding is to-day fortnight."

"I hadn't realised it was so near. However, all the better. It'll be over the sooner, and Iris can remove her Douglas from hence before he has time to begin talking about 'we married men.'"

Lady Rossiter laughed discreetly, but after a little pause she interjected quietly:

"Mr. Garrett is a good sort, really, in spite of his mannerisms."

She had no particular grounds for this charitable assertion, but she made it a matter of principle to utter some kind little phrase on behalf of anybody whom her interlocutor of the moment had verbally slighted or condemned. This peace-making habit was not unapt to have the singular effect of promoting a lively desire on the part of the first speaker to abuse the absent one a good deal more vigorously than before.

Sir Julian, however, was either too old a hand, or else too little interested in Mr. Garrett, to find himself similarly moved.

"I cannot imagine why Iris insists upon being married down here at all," he said, without hostility.

"She couldn't have been married from that tiny flat of hers, and I think it's natural she should want it to be from her brother's house. It will have to be very quiet, as they won't have room for any sort of reception. Besides, it would be very unsuitable, and I'm glad to say that Mark has made her see it."

"How many of 'we Garretts' are going to grace the scene?"

"Mr. Garrett only has a father," said Edna repressively. "He is to stay at the cottage."

"Tell Mark that we can put up anyone he likes, for a night or two."

"Indeed, yes. In a household where every item must count, a guest is rather a serious consideration, I'm afraid. Mark will probably be thankful when it's all over."

Sir Julian felt no doubt of it.

His sympathies with Mark, already lively, became acute the following morning when bride and bridegroom-elect suddenly appeared in his study with the purpose of expressing their gratitude for the extremely liberal cheque that had been Sir Julian and Lady Rossiter's wedding gift to Iris.

"Douglas and I have been nearly quarrelling the whole way here as to how we'll spend it," said Miss Easter candidly.

"Hardly *quarrelling*, have we?" reproachfully asked Mr. Garrett, as usual addressing himself exclusively to his betrothed.

"Oh, we've never really quarrelled yet, have we? At least," said Iris archly, "unless you count the copper tea-kettle time."

"Ah! The copper tea-kettle!" responded Mr. Garrett meaningly.

At which reference they both, according to their wont, indulged in the hearty laughter, naturally unshared by Sir Julian, of those to whom some perfectly obvious allusion is amusingly intelligible.

"We've actually settled the great question of bridesmaids, Sir Julian," observed Iris, an easy victim to the not uncommon bridal delusion that such details must be of major interest to all alike.

"Your friend in London?"

"Oh no! She doesn't approve of marriage, you know. She thinks it a mere servile bond for the woman," explained Iris glibly. "In fact, she's a tremendous advocate for Free Love. She's furious with me for marrying at all."

Sir Julian glanced at Mr. Garrett, wondering how he regarded the rather stupefying gospel preached by the chosen friend and companion of his bride.

The young man appeared more thoughtful than dismayed.

"In a general way," he remarked detachedly, "we moderns are all in favour of abolishing the present rather archaic marriage laws, and re-establishing the whole thing upon the basis of a purely civil contract; dissoluble after a term of years at the wish of either or both of the contracting parties."

Sir Julian had a momentary vision of earnest suburban debating societies, at which he felt sure that Mr. Garrett had formerly launched his eloquence, in words almost, if not quite, identical with his present text. Having no wish to fathom the young man's further views, he merely renewed enquiry of Iris as to the question of bridesmaids.

"Only dear little Ruthie," said Iris. "It's quite odd, but I haven't got an enormous number of girl friends. Somehow I've got heaps and heaps more men friends. I can't imagine why, I'm sure."

Neither could Julian, but he refrained from saying so.

"At one time, I rather wanted Miss Marchrose. Of course, I know she's not quite, absolutely, altogether one of ourselves—but still, as it's all to be so quiet—and then I could have got hold of a cousin to match her—but she wouldn't hear of it. Of course, she *is* older than I am."

"A good deal older, surely," said Sir Julian rather drily, contemplating the youthful blend of prettiness and vulgarity in front of him.

"Douglas," said Iris, with great suddenness, "do go away. I've just remembered that I want to ask Sir Julian something most frightfully particular."

"Secrets?" ejaculated Douglas, with playful reproach.

"Just a tiny, tiny little one. Now do go right away, there's a dear boy."

Thus adjured, it was scarcely possible for Mr. Garrett to do otherwise than to obey, but it would have shown but little knowledge of his capabilities as an engaged young man to expect him to do so without a last mirthful flight of fancy.

"Then I'm weel awa'," he exclaimed, in a Scotch manner that almost compensated for the lack of relevance in his choice of idiom, and swung his long legs over the sill of the low window, scraping the paint with his boots as he did so and annoying Sir Julian.

"It's about Miss Marchrose," said Iris, her head even more on one side than usual.

Sir Julian wondered whether he could possibly stop her before she said anything more.

"At first I liked her awfully. In fact, I think she's sweet. But the story about the poor man she threw over is perfectly dreadful. Of course, she couldn't have cared for him *really*, because any woman—"

"I know all about that," hastily interrupted Sir Julian. "Surely we needn't go into a thing that happened several years before she ever came here, and which is no one's business but hers."

"If it had been Douglas," pursued Miss Easter, fixing an enormous pair of melancholy eyes upon her discomfited listener, "if it had been Douglas, *however* much of an invalid he had to be, I should simply want to marry him all the more. I should want to give up my whole life to him, so as to make up a little."

"Well, I hope you may never be tried in such a terrible manner," said Julian, unable to repress a shudder of horrified sympathy for the invalid who should find his shattered life relegated to the devotion of Miss Easter.

"But of course, she couldn't have loved him really," asserted Iris, apparently unaware of a certain lack of originality in her choice of comment.

"No."

"Or she would have felt that she *couldn't* do enough to make up for it all."

"Yes."

"That's what I should feel if it had been Douglas."

Sir Julian could not think of a reply that should provide any variation upon his previous monosyllabic ones.

"And if it had been *me*, Douglas would have felt just like that, too."

Sir Julian began to wonder how much longer they were to continue this consideration of hypothetical contingencies.

"The fact is, I'm afraid I've been too fearfully silly for anything."

It being impossible to express his own conviction that nothing could be more probable, Sir Julian still sat speechless, looking with growing dismay at his visitor, who was exhibiting every sign of an intention to burst into tears.

"I am afraid," said Iris, beginning to cry, "that Mark has fallen in love with her."

After a pause of extremely uncomfortable consideration, Sir Julian observed, with a sententiousness of which he was perfectly aware:

"If such is unfortunately the case, why should you blame yourself?"

"Because I did everything I could to make it happen. I saw they liked each other, ages ago—oh, long before Christmas! and I had her to dinner and things, and made her sing 'Annie Laurie' because Mark admired her voice, and I told him how she said she liked working at the College with him."

"But why, in Heaven's name?"

"Because," sobbed Iris, "I thought it would be such a beautiful thing for them to defy conventionality and be happy in spite of everything—a *grande passion*—you know. ..."

The extreme perversion of the point of view thus disclosed left Sir Julian, at no time eloquent, more completely deprived of utterance than ever before.

"In those days," Iris continued, with an effect of great remoteness in her manner, "I thoroughly and completely believed in Free Love myself. Of course, I was younger, then."

"Only by two months," Sir Julian gloomily reminded her.

"Oh yes, but those two months have taught me everything. Love is such a wonderful teacher. Ever since I've been engaged to Douglas, it's been like a new heaven and a new earth, and I can see things that I never saw before."

She began to dab at her eyes with her handkerchief, while Sir Julian thought of a great many observations which it was extremely improbable that he would make aloud.

"It was only a day or two ago that I heard about her having been engaged and then jilting the man because of his accident, and it was the most frightful shock you can imagine. What should I feel if she did that sort of thing to Mark one day? Of course, it shows that she's not at all the sort of person to sacrifice herself for anybody."

"I am quite sure," said Sir Julian gently, "that you have no idea what a terrible thing it would be for any man to fall seriously in love with a woman to whom he could never offer marriage. Mark is a married man."

"He hasn't seen that awful creature for years and years," said Iris resentfully.

"That has nothing to do with it. She is his wife."

"It seems so dreadfully hard."

"Yes, but it would seem a great deal harder if he cared for someone else."

"And she for him," Iris added tenaciously.

"I hope that your imagination has misled you," said Sir Julian gravely.

"But what shall I do?"

"Nothing. If you have already ceased your extraordinarily misguided efforts towards bringing them together, you can only leave the whole question alone. After all, Mark knows very well that as long as his wife is alive he's as much bound to her as though she were living at home in the normal way. They are neither of them children, and we have no right whatever to suppose that they cannot tell right from wrong."

"I never told her Mark was married."

"I think she knows."

"I wonder if that would stop her," said Iris reflectively. "I can't help feeling that if by some dreadful Kismet Douglas had been already married when we met, I should have given myself to him just the same. I should simply have had to. I'm sure that in some former incarnation—"

"You know nothing about it," said Julian unceremoniously. "You have been a foolish little girl, and the only thing left for you to do is to forget the extremely poor taste in which you have been behaving. I should like to know what made you come and tell *me* about it, though."

"I thought you could talk to Mark." Miss Easter wept piteously, looking so very youthful that Julian felt inclined to relent.

"That shows how very little you know about it. I have no intention of insulting Mark by doing anything of the kind, and if I did, he would very properly kick me out of the house. Stop crying, please."

"Wouldn't it be better if Miss Marchrose were to leave the College?"

"What for? Now stop being so childish and let me fetch you a glass of water. Mr. Garrett will want to know why you have been crying."

"I always, always tell Douglas everything. We've promised never to have any secrets from one another. Perfect confidence is the only way to married happiness."

"You can tell me about that after you've been married a year or two. But now I want you to listen to me."

Iris looked at him with drowned, forget-me-not eyes.

"I am going to forget what you have told me, as far as it is humanly possible to do so, and you must do the same. Promise me that you won't mention what we have been discussing to anybody else, ever."

"Oh, but Douglas! Oughtn't I to tell Douglas?"

"No, certainly not."

"It seems so awful to begin one's married life with a secret."

Sir Julian had perhaps never before felt so much tempted to resort to physical violence.

"I assure you that it would be exceedingly dishonourable, and that you couldn't do Mark a worse service, than to hint at such a thing to anybody on earth."

"Then," said Iris heroically, "I promise."

Sir Julian relaxed his clenched hand, and opened the door for her.

"I never, never thought," said Miss Easter, "that you and I would ever share a secret, Sir Julian! I used to be so dreadfully afraid of you—but I never shall be again!"

Watching his departing confederate, restored once more to smiling animation, flutter from the room, Julian returned to his seat before the writing-table.

"For a man who professes to dislike officious interference," he reflected ruefully, "I am the recipient of an unfortunate number of disastrous confidences."

XIV

Lady Rossiter, a few days later, put on a comparatively new set of black fox furs, which helped to enhance in her the agreeable conviction of being in a position to be kind to those less fortunate than herself, and drove to Culmouth College.

It was her intention to put the matter of the presentation upon a sound footing without delay, and she had purposely chosen a Saturday afternoon for her visit, knowing that the College would be almost empty and that Fairfax Fuller was generally to be found there alone until half-past two or three o'clock.

The Supervisor, however—the window of whose private office gazed on to that side of the street by which the College was approached—proved strangely difficult of access.

The place seemed almost deserted, but Lady Rossiter encountered downstairs the small and precocious-looking student of shorthand whom she and Iris had remarked at the speed test.

"Do you know if Mr. Fuller is here, little boy?" she enquired of him, with that extra distinct enunciation by which so many people indicate their consciousness of addressing a social inferior, but also with a very agreeable smile.

Edna believed much in the power of a smile, and sometimes quoted a few lines of those popular verses, "Just by smiling."

"Ay," said the little boy.

"Will you go and tell him that a lady would like to see him?" said Edna, who did not think the youth capable of reporting her name correctly.

"Ay."

The messenger departed, whistling shrilly, and presently returned grinning broadly.

"Mr. Fuller, he's so busy as ever he can be. Could you give a message, like?"

"I'm afraid not," said Edna, suave but firm. "Tell him it's Lady Rossiter."

"I told him that," said the youth, looking still more amused.

Edna began to feel that the value of smiles might be overrated.

"Thank you. I'd better go myself. I'm so much obliged to you."

She nodded at the little boy rather distantly and went herself to knock at the closed door of Mr. Fuller's office.

A voice within uttered a short, sharp ejaculation which Lady Rossiter, with an optimism that did more credit to her imagination than to her common sense, interpreted to mean, "Come in!"

The room she entered was thick with the smoke and odour of the peculiarly rank tobacco affected by Mr. Fairfax Fuller, and in spite of an open window, a haze of blue fumes hung over the table at which he sat, his head thrust aggressively forward and his elbows squared.

Few things could have been less expressive of welcome than his unsmiling "Good afternoon," as he rose to his feet and laid his cherry-wood pipe upon the table.

"Don't stop smoking, I'm quite used to it," said Lady Rossiter, gasping a little. "Are you very busy?"

"Yes, very," said Mr. Fuller uncompromisingly.

"Then I mustn't keep you," his visitor smilingly observed. "May I sit down?"

Fuller moved a chair about two inches in her direction and pushed into prominence the broad leather strap and silver watch on his hairy and powerful wrist.

Lady Rossiter affected not to observe this gesture, which she preferred to attribute to the awkwardness of embarrassment rather than to any want of cordiality.

"And is all well with our College?" she enquired brightly, and casting a friendly glance at the papers on the table, all of which Mr. Fuller immediately thrust into the nearest pigeon-hole.

"The College is all right."

"That's good. You know it's very near my heart. I shall never forget how we've seen it grow from the very start, and the interest one's had in every member of the staff. I'm sure you're like me, Mr. Fuller, and care a great deal about the *human* element."

Edna paused, but the sympathetic response which might reasonably have been expected was not forthcoming.

"We've been so like a little family party here, I always think—especially those of us who saw the very beginning of all things. Let me see, I think you and I and Sir Julian, and of course Mr. Easter, are the only ones left of the original committee, aren't we? Oh, and the old Alderman."

Fuller emitted a sound that might conceivably pass for a rejoinder.

"They're all so pleased about Miss Easter's engagement—a wedding is always an excitement, isn't it? Have they," said Edna, momentarily thought-less, "have they told you of their little scheme for making her a presentation?"

"As I happen to be Supervisor of the staff, they naturally came to me in the first place, Lady Rossiter."

"Of course they did. How stupid of me! One forgets all the grades and distinctions, there are so many of them now. But it was really about the presentation plans that I wanted to talk to you."

She waited in vain for some assurance that the wish had been in any way mutual.

"I felt sure that you and I would understand one another," said Edna, almost pleadingly, "if we had a little talk together."

Silence.

Lady Rossiter could no longer disguise from herself that the little talk, if it was to take place at all, must do so in the form of an unsupported monologue. She began courageously:

"I like the idea, you know, and I think it will touch and gratify Miss Easter and her brother very much indeed. Only these schemes are always the better for tactful handling, don't you agree with me? We don't want any little awkwardnesses. And I'm not quite sure that I think the suggestion of having the presentation made by poor Miss Marchrose was a very wise one. Now, Mr. Fuller, I know I can speak to you in confidence, and

I'm going to say something that I should never dream of saying to any other member of the staff. I am sorry to tell you that there are reasons—I needn't go into them, they are very painful ones—why Miss Marchrose should not be selected to offer this little present to a young and innocent girl on behalf of the staff. I know I need not go into details."

Fuller stared at Lady Rossiter with dark, smouldering eyes.

"I'm perfectly satisfied with Miss Marchrose's behaviour since she's been here," he growled at last.

Up went Edna's eyebrows, all too expressively. "That's as it may be, Mr. Fuller. A woman is sometimes a good deal more clear-sighted than a man, in certain matters. But I happen to have heard a good deal about Miss Marchrose before she came here at all, and as a member of the General Committee, and also of Mr. Cooper's little committee for the presentation, I may tell you that I very decidedly veto any suggestion of letting her represent the staff of this College."

The Supervisor looked her full in the eyes.

"Are you telling me, Lady Rossiter, that that girl isn't straight?"

Edna's opaque white skin, that seldom registered alteration, coloured faintly.

"Mr. Fuller, God forbid that I should condemn any woman unheard. I won't pretend not to know what you mean."

"I can put it plainer if you like," Fuller retorted. "But I want yes or no, Lady Rossiter."

"Then," said Edna with dignity, "as far as I can tell, *no*."

"I should damned well think not," exploded Fairfax Fuller, without a trace of apology. "I take my orders from Sir Julian Rossiter, and until he's lost confidence in me, I run this staff the way I think best. You'll excuse me, Lady Rossiter, if I say that I think we've discussed the matter long enough."

Edna stood up, more angry than she had ever allowed herself to be since the days of her girlhood.

"You forget yourself altogether, Mr. Fuller, and I feel certain that you will be the first person to realise that an apology is due to me when you are yourself again."

For all answer, Fuller opened the door and banged it to again almost before she had crossed the threshold.

Lady Rossiter, in the hall outside, found her knees shaking under her in a manner hitherto unknown to her. Fairfax Fuller's temper, displayed after the fashion of his kind, was a return to nature of which she had never before had experience. Not devoid of an instinctive reluctance to being found, shaken and agitated, in the College which had only been allowed to see her as a serene visiting goddess, Edna almost furtively made her way upstairs in search of an empty classroom in which to calm herself.

A general quiet pervaded the upper floor of the building; the smell of soap and water upon newly-scrubbed boards proclaimed the recent presence of the usual Saturday afternoon charwoman. Lady Rossiter, still shaking, felt the imperative need of a champion, and murmured something indignant to herself about a woman alone, which was shortly afterwards disproved by a distant and subdued sound of unceasing voices. Edna reflected that even young Cooper might be of solace, and was also not averse from seizing the opportunity of disclaiming all further connection with the presentation of Iris's wedding-present.

She rose wearily, crossing the lobby in search of the just-audible voice that she judged to come from the smallest and most remote classroom. The door was shut, but through the upper panels of glass Lady Rossiter was only too well enabled to perceive that which struck fresh dismay to her mind.

Miss Marchrose was sitting at a small table in the window, her back to the door, her head bent, and her hands idle in her lap. Beside her sat Mark Easter, his voice still audible, and in front of him a disordered pile of papers at which he made no pretence of looking.

Lady Rossiter drew back almost upon the instant, but she had seen that he was speaking much more earnestly than was usual with him.

From sheer desire to gain time in which to consider these unwelcome phenomena, Edna retreated once more to the room across the landing.

She remained there in thought for nearly twenty minutes, subconsciously aware that the murmur of those two voices went on almost without intermission the while.

The noise as of heavily-nailed boots galloping up the uncarpeted stairs came to distract her, and the little boy whom she had seen earlier in the afternoon burst into the room.

"Were you looking for me?" Lady Rossiter enquired rather severely.

"Mr. Fuller axed me if you were here still."

"It's almost time for my car to call for me," Edna said with dignity. "I am just coming down."

She had entirely regained her usual poise, and faced Fairfax Fuller, who stood at the open door of his room, obviously awaiting her, with perfect composure.

The Supervisor looked very much heated, but spoke with grim formality.

"I must apologise for the expression I used to you just now, Lady Rossiter."

Edna looked at him for a moment, and then let the wide charity of her slowly-dawning smile envelop his very patent anger and confusion.

"But that's quite enough! Perhaps we both grew rather excited; but after all, the best of friends must have their little quarrels. I am more than ready to forget."

"Say no more about it," muttered Fuller, obviously under the impression that he was gracefully bringing matters to a conclusion.

"Ah, but one word more I must say," Edna interposed quickly. "You know, I'm afraid I must hold quite, quite firm about the presentation. Or perhaps I had better tell Mr. Cooper that, much as I appreciate having been consulted, I prefer to withdraw from his committee."

Fuller's bulldog jaw was set hard.

"That's as you like, of course."

If Edna had not expected such a rejoinder, the tremor with which she received it was all but imperceptible.

"I'm sorry we don't see things in the same light," she said sweetly, "and I can't tell you how heartily glad I should be to find myself in the wrong about poor Miss Marchrose."

She hesitated for a moment, but neither the voice nor the expression of Mr. Fairfax Fuller appeared to denote any readiness to resume a discussion previously so much fraught with verbal disaster. So Edna, almost hearing herself pause to think, "Is it kind, is it wise, is it true?" said, "Good afternoon, Mr. Fuller," with perfect cordiality, and descended the stairs, unescorted by the Supervisor.

On the doorstep she encountered old Alderman Bellew, who greeted her with the more cordiality that he had expected to find Sir Julian, of whom he was rather afraid.

"Seeing the car outside, I thought Sir Julian might have run in for a moment on business, and I was anxious to see him. But it'll keep—it'll very well keep. I've had a little walk for nothing, that's all, and it won't do me any harm."

The obese old man was panting.

"May I give you a lift anywhere? I always think that's the best of a car—one can be of use to people who haven't got one."

"Well, I declare that's very kind of you. Would the Council House be out of your way?"

"Not at all."

The Alderman dropped thankfully on to the comfortable seat offered him.

"Did you want to see my husband?" Edna sweetly enquired, not devoid of curiosity.

"Only on a little matter of business connected with the College. It came into my mind that I could get a word with him when I saw the car outside the door. But I daresay I shall see him next week—or I can drop him a line."

"Even Julian," said Lady Rossiter intentionally, "is hardly more interested in our College than I am. You know how I've followed its career from the very beginning and always kept in the closest possible touch with the members of the staff. And I needn't tell you that I've never yet missed a General Committee meeting."

"Have you not, indeed!" responded the Alderman, obviously debating in his own mind whether or not he should take Lady Rossiter into his further confidence with regard to the affairs of Culmouth College.

She maintained a tactful silence.

"The fact is, Lady Rossiter, that a suggestion has been made—this is quite confidential, you understand—for opening a new branch of the College. They're asking for something of the same kind in Gloucestershire, and it appears that the municipal authorities are ready enough to guarantee the funds. I have a very gratifying letter, which I want your husband to see, speaking in most complimentary terms of our little show here. Of course, it's quite understood to be more or less run on philanthropic lines. That chap Fuller has done marvels, and actually achieved a balance on the right side, but the concern isn't primarily meant to be a paying one, as I needn't tell you."

"No, indeed. One's idea was to fit the wage-earners rather more for their task—to help the inhabitants of our little corner of the Empire to help themselves."

"Quite so. And apparently the fame of our little enterprise has spread," said the old man, with great satisfaction. "They actually want me to send a representative to look at the buildings they have in view, and put things in train a bit. Rather gratifying for little Culmouth, eh?"

"Yes, indeed."

"Of course, it all depends on Sir Julian's consent—naturally, that's an understood thing. After all he's done for us, and his position and all."

"I am quite sure you may count upon him," said Edna graciously. "He will appreciate the compliment to our small experiment as much as I do."

If the good Alderman felt slightly puzzled at the extremely proprietory attitude adopted by his listener, he knew better than to give any sign of it.

"There'll be great excitement amongst the staff," he said. "But, of course, they'll know nothing about it for the present."

"There's something rather unsettled about the staff just now," Edna thoughtfully rejoined. "You know how things can be *felt* in the air sometimes, and I've fancied rather an absence of our usual *esprit de corps* lately. I haven't quite known what to attribute it to—"

Being at all events perfectly well aware of what she was going to attribute it to now, Lady Rossiter only paused long enough to make sure that the Alderman, listening open-mouthed, had no theory to put forward.

"May I speak quite frankly, and in confidence?"

"Of course, of course."

"It's a thing that's rather difficult to speak of at all, but, of course, you know Mr. Easter's circumstances as well as I do. He *is* a married man."

Alderman Bellew, looking more astounded than ever, gave a breathless nod of assent.

"And also," said Edna, smiling a little, "he happens to be an extremely attractive person. Consequently, when a young—a fairly young, woman, spends her Saturday afternoons typing at the estate office, and then has herself escorted home afterwards, and keeps all her civility, and all her smiles, and all her conversation, for one particular person—well, one is inclined to wonder a little, that's all."

"Bless my soul!" ejaculated the astonished Alderman.

Edna suddenly became grave.

"You understand that I'm not, for one single instant, hinting at any sort or kind of—of understanding or flirtation between them. I know Mark, I suppose, better than anybody else on earth knows him, and I trust him absolutely. But I needn't tell you—a man is a man."

"Of course," said the Alderman portentously, as one resolved to rise to the occasion, "we really know very little about *her*. I suppose you mean the Lady Superintendent?"

"Yes, poor Miss Marchrose. Don't think that I would willingly say an unkind word about her, for *indeed* I could never cast the first stone. But I've been uneasy for some time, and this afternoon it gave me a little shock to see something—Oh, never mind what! A straw very often shows which way the wind blows."

Having by this reticence left the simple-minded Alderman to infer the existence of a whole truss of straw at the very least, Lady Rossiter leant back and closed her eyes, as though in weary retrospect.

"It would never do to have talk of that kind going about, Lady Rossiter. Demoralise the staff in a moment, you know. I remember rather a similar case, years ago, in the big insurance office where I started life. One of the partners played the fool—nothing wrong, you know, but there was a pretty typist, and he was for ever sending for her to take down letters, and the others got talking—you can guess the sort of thing. The girl had to get the sack, of course."

The matter-of-factness of this conclusion was against all Lady Rossiter's avowed principles of championship of her sex, and consistency would not allow her to assent. But she gave a heavy sigh, and said:

"I know the sort of thing you mean, and gossip spreads so easily in a little community like ours. I can't help knowing, either, that one or two people have already noticed the way in which Miss Marchrose behaves."

"Oh, well, you know," leniently remarked the old man, "it may not be altogether her doing. Easter has no business to forget he's a married man."

"I am afraid," Edna answered with reserve, "that I know one or two things about Miss Marchrose which go to show that she is not exactly an inexperienced person. Besides, women have very strong instincts sometimes, and get to know a good deal by intuition. I will tell you perfectly honestly, Mr. Bellew, that I've never altogether trusted her, although it seems a hard thing to say."

Perhaps the Alderman was somewhat of the same opinion.

"What does Sir Julian think?"

"He has comparatively few opportunities of judging; and besides, I haven't really discussed the matter with him. One does dislike anything of that sort so intensely, it's very difficult sometimes to speak of it."

"Yes, yes, Lady Rossiter—of course. But you mustn't distress yourself, on any account. That would never do. You know, the girl can go."

Edna was sincerely horrified at this ruthless cutting of the Gordian knot.

"Oh, but it's her livelihood! We could hardly turn her away like that, unless there was anything definite. There should always be infinite pitifulness, to my mind. Mine is only a humble little creed, but that's the keynote of it all. Long-suffering. Sometimes a woman can do more than a man in such cases. Much as one would dislike it, perhaps one might say a word or two."

"Well, well, it's very good of you, I'm sure. The poor thing may be in a false position altogether," said the Alderman, with more compassion than Edna, in spite of her creed, thought altogether called for by the possible plight of the Lady Superintendent.

"I know I can rely on you to keep all this to yourself absolutely. Perhaps I ought hardly to have spoken, but it gave me a great shock this afternoon. However, we needn't go into that. There is really nothing to be done, except to be very much on one's guard as to possible gossip amongst the staff."

"We must await developments," said the Alderman solemnly.

On this noncommittal *cliché*, he thanked Lady Rossiter very much for having brought him to the steps of the Council House, and ponderously ascended them, still evidently full of thought as to her hinted revelations.

Edna, deeply reflective, was motored back to Culmhayes. The question of the presentation had almost been driven from her mind by the preoccupation engendered at the sight of Mark Easter and Miss Marchrose in their companionable solitude. Her suspicions, already stirring, were now in a lively state of activity, and her feelings divided between an unconscious satisfaction in having been proved a true prophet and a very real apprehension as to the condition of Mark Easter's affections. She remained, however, carefully compassionate in her thoughts of the chief culprit, and was resolved that no impetuosity of Alderman Bellew's should summarily deprive Miss Marchrose of a good post, and incidentally provide her with a grievance.

Edna's appeal to the Alderman had been as nearly impulsive as any utterance of hers ever could be. She had chosen her words—as she always did—but the instinct that had moved her to speak at all was the age-old and overmastering desire of drawing attention instantly to the failure of a fellow-creature in subscribing to the recognised code.

She consecrated several grave moments of thought to the situation, which she mentally qualified as a problem, although she would have been puzzled to define the exact necessity for a solution.

In her own room, Lady Rossiter became still further conscious of the disturbed state of her spirits.

She rang for her maid.

"Shall I take your furs, m'lady?"

Edna parted with her last shred of calm, in some mysterious fashion, when the comfortable and eminently becoming weight was lifted from her shoulders.

"I am very tired, Mason," she remarked patiently.

"Yes, m'lady? It's rather tiring weather," said Mason woodenly.

"I don't know about that. But when one thinks a great deal about other people—their weakness and ingratitude and folly—it seems to wear one out, somehow."

"I've mended the blue tea-gown, m'lady. Shall I put it out?"

"No," said Edna, with most unwonted sharpness.

It seemed to her that Mason was a woman on whom it was extraordinarily difficult to make any impression. Edna sedulously "took an interest" in all her servants, and made a point of lending books to her own maid, but never had she met with one less responsive to her influence.

She compressed her lips slightly, and made the small, collected pause with which it was her custom to counter such rare tendencies to irritability as she ever experienced.

The instant's recollection was followed, as always, by a flow of larger, more serene charity, enveloping successfully even the recalcitrant Mason.

"I hope you have a nice book for Sunday, Mason. I know it's your great day for reading."

"Yes, thank you, m'lady."

Lady Rossiter's thoughts dwelt tenderly on those copies of Ruskin and Stevenson, in the rather cheaper editions, which she kept for purposes of lending. She had drawn attention to several passages in them by faint scorings in pencil.

"Well, and which is it?"

Mason looked blanker than ever.

"What, m'lady?"

"Which book are you reading, Mason?"

The silence that ensued might, from Mason's expression, have been construed as one both sulky and resentful, but Edna waited with implacable sunniness.

Finally the maid, opening the door for her mistress, replied in a vicious manner:

"Well, m'lady, at the present, I'm reading a sweetly pretty story called 'East Lynne'"

XV

The activities of Lady Rossiter did not altogether cease at her conversation with Alderman Bellew.

She spoke to Miss Farmer, at the back of her mind the conviction that Miss Farmer would think it due to the other members of the College staff to ascertain whether their attention had yet been focussed upon the incipient scandal in their midst.

She made tentative beginning:

"You will reassure me, Miss Farmer, and I can't tell you how glad I shall be. It *is* my fancy, isn't it, that there is—what shall I call it?—something that rather disturbs—in the atmosphere?"

"The—College, do you mean, Lady Rossiter?" Miss Farmer spoke confusedly, evidently quite undecided in her mind as to Lady Rossiter's meaning, and anxious not to commit herself until she had ascertained it.

"Ah, then you do know. I'm sorry," spoke Edna gravely. "One condemns no one—that's understood, of course. But you, who are working there all day and every day—you must know better than anyone how far it's all gone. I mean nothing that can't be spoken—oh yes, you know—after all, we're both women. But there's the staff to think of—my staff that I'm proud of, and care for. Tell me, do they talk about Miss Marchrose and this insane infatuation of hers?"

"No—no, I don't think so—I hardly know …" hesitated Miss Farmer, very red, and obviously feeling her way.

"Thank God for that!" Lady Rossiter piously interjected. "You understand what I mean? It's not that I, of all people, who know Mark Easter intimately, could ever underrate the fact that he is an unusually attractive man. But then, you see—Mark is married. It's so simple, isn't it, to those of us who can see straight? There is just that choice—right or wrong—and one's chosen one's path long, long ago. But this poor girl in whom we're interested, whom one longs, oh so pitifully and tenderly—to help. You see, I'm afraid that her ideals are poor, dwarfed, stunted things. She is very foolish, undignified and unwomanly, but I pray and I believe—I try with all my heart to believe—that it is just *that*—because she knows no better. Only, Miss Farmer—don't let them talk at the College. I know it's very easy—a little staying on after hours, an excuse or two for going into Mr. Easter's office, a hundred-and-one indiscretions of that kind— and the mischief's done."

"Oh, Lady Rossiter! but really, excuse me if I say that I hardly think—"

Edna swept on, sweeping with her the bewildered and embarrassed protests trembling on Miss Farmer's lips.

"No one could ever fear harsh judgments from you, Miss Farmer. I know that, and that's why I've spoken to you. And because I want you to try and prevent others from judging and condemning unheard. ... There'll be talk—oh, I know human nature, and that it's impossible for things to be otherwise—but at least I may count upon you for stemming the tide a little, until the way is rather clearer. Believe me, there will be a crisis—a solution of some sort will come. I *know* that the present state of tension can't last."

It may reasonably be conceded that Lady Rossiter had ample cause for the assertion.

She sent Miss Farmer away, muddle and incoherency on her inarticulate tongue, and in her starting eyes fears visible for all to see.

Edna thought of Mark Easter, and asked herself whether one word from her might not save Mark from endless vexation and discomfort when the inevitable *débacle* should come upon the impossible situation. She had for too long been accustomed to look upon herself as the only feminine element in Mark's mutilated life, to entertain on his behalf fears of a more serious kind.

But Mark was thinking of his sister's wedding and of her many, and essentially unreasonable, attempts to turn his small house into a scene of extensive and prolonged hospitalities for which it was eminently unfitted in every possible way.

Edna postponed the utterance of her one word.

She only offered, very gently and matter-of-factly, to enact the part of mistress of the house when and whenever her services might be acceptable. Mark Easter thanked her very warmly and thought that he could "manage."

That the process of "managing "was not an easy one was descried shortly before the wedding by Lady Rossiter and her husband, inadvertently entering the villa and finding it a sea of frenzied preparation.

Aggressively new trunks stood in the small entrance, effectively blocking the staircase, and from the drawing-room door, propped open by a piano-stool, came the sound of voices raised in considerable agitation.

The form taken by the *boulversement* of the five occupiers of the drawing-room appeared to consist principally in their each and all having taken a seat upon some piece of furniture not primarily intended to be sat upon.

Iris, very dishevelled, was perched upon the piano; her *fiancé* bestrode a small table; Mark, looking harassed, sat on the corner of the lowest bookcase in the room; and Ruthie and Ambrose, their respective boots drumming a lively quartette against the wainscoting, disfigured either end of the writing-table. Iris turned in instant appeal to the entering visitors.

"We're simply fearfully worried," she declared penetratingly. "Do help me to settle. Oh, do sit down, Lady Rossiter!"

Edna smilingly selected the corner of the sofa least encumbered by cardboard boxes and crumpled tissue paper.

"It's old Aunt Anne. We don't know what to do about having her at the wedding. We never, never thought she'd want to come."

"She's seventy-nine," said Mark.

"And perfectly *awful*," moaned Iris.

"One had hoped, and meant, to avoid a conventional gathering of relations altogether," mournfully interjected Mr. Garrett's deep tones. "I myself have had to be extraordinarily careful. We, who are members of the Clan, have to reckon with such immense feudal feeling and that kind of thing—the sort of old-time loyalty one hardly sees on the wrong side of the Border—and finally we decided to eliminate all but the very nearest.

The dear old pater is going to represent the family, and the old pipers and gillies and—er—dependents generally."

"I am afraid he has a long, cold journey before him, then, in this bitter weather," said Edna civilly.

"The pater is not actually in dear old Scotland at the moment," said Mr. Garrett, in a tone of reserve.

"But Aunt Anne!" wailed Iris. "Will you believe it, she's written to ask if we're expecting her here to-morrow—just two days before the wedding. And, of course, we're not. We never thought of her coming at all, did we, Mark, at her age?"

"And she's only sent you salt-cellars, at that," said Mark, with a rueful grin.

"We should be delighted to receive anyone at Culmhayes if it's a question of room," began Sir Julian, in voice wherein delight was not the most prominent emotion discernible.

"Thank you, Sir Julian, it's most awfully good of you. But it's not that. Douglas' father will insist on going to the hotel, with him, so we shall have a spare bed. But Aunt Anne wants such a lot of looking after; and then she'll be old-fashioned, and hate everything and disapprove of my frock, and—I can't *bear* it if she's to come and spoil everything," said Miss Easter, in an outburst of passionate resentment.

"My dear, what can it matter what other people think? One takes one's own line, without hurting or vexing anyone—that, never—but just quietly, without wondering what others may say—" But Lady Rossiter's generalities proved of no avail in soothing Iris, although they gave Douglas an opportunity for uttering a small effective Gaelicism.

"Dinna fash yersel', Iris, as we Kelts say at home."

"It's all very well, but how can I write and tell Aunt Anne not to come—that we aren't expecting her? It would look as though we didn't want her."

The truth of this implication appeared in such blatant obviousness to at least three of Iris's listeners that none of them spoke a word.

At last Sir Julian said drily:

"In fact, it's one of those disconcerting situations that look exactly what they really are."

"And one wishes they didn't," concluded Mark.

"The modern wedding," said Mr. Garrett suddenly, "I look upon as the surviving relic of a barbarous age. It is iniquitous that a contract between two private parties should be made the excuse for a public display, an incontinent gathering together of incongruous multitudes, for the mere purposes of gaping and staring. To my mind, there should be no other ceremony than the verbal plighting of troth, given in the presence of two witnesses, upon the bare, open heath—"

"We haven't any bare, open heaths round Culmouth," interposed Julian hastily.

"I was thinking of the customs in my ain countree," said Mr. Garrett morosely.

A rather blighted silence fell upon the room.

It was broken by the wailing voice of Ambrose, whom everyone had forgotten.

"Aren't we *ever* going to have tea?"

"Good gracious, I'd forgotten all about it!" cried Iris, exaggeratedly aghast. "Ruthie darling, do go and see if Sarah can let us have tea at once. We shall be seven."

Sir Julian made earnest attempts and Lady Rossiter polite feints, at leaving the villa on the instant.

"You must stay," said Iris piteously, "because everything is so awful that I know I'm going to scream presently."

On this inducement or another, the visitors remained throughout a strange, Passover meal, in the course of which Iris leapt up and wrote and destroyed three successive telegrams alternately telling Aunt Anne that she was or was not expected on the following day, and Mr. Garrett discoursed further on the marriage laws of England, regarded by him with the extreme of disfavour, and the children took advantage of their father's usual leniency and their aunt's roving attention, to dispose of immense quantities of cake previously smeared with jam.

Edna, remembering the quasi-maternal rôle adopted by herself towards

Ruthie, fixed a look of grave surprise upon the child from the other side of the table.

Ruthie ate on.

Lady Rossiter deepened the look and sought to convey its full inner meaning by dropping a pained glance at the jam-laden slab in Ruthie's hand and then raising her eyebrows and slightly contracting the corners of her mouth.

These signals being stolidly disregarded, there only remained to say in very gentle accents:

"Are you always allowed cake and jam together, dear?"

"*Always,*" said Ruthie, with a face of brass, and in her voice an intensity of assurance that conveyed with certainty, to anyone as well conversant as was Lady Rossiter with the extremely low standard of truth prevailing in the Easter nursery establishment, that she was lying.

Edna turned her gaze upon Ambrose.

His face already bore the peculiarly glazed and pallid look that characterises over-eating, but on meeting Lady Rossiter's eye he made a mighty effort to cram his remaining cake into an already bulging cheek.

"You'll choke, Peekaboo," warned Ruthie, with only too much reason.

Thereafter the conversation was adjusted to the accompaniment of the exceedingly distressing sounds proceeding intermittently from Ambrose.

"Dear, dear—a crumb gone the wrong way?" said the unobservant Iris. "You'll be better in a minute, dear."

"I choked—" began Ambrose wheezingly, obedient to the unwritten law which decrees that the victim of a choking fit should add to his own discomfort and that of other people by entering into a gasping analysis of the phenomenon.

"Look at the ceiling, Ambrose," advised Mark.

Everyone in the room immediately set this desirable example by a sort of mysterious instinct, while the unfortunate Ambrose kept his head well down over his plate and continued to emit hysterical crows.

"Look at *me*, Peekaboo!" shouted Ruthie. "*I'm* looking at the ceiling!"

She hung backwards over her chair, glaring upwards with starting eyeballs.

"Don't do that, Ruthie," said Mark, Iris and Lady Rossiter simultaneously.

"Try and get your breath, laddie," advised Mr. Garrett kindly, if with some superfluity.

"He'll be better in a moment. Go on talking," was Lady Rossiter's tactful suggestion, which had the immediate effect of paralysing the assembly into a silence upon which the paroxysms of Ambrose struck with greatly enhanced violence.

Sir Julian threw himself into the breach, addressing himself to Mark Easter with an air of unconcern which he felt to be overdone.

"Have you talked to Walters about the car for Tuesday? I told him you would let him know what time—"

"Let's pat Peekaboo on the back," cried Ruthie hilariously.

"Gently, then. Yes, Sir Julian, thanks very much, I ... No, no, Ruthie— stop that—can't you see you're making him worse?"

"Daddy, I just choked—a crumb—"

"For goodness' sake don't talk, Ambrose. You'd better go upstairs."

"I'm sure the child will have convulsions in another minute. Do look at his face! Douglas, don't you think he's turning black?"

This last contribution of his Auntie Iris's to the sum of calamities already overwhelming the distressed Ambrose caused him to burst into tears.

"*Do* drink some tea, dear," urged Lady Rossiter.

"Take him upstairs, Ruthie," said her parent wearily.

The victim was removed, protesting inarticulately at the mirthful ministrations still insisted upon by his sister.

Everyone was conscious of relief, and Lady Rossiter said tolerantly, "Poor little boy!"

"He feels the wedding *dreadfully*," Iris observed.

"Feels the wedding?"

"Yes, you know, he's afraid that it means losing me. I've always been so much with the dear kiddie-widdies."

"You've always been very fond of them, my dear, and they of you," said Mark gratefully.

"I should have liked little Peekaboo for a page," said Iris sentimentally, "but he's just the wrong size. And besides, poor darling, he hasn't got his front teeth. Ruthie's bridesmaid frock has come, Lady Rossiter."

Under cover of the polite interest evinced by Edna at the information, her husband made his escape from the room.

He and Mark, smoking in the garden, turned with undisguised relief from the topic of the hour, and discussed instead the affairs of Culmouth College.

"What about this Gloucester business? Old Bellew is patting himself on the back all right. He thinks there's likely to be an opening in Cardiff, too."

"All the better. We always hoped the scheme would spread, Sir Julian."

"I know. Who could have guessed it would come so quickly, though? Look here, Mark, have you thought who ought to go and see these Gloucester fellows and start them off in their new premises?"

"Well—I left that to you," said Mark hesitatingly.

"Of course, you're the man to send, but I don't know that we can spare you at the minute."

"I'm quite at your disposal for anything," said Mark cheerfully.

"Would you go? After all, it could only be a matter of two or three days."

"That's all. But the only thing I'm thinking is, whether it wouldn't be a good thing to take one of the actual staff—someone who's really been working the thing from the inside."

For an insane moment, a surmise worthy of Iris herself crossed Sir Julian's mind. Could Mark Easter be about to adjudicate to himself Miss Marchrose as a travelling companion?

"What about Fuller?" said Mark. "He's a good man of business, and got all the facts and figures at his finger-ends."

"He could be spared, I suppose?"

"I think so. Miss Marchrose could quite well take on for a day or two. She's won golden opinions from Fuller."

"H'm. The misogynist," said Sir Julian reflectively.

Interruption came only too soon.

Sir Julian heartily wished that he had taken the more drastic measure of returning outright to Culmhayes when the garden was invaded not only by the lovers themselves, Edna walking slightly behind them with a rather consciously unconscious expression, but also by a triumphantly whooping Ambrose, glorying in his restored ability to render the day hideous with sound.

Ruthie was for the moment, unwontedly enough, both invisible and inaudible.

Iris instantly attached herself to Sir Julian. He had been regretfully compelled to realise that ever since the day, regarded by him with horror, of their conversation in his study, Miss Easter had assumed the existence of some intimate understanding between them, such as caused her to make him the recipient of many small personal confidences that filled him with embarrassment.

"You know I wanted Douglas to be married in a kilt?"

"Did you?"

"But he's so ridiculously shy. And what's that other thing they wear?"

Sir Julian looked unintelligent and Mr. Garrett's deep voice behind him made suggestion.

"Is the lassie thinking of the tartan?"

"Ye-es," said Iris doubtfully. "Or do I mean a plaid?"

Sir Julian felt quite unequal to enlightening her.

"I see that I shall have to teach you many things," said Mr. Garrett gloomily.

"Do you expect ever to live in Scotland?" Sir Julian enquired.

"We toilers and sowers gravitate to London instinctively. I always say," Mr. Garrett observed, in tones of great interest, "I always say, that London is the modern Mecca. Pilgrims come there from all parts. It is, in many ways, a city of freedom. London, someone has said—the name of the writer has escaped my memory—is the only capital in the world where a man can eat a penny bun in the streets without exciting comment. Now, that seems to me quite extraordinarily descriptive."

It seemed to Sir Julian, on the contrary, quite extraordinarily futile, and he wished, not for the first time, that Iris would make her appeals to some other source, when she murmured in a trustful way:

"Isn't Douglas rather wonderful? You know what I mean—I think he's wonderful, sometimes. The things he says, I mean."

"We shall live in London for a time," Mr. Garrett pursued. "My journalistic work will keep me there, and then we have to think of Iris's literary career. I immensely want her to meet some of the great thinkers of the day."

Iris looked awestricken, clasped her hand, and said in a small, hushed voice:

"Just think of the vistas and vistas and *vistas* that it opens up!"

Sir Julian did so, and barely suppressed a visible shudder at the phalanx of journalistic luminaries, of whom he felt certain that the great thinkers of the day, as known to Mr. Garrett, consisted.

"How is your book going?"

"The sales haven't been very large, but it's been tremendously *noticed*, for a first novel," said Iris hopefully.

"You must help me to persuade Iris," said Mr. Garrett, also adding his mite to the quota of appeal so ill responded to by the unfortunate Julian; "You must help me to persuade this little woman, that big sales matter very little in comparison with the meed of recognition that 'Ben' has received from the *thinking* section of the reading world."

"Ruthie is up that tree," announced Ambrose loudly and suddenly, thereby for the first time becoming the unconscious object of Sir Julian's brief and passionate gratitude.

Iris, Douglas and Sir Julian all gazed upwards and became aware of Miss Easter, perilously grappling the bare limb of a leafless tree.

Followed Ruthie's inevitable discovery that the position so recklessly attained was both uncomfortable and insecure, her proclamation of immediate and excessive peril, and the issuing of annoyed ejaculations and peremptory advice from the up-gazers gathered below.

"Better fetch a step-ladder at once. She'll only fall and hurt herself," said Iris.

"Where?"

"Oh," said Iris distractedly, "I don't think we've got one anywhere."

"Better abandon the project, then," Mark observed mildly. "I'll go up after her."

"The tree will break," wailed Iris.

"Not it! Wish it would, and give the kid a lesson. Sorry to treat you to such a series of domestic calamities, Lady Rossiter."

"No, no," said Edna, smiling. "You know I take things as I find them."

They waited to see the rescue effected, and left Mr. Garrett serenely observing, "You should remember to look up, and not down, when you climb, lassie."

"What a household!" said Julian.

"One wonders what those unfortunate, motherless children will grow up into," his wife responded thoughtfully.

"It doesn't seem to me that there's much room for wonder."

"When this wedding is over I shall talk to Mark again about sending Ruthie to school. It would really be a great mercy if the boy could go too."

"Why shouldn't he?"

"He's really not at all strong, I believe. But I'll talk to Mark," repeated Edna.

Some subtle hint of complacency in her voice kept Sir Julian obstinately silent. He really did not know whether or not his wife's influence with Mark Easter was as strong as she assumed it to be. Mark was of all things easy-going, and Julian did not know that the question of his children preoccupied him very deeply. Not improbable that he might even sacrifice Ambrose and his problematical delicacy of constitution for the sake of peace, and the satisfaction of Lady Rossiter.

It remained to be seen, Julian thought, whether there were anything to which Mark attached sufficient importance to fight for it. Julian was oddly obsessed by the conviction that contest was in the air.

XVI

It was always felt that the great disappointment in connection with Iris Easter's wedding was the shock unconsciously caused by Mr. Douglas Garrett's father.

The representative of the Clan appeared in the guise of a stout, handsome old man with waxed moustache, in rather smart, tight, black clothes, wearing a top-hat, a white carnation buttonhole, and white spats, and speaking with an accent that, though exceedingly pronounced, was not to be recognised as that of any known part of Scotland.

The conviction gradually filtered through the assembled guests that Mr. Garrett senior spoke with the tongue of Swindon. The blurred vowels and resonant *r* were unmistakable.

But old Mr. Garrett made no pretence at the Keltic atmosphere so fondly affected by his son.

"My dearr boy," he affectionately apostrophised the bridegroom, "I've left the business to take cayurr of itself, for the first time in nearly twenty years. You don't know what business is, loafing about London doing a little scribbling heerr and therre the way you do, otherwise you'd appreciate my presence heerr to-day at its full value."

Douglas Garrett made no audible response that could be interpreted into the required assurance, but old Mr. Garrett spoke so loudly and confidently that it was almost impossible to believe his observations to be anything but a sort of impromptu rehearsal of the speech that he would deliver at the wedding-breakfast.

The interval of waiting in the church appeared likely to be of indefinite duration, and everybody heard old Mr. Garrett express to his son the hope that the "gurrel" hadn't thought better of it at the last minute.

"Therre have been such cases known, my dearr boy," he dispassionately remarked, "and your I-ris looked to me a highly nervous sort of gurrel."

Lady Rossiter, in the front bench, sank on to her knees, less from a sudden access of prayerfulness than from a very obvious desire to make evident the unsuitability of old Mr. Garrett's behaviour to his surroundings.

"*You're* not feeling hysterical, are you?" suspiciously demanded Mr. Garrett, whisking round on the instant at this demonstration. "I know what you ladies are. It's a very trying wait for all of us, and I'm afraid my poorr boy may break down if it goes on much longer. Don't let yourself get upset on any account."

At last the sounds of arrival made themselves heard without the church, the bridegroom's expression relaxed, and his father gave a loud gasp of relief.

An explanatory murmur, of the kind that has an origin destined to remain for ever unknown, pervaded the church.

"She's been crying—dreadfully upset—no mother—poor little thing. All right now."

"I said the gurrel looked to me nervous," remarked the elder Mr. Garrett, with conscious triumph in his own omniscience.

"How like Auntie Iris!" thought Julian, for the hundredth time.

At all events, the bride's pretty little face showed no trace of tears now, as she came slowly up the aisle on her brother's arm.

Following her, and casting triumphant and self-satisfied glances from left to right, was the solitary bridesmaid.

Ruthie was a plain little girl, and it was impossible not to feel that attempt at embellishment had done much towards making her still plainer.

Her short white skirts stuck out to ungraceful dimensions above brown-stockinged legs and strapped shoes that, to Julian's disgusted perceptions, had never appeared of more solid proportions, and the broad sash tied firmly round her person was of a disastrous shade of salmon pink.

A second edition of the sash reappeared round the wide straw hat that Ruthie, *more suo*, wore upon the extreme back of her head.

Her thick, stiff brown hair showed only too evident manifestations of having been severely treated by Sarah, in the manner known as "damp-plaiting" on the previous evening.

The whole effect was rather that of a young South Sea Islander introduced for the first time into European garb and aware of novelty.

The College staff was sufficiently well represented. Iris had expressed a sort of whole-hearted wish to see "*all* the dear people from Culmouth College" in the church, and this rather reckless aspiration had not been left without response.

Cooper was prominent in immaculate gloves, with Miss Sandiloe beside him, coy and alert both at once and poised first on one foot and then on the other, as though her shoes hurt her feet. Julian saw Miss Marchrose, looking better than he had ever seen her, in a bench at the bottom of the church. She wore a soft felt hat that became her, and her changeful face was full of colour.

"She looks happier," thought Julian, and immediately felt a doubtful foreboding as to the source of that look.

He remembered that Miss Marchrose, on the day before the wedding, had officiated at a small ceremony at Culmouth College, when she had presented to Iris, on behalf of the staff, a silver mirror.

Neither Sir Julian nor Lady Rossiter had been present, but Mark had described the occasion afterwards to Sir Julian alone.

"Fuller did all the speaking, and did it uncommonly well, too. I didn't know he had it in him, but it was just right—awfully good little speech. Miss Marchrose presented the thing, and looked very pretty. Blushed like anything, too, when Fuller began something about her having been chosen to represent the staff. Fuller thinks she's his discovery, you know, and he's no end proud of her."

Julian was not a little inclined to wonder whether Fairfax Fuller, emphasising the claims of the Lady Superintendent, had not taken his stand upon the lines of championship. Nor did he care to dwell upon the actual or threatened attacks which should have aroused the never very deeply dormant combative instincts of Mr. Fuller. If Miss Marchrose should need an ally, she had at all events assured herself of one to whom half-measures were unknown. Julian only returned to the present when the bridegroom, in a voice which seemed full of deep protest against the archaic formula required of him, repeated after the clergyman the vows appointed to him. Iris was inaudible.

The exodus to the vestry, and the usual rapturous displays of enthusiasm therein, duly took place, and Mr. Garrett gave his arm to his bride and conducted her down the aisle to the triumphant strains of the wedding-march from *Lohengrin*—the characteristic selection made by Iris on the grounds of originality.

There was to be no reception, and it was undeniable that a certain sense of anti-climax pervaded the villa when old Mr. Garrett, Sir Julian and Lady Rossiter, accompanied by Ruthie and Ambrose, found themselves at the gates, over which a slightly perilous triumphal arch wavered in the cold wind.

"Mr. and Mrs. Garrett is in the drawing-room!" quoth Sarah excitedly at the entrance.

"My dearr children!" exclaimed Mr. Garrett senior, and thereafter carried off the whole situation with a high hand.

He kissed Iris, clapped his son on the back, and stood for some time with his large old hand kindly and weightily gripping the younger man's shoulder; he made jokes about "giving away the bride" that had no merit save that of extreme antiquity, he became exceedingly solemn and alluded to Douglas' sainted mother, and then by a natural transition to Douglas' probable offspring, which discomposed Iris to the extent of sending her into the dining-room forthwith where luncheon awaited the party.

"That dearr child is the least little bit nervous, rushing away like that," Mr. Garrett remarked in an explanatory way, and paternally ushered them all out of the room.

The wedding-breakfast in no way defeated him. Mark, in something less than his usual radiant good spirits, yet muttered to Julian under his breath, with a laugh in his eyes:

"*Ain't I volatile?*"

Volatile Mr. Garrett certainly was. He made two speeches, one when

Iris tremulously cut her wedding-cake, and another at a later stage of the proceedings, when he judged the drinking of healths to be apropos.

"I am nearly seventy," he earnestly told them, with a good deal of emphasis, "and the day may be with us before some of us look for it, when my boy here, and his wife and—shall I say, I hope otherrs as well?—will step into my shoes. And those shoes—I say it in all seriousness, although my speech may be a jesting one, as it were—those shoes, I hope, will not be the proverbial shoes that pinch."

Mr. Garrett paused for a more lengthy appreciation of his own humour, while everyone made polite and rather mirthless sounds of amusement, with the exception of Iris, still blushing, and Douglas, wrapt in impenetrable gloom. Ruthie and Ambrose, indeed, laughed loudly, and at sufficient length to draw down upon themselves a reprehensive glance from Lady Rossiter and a murderous one from the bridegroom.

"The fact is, my dear son and daughter," said old Mr. Garrett impressively, "that there is a future before you. Not only that future of domestic joy and happiness which we see foreshadowed to-day—that circle of home faces"—everybody looked apprehensive—"which I hope will gather round your hearth as the yearrs go on, but also a future in business. Of that future, *I* have laid the foundations for you. Douglas, my dearr boy, you have seen the business at Swindon?"

Douglas looked infinitely depressed.

"That business," said his undaunted parent, "I have built up from the very beginning. You will have nothing to do but follow the lines I have laid down. There's the old home waiting for you, the dear little old house in Cambridge Road West that you know so well, and that I hope that pretty creature here will soon know as well as you do."

Sir Julian, aware that everyone in the room was by this time obsessed by a vivid recollection of the flight of imagination which had led Iris's husband to date his ancestral reminiscences from Scotland, avoided meeting the eye of anyone present.

This exercise, indeed, was freely indulged in by the majority of those who sat and listened to the eloquent speech of Mr. Garrett senior.

It came to an end at last, and Iris ran away to change her dress, a sudden access of skittishness superimposed upon her shyness.

Douglas simultaneously took the opportunity of disappearing, and Sir Julian found himself enabled to put the question that had been making its way to his mind almost irresistibly all the morning.

"What does your business in Swindon consist of, Mr. Garrett?"

"Printing and stationery, Sir Julian," said the old man, proudly and simply. "A go-ahead little concern on the small scale, though I say it that shouldn't. It's enabled me to give my only son an allowance, so that he could see life in London for a while before settling down in Swindon like his father and grandfather before him."

"Your family has an old connection with Swindon, then?"

Sir Julian, interested, had forgotten the Keltic aspirations of Douglas until they were recalled by Mr. Garrett's answer.

"Two generations, Sir Julian. My grandfather came from the North, I believe, but he married a London gurrel, and they settled in Swindon after a year or two. Swindon is a fascinating town, I can assure you, and if ever you make a visit there I shall be happy to show you some of the glories of the dear old place."

Mr. Garrett wiped his glasses and walked about the room, talking gaily and persistently to while away the time of waiting for the bride's reappearance.

"And what's your opinion of a wedding, my dearr little fellow?" he genially enquired of Ambrose, who wore a rather forlorn aspect.

"Eh?" said Ambrose, with more dejection than usual in the delivery of his objectionable exclamation.

"What do you think of a wedding, now you've seen one? This is your first experience, I presume?"

Ambrose looked absent-minded, gazed up enquiringly through his spectacles for a moment, and then said, "Eh?" all over again.

"My dearr child, don't say 'eh,' like that!" rather testily exclaimed the old man, a prey to the universal impulse of annoyance which almost invariably assailed everyone entering into conversation with the unfortunate Ambrose.

"What does your little sister say?"

"I like being bridesmaid," Ruthie announced in self-satisfied tones. "Uncle Douglas gave me a bangle." She thrust the trinket forward for inspection, and old Mr. Garrett admired it gravely.

"I suppose that's what you call a sweet thing? Isn't that the great word? Well, my dearr child, I'm glad you're satisfied."

Ruthie looked at him intelligently.

"I only hope that Auntie Iris will have a baby soon, because then Sarah says it will be my first cousin, and I haven't got any."

On this delicate aspiration of Miss Easter's the conversation came to a rather abrupt conclusion.

"Iris ought to be ready now," said Mark; "they won't have too much time to get to the station."

He went upstairs.

Presently the bridegroom wandered into the drawing-room again, evidently self-conscious, and endeavouring to conceal it by an excessive display of anxiety as to the probability of missing the train.

"Here she is!"

"The car is waiting," proclaimed Ruthie.

Old Mr. Garrett gazed at the white favours adorning the motor.

"Isn't there a shoe tied on behind?" he demanded sharply.

"I—I don't see one," said Sir Julian, rather feebly, and with an unaccountable sense of having been remiss in omitting to provide this emblem of good fortune.

"Don't let them drive away without an old shoe!" pleaded Mr. Garrett. "My dearr child—Ruth, if that's your name—run up to the bedrooms and see what you can find. I couldn't let my boy go off on his wedding trip without a shoe for good luck."

In eager obedience to this flight of sentiment, Ruthie triumphantly rushed upstairs, the successive sounds of burst-open doors, hasty explorations, and triumphant pouncings conveying the rate of her progress with great accuracy to those in the drawing-room below.

In the excitement which Mr. Garrett diffused round the whole question, there was no possibility of an emotional farewell.

Mark put Iris into the motor—a radiantly pretty bride—and Douglas got in beside her, after muttering something about the old man being in extraordinarily good form to-day and inclined to get above his boots.

"We of the younger generation—" began Mr. Douglas Garrett, quite in his old manner, and then looked as though he had suddenly recollected the advanced years of Sir Julian himself, and subsided into the shelter of the motor without another word.

His father, having already hurried to the back of the car and affixed there a white satin shoe and a bedroom slipper, with much boisterous assistance from Ruthie, proceeded to deliver a valedictory harangue from the step.

"God bless you, my two dearr children, and shower upon you all the blessing of the married state. Send the old man a postcard from your first stopping-place, and, Iris, my dearr new daughter, you'll keep my son up to writing, and I shall be ready for you both in the dear little house at home, whenever you like to come there. Also," said Mr. Garrett hopefully, "we shall meet in London. I think nothing of running up there. Good-bye—good-bye—bless you both."

He stood at the door waving a large clean handkerchief delicately scented with eau-de-Cologne, his shiny top-hat rather to one side and the ends of his beautifully waxed moustaches standing out stiffly. His kind old eyes shone with emotion.

"Yourr loss," he remarked, with simple sententiousness, to Mark Easter, "your loss, is ourr gain. That's a pretty gurrel and a good gurrel, I feel sure. I appreciate my boy's good fortune, I assure you."

He shook hands with them all, begged them to visit Swindon, thanked them again and again for their kindness to himself and his dearr boy Douglas, and took his leave.

"I will not intrude upon you any further," was all his reply to Mark's cordial invitation to remain. "You have been goodness itself to an old man. Good-bye to you all, good-bye."

"I think, in Auntie Iris's place, I should have preferred the father to the son," said Julian, as he went homeward with his wife.

"Poor old man! There's something very genuine about him, in spite of his vulgarity," replied Lady Rossiter, with that leniency of tone that most successfully drapes a rather disparaging utterance.

"I wonder," observed Julian, for once in a loquacious mood, "what the next production will be from Auntie Iris's pen? And whether the influence of Mr. Douglas Garrett will be very obvious."

"That might not be a bad thing."

"It couldn't be a much worse thing than 'Why, Ben!' was."

"Silly little girl! I wish she would stop writing altogether. I have locked up my copy of 'Why, Ben!' on account of the servants. I always hold that one is so wholly responsible for the books one leaves about, with either children or uneducated people in the house, to whom they might do so much harm."

"I shouldn't have thought that Mason's head was very easily turned," thoughtfully rejoined Sir Julian, who was aware of his wife's protracted and unsuccessful wrestlings with the recalcitrant spirit of Mason.

"I sometimes think that I shall have to get another maid," sighed Edna. "One goes on so gladly and willingly from day to day when there is the least little sign of any response, but Mason is at a very, very elementary stage. Of course it's all a question of soul-growth—hers is just a young, blind, struggling soul, and there is only the most pitying tenderness to be felt for that, but I suppose poor human nature is impatient, and longs to see a little dawning of that Divine Spark which one knows so well is there all the time."

But to this gently-spoken plaint Sir Julian, suddenly become silent, made no reply whatever.

Edna went into the morning-room rather dejectedly. An unsympathetic atmosphere, she often felt, wearied her more than any physical strain. She was unaware that this conviction is a singularly widespread one amongst those who have never been called upon for any excess of bodily toil.

Iris was married. There was no further occasion for matronly tact and tenderness, nor for the beautiful tolerance of maturity towards the crudities of youth.

Douglas Garrett had achieved his object, and returned to London with his bride. The necessity therefore no longer existed either for overlooking and graciously ignoring his many shortcomings, or for dropping those little kindly sayings that should serve to remind others, too rashly condemning Mr. Garrett, of that great question, "Is it kind—is it wise—is it true?"

Mr. Garrett's father, who might certainly have served as a substantial peg upon which to hang many a word of gentle forbearance, had gone away, and even the most determined philanthropy could see no hopeful outlet in the direction of Ruthie and Ambrose Easter.

Lady Rossiter began to think of Mark. This she did almost instinctively whenever her sense of the need for "giving out" was at a loss for an object. The situation of Mark Easter was one of such obvious tragedy, and daily reiterated pathos, that the consideration of it could minimise the rather incongruous light-heartedness with which he himself faced it. One could always help Mark.

His children needed help.

His whole household required the supervision of a feminine eye at the shortest possible intervals, and Edna had for years regarded herself as the only woman with eyes available for the purpose. Yet when, on leaving the villa after the wedding, she had suggested, with a very gentle hint of compassionate understanding in her voice, that Mark should come and dine at Culmhayes that night, he had replied, without confusion, that he was going straight up to the College and should remain there late.

It was tragically inevitable, Edna told herself, that one should realise what this implied.

Edna sat in reflection for some time, her face shadowed and saddened, but with that absence of mobility of expression that had left her smooth skin almost altogether unlined throughout her life.

At dinner that night, notwithstanding, she met Sir Julian with an unclouded brow. She often said that part of her rule of life was to leave all her cares locked up in her own room, so that she might always diffuse serenity when with others.

By some perversity of fate, however, Edna's effect upon her husband was never the one at which she so carefully aimed. On this occasion the diffusion of serenity engineered by Lady Rossiter appeared only to leave Sir Julian rather more satirically ill-tempered than it found him.

"Julian, you've thought about the question of sending someone from the staff here to Gloucester, haven't you? It will be rather a big responsibility."

"For Gloucester?"

"For the representative of our College," said Edna, with a little low laugh, quite obviously meant to imply that she thought it best to look upon Sir Julian's captiousness as having been humorously intended.

"There won't be very much in it. Only a question of looking at the buildings, and answering anything the local authorities may want to ask."

"Would that young Mr. Cooper be competent?"

"Anyone would be competent."

An all but imperceptible smile hovered on Lady Rossiter's lips.

"Then, Julian, why don't you send that unfortunate Miss Marchrose? If a break is made, easily and naturally, she can begin again at the College on a different footing. You know there's a certain amount of talk going on there?"

There was a long pause. Sir Julian did not ask, "What about?"

Finally he said: "It's Fuller's business to decide who's going to Gloucester. I'm not responsible for the details of running the staff there in any way. Nor is the question an important one."

"Ah," breathed Edna, "you know that I can't quite think with you there, Julian. To me, they are all immortal souls."

"How will Gloucester affect the immortality of their souls?" Sir Julian enquired.

But his wife gazed at him very earnestly.

"A woman's instinct is not very often wrong. There's tension in the air, and—why shouldn't I speak out?—I want to put out a helping hand—to save Mark, before things come to a head and he is faced with a crisis.

"In that case," said her husband blandly, "I had better arrange that Mark should be the person who goes to Gloucester."

XVII

"A very cold north wind," said Sir Julian, entering the room set ready for a General Committee meeting.

"Damnably cold," said Mark Easter, who never swore.

Sir Julian made an elaborate rearrangement of the pencils and blotting-paper on the table in front of him and then looked at Mark.

They were the first arrivals.

Mark's gaze met Sir Julian's, but it was unusually clouded.

"I don't know what's the matter with the place," he said irritably.

"What's happened?"

"Nothing at all, that I know of. It's just in the air. Fuller's like a bear with a sore head, and those two women—Farmer and Sandiloe—whispering together in corners and exchanging glances like conspirators in a gunpowder plot. What on earth is the matter with them all?"

There was silence, and then Mark said, still in the same irritable voice:

"I suppose they think one's a perfect fool. If I've had one of them into my office this morning, I've had half a dozen—on the flimsiest excuses you ever heard of in your life. I don't know what they expected to find there, I'm sure."

If Sir Julian could have enlightened his agent on the point, he did not do so.

But he became himself very acutely aware of the state of tension pervading the College during the course of the committee meeting. Mark, contrary to his usual habit, scarcely spoke at all; Mr. Fuller sat with a face like a thundercloud, and, looking up occasionally under his closely-knitted black eye-brows, fixed inscrutable eyes upon Miss Marchrose opposite.

She looked tired and nervous, and Sir Julian remembered that it was less than a week since he had thought her looking beautiful at Iris Easter's wedding.

Edna, he noticed, did not glance at Miss Marchrose, but from time to time her eyes rested thoughtfully upon Mark Easter.

Even Alderman Bellew, far from susceptible to shades of atmosphere, struck Sir Julian as being vaguely and uneasily watchful.

The meeting was poorly attended, and when it was over Mark said rather doubtfully to Lady Rossiter:

"You'll have some tea before you go, won't you?"

"Thank you," she said graciously. "Only if you're quite sure that it wouldn't put anyone out, give any extra trouble."

"I can find out the state of the commissariat first, if you like," he rejoined, and left the room.

Miss Marchrose had gone already.

Edna's manner altered to one of businesslike determination on the instant.

"I'm going to make a little suggestion," she said clearly.

The Alderman looked up, and at the same instant Fairfax Fuller took two steps forward.

It isn't, perhaps, a very easy thing for me to say," Lady Rossiter said unfalteringly, "but we all know one another here. And I believe—oh, so intensely!—in having courage. But never mind that. I needn't go into any details, but it's this—I think the general feeling amongst the staff is that there might be some slight alteration in the duties of the Lady Superintendent. They don't altogether like her doing so much. It's natural enough, isn't it? Perhaps they feel that inordinately long hours kept by one person cast a slur upon the others, who don't seem to be quite so devoted. Perhaps she hasn't been very tactful about it. I don't know about that. But at all events, couldn't we give her a holiday from evening work for the present? Let her go at about four o'clock?"

The Alderman's prawn-like eyes were fixed admiringly upon Lady Rossiter, but he said nothing.

Sir Julian spoke.

"You can't make an invidious distinction of that sort, Edna. It would be impossible."

"But she looks very tired," said Edna smoothly. "She has certainly been doing too much. We can put it on that score."

"Who has been objecting to the hours that Miss Marchrose puts in?" demanded Fairfax Fuller bluntly.

Edna's little smile admirably blended a protest at the question and a quiet determination to leave it unanswered.

"Because," said Fuller, "if you'll be good enough to tell that person to address his or her complaint to *me*, Lady Rossiter, I will deal with it in the proper way. I never yet heard of a good worker being sent off duty early because a slack one didn't like the sight of over-work."

"Come, come, Fuller," said the Alderman uncertainly.

Fairfax Fuller turned a black gaze upon him that actually caused the old man to move his chair backwards.

"Leave it alone, Edna," said her husband. "If there's jealousy amongst the staff, Fuller is quite right in saying that he's the person to adjust it. They had no business to appeal to you."

"You force me to speak plainly," said Lady Rossiter. "It isn't only a little jealousy, though there is that as well. But—to put things exactly as they are—the staff doesn't like the habit that Miss Marchrose has fallen into of staying on over-time till all hours, and then being taken home. And, frankly, I don't think you can blame them. That sort of thing isn't done. It makes talk at once."

"Evidently."

The fury in Fuller's voice was hardly suppressed.

"I believe that I am not censorious," said Lady Rossiter. "It is utterly foreign to my nature, and I would sooner blind myself to evil than look out for it—yet there are things which go against one's every instinct. This is a very little community and has always been a very peaceful and happy one. It hurts me very much, somehow, that there should be talk of the kind that I know has been going on lately."

"Mischief-making—" muttered Fuller fiercely and without completing his sentence.

"Officiousness is the curse of the age!" exclaimed Sir Julian, neither for the first nor the second time. "Why can't people mind their own business? What has it to do with them?" As he spoke, some part of his mind commented upon the futility of these disjointed exclamations, and the irrationality of the desire to gain time that had caused him to utter them.

The three men gazed at Lady Rossiter.

"Oh, how I hate saying it!" she cried in an impulsive manner. "It isn't that I think there's any harm in it all—indeed, I don't. But I myself have seen little things—tiny, infinitesimal incidents, if you like—that somehow seem to carry significance by repetition. That sort of thing *doesn't* do."

She looked at her listeners for an instant, and made inevitable selection amongst them.

She turned to the Alderman appealingly.

"I'm only a woman, but I know that sort of thing doesn't do in business offices. Isn't it true?"

"Quite true, Lady Rossiter," said the Alderman instantly. "It's an undesirable sort of element altogether. And once people start talking— especially a lot of girls, if you'll excuse my saying so—it's hopeless. It ought to be got rid of."

Edna hesitated a moment. Then she said:

"Shall I—shall I speak to poor Miss Marchrose? It might be easier, for another woman to do it, and I don't think she would resent it from me."

Two, at least, of those present might reasonably have received this assertion with a considerable amount of surprise, in view of certain past incidents apparently shrouded in complete oblivion by the forgiving Lady Rossiter.

The Alderman was less responsive this time.

"It's very good of you, Lady Rossiter—very good indeed. I'm sure we all appreciate your keen interest in the welfare of the College and the staff. But at the same time—I don't know—" He stopped rather helplessly.

"You mustn't think of me," gently said Edna. "Just speak out, quite frankly, and tell me what would be best for everyone. Anything I can do, you know—"

"The fact is, it's least said soonest mended, in these cases," burst out the Alderman. "The girl had better go. Don't you agree with me, Sir Julian?"

"It will probably end in that."

There was a certain surprise visible on Lady Rossiter's face as she heard her husband's reply.

"It's her livelihood," she reminded them; "we mustn't forget that. But at the same time, the College interests come first, and the one thing to be avoided, at any cost, is a crisis. So much can be done by staving things off."

"The doctrine of expediency," inaudibly muttered Julian through his teeth.

It was a doctrine that had never failed to rouse him to wrath.

Fairfax Fuller's deep, angry voice broke out suddenly:

"I should like to know what the girl is being accused of, that we should send away the best worker we've ever struck."

No one replied, until Edna said solemnly, "I accuse no one."

"I beg your pardon, Lady Rossiter, but it is too late to say that now. The girl *has* been accused, and she knows it, and everyone else knows it. The whole thing is in the air. The place stinks of it," said Mr. Fuller with reckless candour. "There was some talk of my being sent off to Gloucester on business, but I don't leave this place until this mess is cleared up. Why, the atmosphere is like a barrel of gunpowder, simply waiting for a lighted match."

"Then why light it, Mr. Fuller?" sweetly enquired Lady Rossiter. "Why insist upon having things put into words?"

"Because it's common justice," said Mr. Fuller doggedly. "We can't send the girl away without giving her a reason, and there isn't a reason to give, that I can see."

"That question will rest with the directors, surely," Lady Rossiter reminded him. She looked straight at Alderman Bellew.

"She'll know fast enough what the reason is, without being told," the Alderman gloomily supported the lady. "She's not a chicken. A girl with any business experience knows very well that this sort of thing isn't tolerated in any office. Nothing serious, of course, as Lady Rossiter has just said, but it makes talk, and it won't do."

Fuller swung round and faced the Alderman.

"I'd like to have the sort of thing you've just alluded to, specified. I'm Supervisor of this staff, and I've nothing against Miss Marchrose."

"As you have just been reminded," pointedly said the Alderman, also becoming heated, "the question rests ultimately with the directors."

"Then my position here is a farce," the Supervisor retorted.

"Anything but that, Mr. Fuller," said Edna earnestly, and with the evident intention of laying a soothing hand upon his arm.

Fuller almost backed into the wall in his avoidance of it.

"Indeed," said Lady Rossiter pleadingly, "no one minimises your position here, nor the responsibility that rests upon you with regard to the staff. But you force me to say something that I would much, much rather leave unsaid."

Sir Julian wondered whether it would be of any use to ask her to do so, and decided that it would not.

"I used to hear about this poor creature years before she ever came here. It isn't the first time that there's been—trouble."

Sir Julian's eyes almost involuntarily met those of the Alderman as this pregnant announcement fell upon the air. He interposed in a level voice:

"My wife means nothing that is derogatory to Miss Marchrose, Mr. Bellew. We are, however, in a position to know that a few years ago she broke off an engagement of marriage under circumstances that were certainly painful, but perfectly honourable to herself. That matter, of course, concerns her private life, and has nothing whatever to do with the point at issue."

"Excepting this, Julian," his wife said resolutely, "that a girl who has once put herself into a false position of that kind is liable to do the same sort of thing again."

"She may get engaged to the whole office one after another and chuck them next day, for all I care, so long as she does her work properly," said Fuller, quite as resolutely as, and a good deal more vehemently than, Lady Rossiter.

"It would scarcely be good for the office generally," replied Edna drily.

"Now, my dear fellow," began the Alderman, "you must look at this matter in the light of reason. The greater good of the greater number, you know. This young woman mustn't be allowed to upset the office."

"She hasn't done so."

"On your own showing, Mr. Fuller," said Lady Rossiter, very much in the tone of one endeavouring to reason with an idiot, "and to quote your own words of a few moments ago, the whole thing is in the air. Everybody is upset and disturbed, because it is impossible for anybody to give out reckless and excited and undisciplined thoughts and emotions without their having an effect upon his or her surroundings. It is—"

"I've yet to learn," Mr. Fuller interrupted, without the slightest ceremony, "that a first-class worker can be dismissed on account of thinking."

"Fuller, Fuller, Fuller!" bleated the Alderman, in an expostulatory tone.

"We can discuss this later on, Fuller," said Sir Julian wearily.

"Sir Julian, I prefer to make my attitude perfectly clear to you at once—" began Mr. Fuller with great vehemence, when Mark Easter came back into the room.

Although the inopportuneness of an abrupt silence striking through the excited conversation that had raged a moment before was evident to the point of blatancy, an immediate dumbness fell upon everyone as the door opened before Mark.

To Sir Julian's perception, it was oddly significant that Mark, after one quick glance from face to face, should remain silent and unsmiling, asking no question.

It was the woman present who haltingly broke through the awkward pause.

"We were just wondering if—if there was to be any tea for us. A Committee meeting in the afternoon is so unusual for the College, isn't it? We hardly know ourselves, when it isn't the ordinary eleven o'clock meeting."

"There is tea in Miss Marchrose's room," said Mark.

He spoke without expression.

"Oh, thank you," said Edna, from pure nervousness, and walked out of the room.

Sir Julian followed her, partly from sheer desire not to be confronted with his infuriated Supervisor, and partly from a wish to see Miss Marchrose herself.

She passed them in the passage, and Edna inclined her head without speaking, and walked on.

Sir Julian stopped.

"Are you coming to give us some tea?" he asked her.

"Yes—No. No—I don't think so," she said confusedly, her pale face colouring unmistakably.

Sir Julian felt vaguely disappointed. He had expected that the consciousness of antagonism in the air would have roused in her a certain latent defiance already dimly foreshadowed in her erect bearing and abrupt, defensive phraseology. But she was looking tired already, and frightened, as though she realised herself to be very much alone.

"Are you busy?" he asked.

"I am, rather."

She looked at him doubtfully, and once more he saw the shadow of fear, unmistakable, in her dark-circled eyes.

He did not know what else to say, although he felt very sorry for her, and he thought that for a moment she seemed about to say something further.

But she only opened her lips for an instant and then turned away without speaking.

"Good-bye," said Sir Julian lamely.

"Good-bye."

He waited thoughtfully outside the College for Lady Rossiter, nor did the entertainment of afternoon tea prolong itself.

She came out, followed by Mark Easter.

"Will you have a lift, Mark?"

"Thank you, I've got one or two things to finish here."

Julian, being well aware that at this Edna was endeavouring to exchange with him a sudden, meaning glance, became instantly absorbed in the mechanism of the car.

"Mark, don't do that. Do come back with us now," said Lady Rossiter earnestly, and irresistibly and quite involuntarily reminding Sir Julian of the heroine of a certain type of fiction, pleading at the door of the public-house, "*Bill, come home with me now.*"

He stifled the ribald association and started the engine.

"You'll walk back then, later?"

"Come back with us, Mark," repeated Lady Rossiter.

Sir Julian opened the door of the car.

"Why are you in such a hurry?" demanded Lady Rossiter resentfully, in an undertone.

"Perhaps we could wait for you, Mark, if you're only going to be a little while."

"I'm afraid I shall be longer than that," said Mark, looking harassed.

"That's all right," said Sir Julian firmly, and took his seat in the driver's place.

Lady Rossiter reluctantly stepped into the car beside him.

They saw Mark turn into the College again as the car moved from the door.

"I am utterly exhausted," said Edna.

Her husband, according to his wont, made no response, and she presently spoke again.

"Couldn't you *feel* the tension in that place, Julian?"

"Yes."

"You are not a fanciful person, perhaps not even a very perceptive one, and certainly Mr. Fuller is neither. Yet both you and he were on edge. I could see it and feel it."

"And hear it too, I imagine, so far as Fuller was concerned," said Sir Julian, not without reason.

"One does not expect very great self-command from a man of his type. But I'm frightened, Julian, I tell you honestly. You know how extraordinarily susceptible I am to the influence of a thought-form?"

"Of a *what*?" said Sir Julian, having heard her perfectly, but being desirous of venting his own sense of uneasiness in ill-temper.

"Perhaps I used an out-of-the-way expression. But you know what I mean, surely. On another plane—one that is perhaps not so far removed from our own as we sometimes think—these things are classified. I have no psychic gifts myself," said Edna, in a modest way that positively seemed to imply a certain distinction in the absence of those attributes, "but undoubtedly there are those amongst us who can absolutely *see* and translate into terms of colour and shape for the rest of us."

"I feel sure that the colour and shape of any thought-form belonging to Fuller at the present moment would repay inspection," said Sir Julian grimly.

"Ah, poor Mr. Fuller! It hurt one, didn't it? Prejudice and violence and ignorance—the three foes that we, who can see a little further into the great, wonderful Heart of Life, have to fight against all the time. But sometimes it does feel as though all one's love and pity were being flung back upon oneself again, as though a hard wall of resistance were opposing everything."

Edna gasped a little.

Her husband wondered so much whom she supposed herself to have been loving and pitying that afternoon, that he felt constrained to ask the question aloud.

"But all—all of them!"

Edna, usually undemonstrative, flung apart her hands in an expressive gesture.

"How can you ask, even? The pity of it all, Julian! That was what wrung my heart. … Oh, Julian! be careful."

Sir Julian, most skilful of drivers, had sent the car swerving recklessly round the sharp corner of Culmhayes drive.

"I beg your pardon, Edna."

Both were silent till the house was reached. The topic that occupied them both, however, was revived that evening.

This time Edna approached it from a less exalted point of view.

"It's very curious how much these people absorb one's thoughts. And yet, of course, it's not curious at all. They're fellow-creatures, after all. Sometimes I think the old Alderman is quite right. The best thing would be for Miss Marchrose to go. I wish she would resign of her own accord."

"I think," said Sir Julian, "that there is every chance of your wish being realised."

"Why?"

"It's a question," said Sir Julian, very distinctly "of exactly how long she can stand her ground. She is a very intelligent person, and, unless I am greatly mistaken, a very sensitive one, and my own opinion is that she will be defeated early in the day by the mere atmospheric pressure against her."

"You mean that she will *feel*, without having it put into words, that things can't go on as they are at present?"

"It wouldn't need very keen perceptions to have come to that conclusion already."

"Perhaps not." Lady Rossiter spoke thoughtfully. "You see, the one thing one doesn't want, is to have things put into words."

Sir Julian, disagreeing with her even more completely than he usually did, answered nothing.

"It's Mark I'm thinking of principally. At the present moment I honestly believe that Mark, who is exceptionally simple, hardly realises that anything has upset the College. Certainly he won't attribute it—yet—to the way in which that unfortunate young woman has been behaving."

"Why should he attribute it to her behaviour any more than to his own?" Sir Julian reasonably enquired. "It usually requires the behaviour of two people to start this sort of idiotic gossiping."

"Mark has been foolish, I daresay," coldly said Lady Rossiter. "All men are alike in these matters, and when a woman hurls herself at a man's head you can't expect him not to take a certain amount of advantage."

"Of what, exactly, has this hurling consisted?" demanded Sir Julian, with an air of judicial impartiality.

"You have seen quite as much as I have," Lady Rossiter mistakenly informed him; "she never has a civil word for anyone else, and she is perfectly brazen in boasting of the amount of extra work she does for him. She haunted the estate office when that other girl was ill, and took over her typewriting work in the calmest way. Of course, it was practically impossible for Mark to refuse, when she insisted. And, of course, there's her fashion of getting him to walk home with her after dark every night."

"And all this would be perfectly legitimate and desirable if only Mark's dipsomaniac was in a better world instead of in this one," was the thoughtful *résumé* of Sir Julian—a *résumé* of which the wording, if not the substance, found so little favour in his wife's hearing that she had instant resort to the inevitable Roland with which it was her custom to counter his time-honoured Oliver.

"If you remember anything at all of that miserable affair that went so near to wrecking poor Clarence Isbister's life, you can hardly say that."

Sir Julian wished for no recapitulation of the oft-told tragedy alluded to.

"I remember perfectly. He battered his head against the walls of his nursing-home, and I think any girl was well rid of him on that account alone."

Lady Rossiter rose with great quiet.

"I am going to bed. It has been a strain, altogether. But, after all, I shall feel it's been worth anything—whatever it may cost me—if only one can stave off any sort of disastrous crisis. It seems to me that, at the moment, the one thing to be avoided is definitely putting things into words."

"Plain speaking?" enquired Sir Julian. "It is, on the contrary, the one thing that I should really like. But don't be afraid, Edna. We shan't get it—unless it's from Fuller."

XVIII

Sir Julian's desire for plain speaking was more amply gratified on the following day even than he had anticipated. He had purposely made an early appointment at the College, in order to discuss with Mark and the Supervisor the question of the journey to Gloucester, but he was aware that a curiously strong sensation of anxiety constituted an underlying motive for his presence there.

There flashed across his mind the dim recollection of a conversation in which he had taken part, with Mark Easter and Miss Marchrose, one afternoon on the way from Salt Marsh to Culmhayes.

They had agreed in their estimate of the potency of an atmosphere. He thought it was Miss Marchrose herself who had said that "the worst times are when nothing at all has happened, and yet everything is happening."

Prophetic, reflected Julian, half amused. He made his way slowly to Mark Easter's room.

A feminine voice, lowered to that penetrating sibilance which most infallibly attracts the attention which it is designed to escape, reached his ears.

"—And she knew I was looking at her, too. I could tell she did, by the way she coloured. You know. And I never said a word. Simply looked at her, you know. 'Don't let me disturb you,' I said. Like that, quite quietly."

Sir Julian pushed the half-open door. Miss Farmer and Miss Sandiloe stood in close confabulation just inside the room.

"Oh, good morning, Sir Julian." They both looked much confused.

"Good morning," he said gravely. "Mr. Easter has not arrived yet?"

"No," said Miss Sandiloe, ever ready of speech, in spite of her manifest discomfiture.

"No, he hasn't. He very often gets in rather later these mornings."

"I can wait," said Sir Julian. "It's not ten o'clock yet."

Miss Farmer began to sidle towards the door. Her companion followed her, but was inspired to turn round and add an unnecessary rider to her last observation.

"Mr. Easter is always here so late in the evenings now, too," she remarked artlessly, as she went out of the room.

Sir Julian heard a nervous giggle as the door closed behind them both, and he thought that Miss Farmer ejaculated something that sounded like, "However you could, Sandiloe!"

"If Miss Marchrose has been up against *that* sort of thing for the last week ..." was his unformulated thought.

A further example of "that sort of thing" confronted him in the entrance hall, where he presently betook himself restlessly.

Three girls, all of them pupil-teachers of the College, with young Cooper, the Financial Secretary, stood near the notice-board. Their necks were craned forward, and their eyes, expressive of curiosity, suspicion, and a certain excitement, were unanimously following the tall, slight figure of Miss Marchrose as she disappeared towards a distant classroom.

"Good morning," said Sir Julian, with extreme abruptness, and in tones not usually associated with a morning greeting.

Everyone jumped violently.

The three pupil-teachers disappeared with celerity, and Mr. Cooper turned a brick-red countenance upon his chief.

"Just looking at the notice-board," he said, in an affable manner.

"There appears to be nothing on it," Sir Julian made rejoinder, with equal obviousness, but in a voice that was not without point.

"Nothing at all," agreed Mr. Cooper, rather feverishly, and running a hand across the green baize square as though further to demonstrate its bareness.

"I see you're in early, Sir Julian."

"I have an appointment with Mr. Easter, but I'm rather too soon. Fuller is in class, I suppose?"

"Yes, Sir Julian. Let me see," Cooper produced his wrist-watch. "I'll look at the time. Yes. He'll be in class for the next three-quarters of an hour. Shall I send for him, Sir Julian?"

"No, thanks. I'm in no hurry. There's just the question of the place to be opened at Gloucester. You've heard about it, haven't you, Cooper?"

"Oh yes, Sir Julian. The whole staff has been much interested, and very proud too, if I may say so. I'd even thought—I don't know if I may venture—"

"Are you a candidate for the job of going down there next week?" Sir Julian asked, smiling.

"Not myself," said Mr. Cooper. "I may even say, Sir Julian, that I doubt if I could be spared at the moment. We have one or two French scholars, and the accountancy is particularly heavy just now. Of course, it's what you wish, Sir Julian, but I hardly think I could leave at present, even for a day or two. But I was wondering whether I might venture a suggestion."

"Certainly," said Sir Julian, rather astonished.

"It has occurred to me," remarked Mr. Cooper, with a certain pompousness, "that Miss Marchrose would not be at all unfitted to do what's required. And a little change might be rather a good thing for her, in its way, Sir Julian."

"Indeed?"

"There's been a certain amount of feeling, I'm afraid, just lately."

"I should like details, if you please."

"One hardly likes to say anything," Mr. Cooper began, with great and evident satisfaction. "She's a splendid worker, as you know, Sir Julian, and the other young ladies took to her quite wonderfully from the start. Quite foolish, one or two of them were about her. But the fact is, if you'll excuse my mentioning it, she's been rather indiscreet of late."

"Go on," said Julian in level tones, as Cooper waited, apparently for some sign of encouragement.

"The fact is, to put the whole matter in a nutshell, some of them have got talking. You know what that means, especially with one or two rather excitable young ladies."

There was a pause, during which Julian recollected Mr. Cooper's old-time predilection for the society of Miss Sandiloe.

"She hasn't made any secret of liking Mr. Mark Easter's society very much, and she's given him a good deal of hers. That's all it amounts to," said Mr. Cooper, with a great effect of frankness.

"He has found her useful for some of the extra work."

"No doubt, Sir Julian. That's all it is. But she's in that office of his nearly as often as she's in her own, and then they've been late a good many evenings and stayed on here working after the College was supposed to be closed. It was also known, Sir Julian, that the present Mrs. Douglas Garrett—Miss Easter that was—used to ask Miss Marchrose to her brother's house a good deal while she was home."

"We are not in the least responsible for what the staff may do out of hours."

"Certainly not, Sir Julian. And of course we all know and like Mr. Mark Easter, and I've no doubt that he's never said a word to her that we mightn't all have heard. But somehow," said Mr. Cooper, with a fatalistic expression, "somehow, the staff have got talking."

"It doesn't concern them in any way whatever."

"Those were my very words," Mr. Cooper replied impressively, "my very words, when one of the young ladies approached me on the subject. This is an affair which concerns no one but Mr. Mark Easter, I said, and you may be sure that he will deal with it in the best manner possible. In fact, I said, if this unfortunate young lady has forgotten the circumstances of the case, we may be quite sure that Mr. Easter will himself take an early opportunity of reminding her."

Mr. Cooper's tone implied that no more triumphantly satisfactory *dénouement* could be hoped for.

"And do you suppose that he has done so?" enquired Sir Julian, from sheer curiosity to hear Mr. Cooper's reply.

Cooper shook his head from side to side.

"I couldn't say at all, Sir Julian. There's been a very uncomfortable state of things prevailing for the last few days, altogether. I couldn't put a finger on any one thing not to give a name to it, but there's constraint, Sir Julian, and we all feel it. This has always been such a friendly little party, that one can't help noticing, like."

"I shall be greatly obliged, Cooper," said Sir Julian with deliberation, "if you would check this tittle-tattling, as far as possible. It is extraordinarily objectionable."

Cooper looked far from hopeful.

"She'll have to pull herself up, as it were, or else leave altogether, Sir Julian. Otherwise I don't see what's to prevent the staff from getting talking."

Sir Julian perceived that no amount of words would remove from Mr. Cooper his conviction of the inevitability of the calamity which he described as the "getting talking" of his fellow-workers.

"I shall think the matter over. Certainly we can't have this sort of atmosphere in the place. It's upsetting everyone."

"That is so, Sir Julian. It's the talk that's doing the harm," said Mr. Cooper solemnly.

"Certainly it is. I hope there will be no more of it."

Sir Julian's hope was uttered for rhetorical purposes merely. His never very sanguine outlook had been in no way illuminated by the eloquence of Mr. Cooper.

"Don't let me keep you any longer, Cooper; I know you're busy."

"Thank you, Sir Julian. If you'll excuse me. My watch—ten minutes past—then I'll go straight to Classroom III.—up the stairs."

Mr. Cooper hurried away, taking two steps at a time.

Sir Julian's discussion with Mark was completed rapidly enough.

"I'm quite ready to see this Gloucester affair through," said Mark, looking out of the window, "Fuller doesn't seem anxious to take it on."

"Can you spare the time?"

"Easily."

"To-day is Friday. What about Monday?"

"Right."

Mark said nothing more. The tiny furrow between his eyes had deepened a very little.

They spoke of business for a little while and then Sir Julian left Mark in solitary possession of the small office.

As he came away he encountered Miss Marchrose.

Her observation was worthy of Mr. Cooper.

"I'm going to the High Speed room," she said, with evident nervousness.

"Are you giving another test there?"

"Oh, no. We're very slack at present. The last lot have gone out, and we mostly have beginners. But I want to put some things away."

She was quite evidently defending herself against some unspoken accusation.

As she turned away, she looked back at Sir Julian, again with that suggestion of wishing to say something further.

"What is it?" he asked, almost involuntarily.

"Nothing," said Miss Marchrose, her voice catching in her throat.

Sir Julian walked away slowly.

"Sir Julian!" she said, rather breathlessly.

He turned at once.

"Are you—are you just going?"

"I am in no hurry."

He reflected for an instant and then decided to take her wishes for granted.

"You will find me in the annexe. There's no hurry, so take your time about putting the papers away. I'll wait for you there," said Sir Julian calmly.

He waited barely five minutes.

She came into the room, very erect, with tension in every line of her face and figure, and a little dent coming and going at the corner of either nostril.

She shut the door quietly behind her.

"Sit down," said Sir Julian, placing a chair for her, so that she could lean both arms on the table, and steady a certain tremulousness of which he suspected the existence.

In order to give her time, he slowly and carefully took out and lit a cigarette. He was conscious of a sensation of surprise in the midst of his mingled annoyance and compassion. He had not expected her to acknowledge defeat so quickly, and he wondered whether some element of which he knew nothing had been introduced into the invisible contest against her.

"I think I shall have to ask you to accept my resignation," she said at last, in a sort of rush.

"I'm sorry," said Sir Julian carefully.

"I've spoken to Mr. Fuller about it, but he—he was a little bit difficult."

"I can quite believe it."

"I couldn't get him to accept my resignation at all," she said, smiling rather forlornly.

"Fuller is not easily defeated."

She interpreted his thought rather more accurately than he desired, in her quick rejoinder.

"And I *am*. I haven't been able to cope with the last few days at all. Do you remember how we talked about atmosphere one afternoon before Christmas?"

"On the way back from Salt Marsh? I was thinking about it not so very long ago."

"Then," said Miss Marchrose slowly, "you knew about—this place?"

Sir Julian made no pretence at not having understood her.

"I know that it has afforded a rather poignant example of the very thing we discussed that afternoon," he replied.

"I thought you knew," she said, pushing her hair away from her forehead with a rapid, nervous movement. "But you see *I'm* in the dark. No one has said a single word to me. I'd so much rather they did."

"Yes, I can understand that. But you see no one is in a position to say a word to you, except—officially—Mr. Fuller as Supervisor."

"Then why hasn't he?" Miss Marchrose demanded, a sudden colour flooding her pale face.

Sir Julian said nothing, for the conclusive reason that he could think of absolutely nothing to say.

"He told me to-day that my services had been perfectly satisfactory, and that he didn't want me to leave."

"I know he doesn't."

"In that case," said Miss Marchrose, "I must place my resignation with you direct, Sir Julian."

"Have you definitely decided to resign?"

"I'm afraid so," she said, again colouring suddenly.

Sir Julian once more kept silence from a helpless sense of the impossibility of any discussion, although intuition told him that she was more or less blindly in search of a safety-valve for her perplexities.

She remained in her chair for a minute or two, looking down at the table, and only a very slight, involuntary movement of her fingers betrayed the tension of waiting.

Sir Julian paid the penalty sooner or later exacted of all those whose perceptions are acute, in realising with vividness her sense of bafflement as he remained mute.

With a sort of remnant of the pluck that he had always credited her with, she rose at last and said, "Thank you very much, Sir Julian," quite steadily.

He rose also and opened the door, and she went out.

Sir Julian remained more than ever convinced that some very forcible factor, of which he was still unaware, had entered the lists against her, and definitely defeated her.

"It's no business of mine," he reflected to himself, almost violently.

Nevertheless, he had more to hear upon the subject that same afternoon.

He met Alderman Bellew, whose discursive comments were not to be stayed.

"Easter's a very nice chap, you know," said the Alderman sapiently. "I don't like the idea of this young woman making a fool of him. He's not been looking himself for the last day or two. Didn't you think him a bit off colour at the General Meeting yesterday, now? I can assure you that he didn't look himself, to me. He looked"—the Alderman lowered his voice in a very impressive and mysterious manner—"he looked *worried*."

Sir Julian felt inclined to ejaculate, "You don't say so!" at this bit of penetration, but the Alderman went on:

"It's not to be wondered at, either. I don't know whether you've noticed a sort of disturbance lately in the College—something in the air?"

"I know what you mean," Sir Julian said truthfully, but noncommittally.

"Exactly. Just what Lady Rossiter was speaking of the other day. Well, now that sort of thing won't do, will it? It upsets the staff—upsets the work—upsets that chap Fuller, badly. Took it very much to heart, didn't he? I suppose he thinks it reflects upon his credit as Supervisor, when things go wrong with the staff. However, it's all quite easily put right, when all's said and done."

Such not being the comfortable conviction of Sir Julian, he waited for further enlightenment.

"The girl can go."

"Oh," said Sir Julian. "Yes. The girl can go, of course."

"It needn't affect her references in any way," said the Alderman, apparently made uneasy by something in Sir Julian's tone.

"Certainly not."

"There's no harm in the girl, I daresay, though I don't like what I hear of those antecedents of hers."

Sir Julian was perfectly well aware that Miss Marchrose's antecedents, so far as Alderman Bellew's knowledge of them was concerned, rested upon the slender fabric of the hints thrown out by Lady Rossiter on the subject. He therefore remained unresponsive, and Alderman Bellew presently, with an air of rather puzzled reluctance, abandoned the subject.

"It's no business of mine," Sir Julian told himself with increasing vehemence, as his perception grew of the strength of the league that was so successfully fighting the shadow of a possibility.

Even Culmhayes was pervaded by unrest.

Edna was silent all through dinner, except when the servants were in the room, when she discoursed in an elevating way about the first breath of spring, and a tiny twitter which she said that she had heard in the beech-wood that afternoon.

Sir Julian heard about the twitter towards February or March every year, and received the news of it with modified enthusiasm only.

As soon as they were alone, Edna drew a long breath, flung her head back, and said with a sort of restrained ardour:

"Julian, whom do you suppose I met this afternoon in the beech-wood?"

"The first squirrel of the year," suggested Sir Julian, with perfect indifference.

"I am not laughing."

"Neither am I. Do you mean a human being, or a harbinger of spring?"

"I met Mark," said Lady Rossiter very gravely.

Sir Julian peeled a walnut attentively.

"It seemed—I say it in all reverence—like an answer to prayer, for I had prayed over it all. Julian, I was miserable. I could see all the tangle and perplexity so clearly, and yet I felt bound and helpless. I could do nothing to help or to hinder."

Julian reflected detachedly that his wife did herself less than justice.

"And then I met Mark. And I knew as soon as I saw him that it was my opportunity for helping. It is so curious, when one has formed the habit of looking for little opportunities, how the big one is sure to come sooner or later. Mark wanted help badly, Julian."

Lady Rossiter waited for a moment, during which her husband remained motionless, and then went on speaking in slow, even tones.

"I believe in courage, as you know, most intensely. It is so difficult, sometimes, to break through our conventional reserve. It was so to-day. But I spoke. Mark has no woman in his life."

"I can hardly agree with you, in the circumstances," muttered Julian grimly, but his wife disregarded the interruption.

"And there are times when a man wants a woman to whom he can speak freely. Oh, I didn't hurt his chivalry in any way—I respect it far too much. Nothing was put into words between us, practically—but everything was implied."

"At the moment, Edna, I prefer words to implications, as I am very much more likely to understand them. What did you say to Mark?"

"Very little," said Edna, with a dignified simplicity that failed entirely to convince Sir Julian of the accuracy of her statement. "But, thank God, I believe I have made certain that there will be no *débacle* such as one could not help dreading. I was in terror that that unfortunate girl should try to force an issue."

Sir Julian realised, with a slight shock of surprise, that his wife's estimate of Miss Marchrose's capabilities of enterprise were identical with his own. Edna, he reflected, did not yet know that Miss Marchrose had, to all intents and purposes, most unmistakably hauled down her colours when she had tendered her resignation to him that morning.

"How are you to prevent her from forcing an issue?" he asked.

"It's so simple. Mark is going away on business, and he leaves on Saturday instead of on Monday. A week makes a long break, Julian, in a case like this, and she will either understand why he has gone without being told, or she will find her position intolerable, and leave the College. Even if she stays on—though I think it impossible that she should—they will begin again on a very different footing. Mark understands now."

"Understands what, in Heaven's name?"

Edna raised her eyebrows and made a significant gesture.

"Mark goes to-morrow?"

"Yes. Thank Heaven, I made him see that there is greater courage in turning one's back, sometimes, than in facing a danger. Every day that passes, as these last days have passed, the risk of an explosion becomes greater. It's like skating over a volcano."

"Nobody ever does skate over volcanoes," said Julian, almost automatically. His mind was working rapidly.

Mark was turning his back.

As Edna had said, it might be the greater courage.

There would be no crisis. Nothing had happened and nothing would happen. A crisis, indeed, must have spelt disaster, Sir Julian told himself mechanically, all the while with a sense of having somehow missed a clue.

The next moment he had found it.

His original instinct with regard to Miss Marchrose had been right. She had in all probability known whither she was drifting, and she had been prepared to face the rapids gallantly. But Mark ... Julian dropped his metaphors and envisaged crude facts—Mark, after all, had himself been responsible for the determining factor that alone could have vanquished her courage utterly.

Fully alive to an awkward situation, Mark Easter had inevitably conveyed to the girl, whom Sir Julian, more than ever, qualified as an incurable romanticist, the illimitable difference in their scales of relative values.

And it was that certainty that, reaching her in the atmospheric tension of the last few days, had defeated Miss Marchrose.

XIX

"You're going this afternoon, Mark, after all?"

"If you've no objection, Sir Julian."

"My dear fellow, I'm always trying to persuade you that Saturday afternoon and Sunday were not meant for work."

Mark laughed, not sounding very much amused.

"Report progress after you've got there and let me know when you're likely to be back."

Mark nodded.

Sir Julian put his hand upon the younger man's shoulder with a gesture of intimacy unusual to him.

"Don't hurry back."

"Thanks very much," said Mark, with equal brevity and sincerity.

As Mark Easter went into the estate office, whither Sir Julian had driven him, he looked round with the smile that, after all, never altogether failed him.

"I might get some good golf down there."

"Yes," Sir Julian assented gravely, after an instant's pause. "You might get some good golf down there. I hope you will."

He did not go near the College that morning, but found himself wondering very much whether or not Mark had done so.

Instinct, rather than conscious volition, took him that afternoon down to the sea-wall, to find Miss Marchrose.

Mark had gone, and she herself would leave the College, probably before his return, and Sir Julian thought that it would not matter very much now if he offered her such solace as could be afforded by his understanding, complete as he felt it to be, of their wordless drama.

It was an afternoon of west-country weather, and the very spray was misty and soft as it curled upwards from a grey, still sea. This time there was no high wind to contend with, as on the day when they had walked the length of the sea-wall, and she had told him about her life in London and the story of Clarence Isbister.

He could discern her slim figure braced against the wall as he crossed the sand-dunes and came towards her.

When she turned her face to him, he saw with a shock, that was not altogether surprise, that it was pale and blurred with crying and that her eyes looked as though she had been weeping all night.

The faint elusive beauty, such as it was, had left her face altogether; but her voice, veiled with exhaustion, retained all the quality that gave it charm.

She said, with rather tremulous directness:

"I thought that perhaps you'd come. I was hoping you would."

"Then I'm glad I came," said Sir Julian. "Are you warm enough, sitting here?"

"Yes, I think so. I don't want to walk, I'm tired."

It was obvious that she was very much tired indeed.

"I am very sorry," said Julian simply, and his tone implied a deeper regret than the compassion that he felt for her evident fatigue.

"You are going to let me talk about it now, aren't you?" she asked, with a sort of childish urgency in her voice.

"Anything you like, or that is of any use to you," he replied levelly.

The necessity of self-expression is singularly strong in human nature. Sir Julian surmised that the only outlet in the case of Miss Marchrose's vehement and highly-strung personality lay in the exercise of a certain gift for elementary sincerity that made of her words something more than self-analytical outpouring.

"He has gone away," she said tonelessly. "But even before he went away I knew how it all was. I have been the most utter fool. You could hardly believe what a fool I've been. You know I told you the other day that I'd hardly ever been happier than I've been here?"

"I remember."

"Well, even then, I half knew that it was because of him. And very soon afterwards I knew it quite. And it seemed to me that I couldn't stop myself.... The thing I cared about was doing work for him, and being with him, and just at first it didn't occur to me that it would ever be anyone's business but mine. I mean, I never thought that anyone would notice, or that it would matter if they did."

Sir Julian thought of his own crusade against the thing that he termed officiousness.

"But of course," said Miss Marchrose, "I've had experience of business life, and I knew that in any office, the—the sort of things that make talk can never be tolerated for a minute. It's always stopped at once. Generally they send the woman away. And I thought that very likely that would happen to me, sooner or later."

"And you didn't mind. I understand," said Julian.

"No, I didn't mind," she repeated forlornly enough. "I seem to have got to a place where I can't feel ashamed of anything—otherwise I suppose that I shouldn't be telling you this."

"I think," said Julian slowly, "that you can put that idea of shame quite out of your mind. It has always struck me as a very much misapplied emotion. There is nothing to be ashamed of in anything that is true. The only thing that is shameful is pretence. You are talking to me now on a plane where pretence can have no possible existence, and therefore, if it is of any help to you, go on speaking what is in your mind. I can do nothing for you, but I am here, and I will listen to you. And I shall never repeat to any living soul those of your thoughts which you choose to speak aloud in my hearing."

He leant over the wall, gazing with absent eyes at the grey expanse of sea that his soul loved, and remained immovable.

"You're quite right," she said, "I want to speak about it. I do want to speak about it. Rather like that day when I wanted to talk about Clarence Isbister, and you let me.

"You do understand, don't you? I knew that Mr. Easter was married. He told me so himself, quite soon. And I heard about his wife, a little, you know—from other people at the College as well. At the very beginning I was only just sorry, and then I minded very much, and then, after a little while, I thought it wasn't going to matter. To him, you know."

"Tell me what you mean," said Julian gently.

"I suppose I mean that, anyway, it wouldn't have mattered much to me. I know that there are these standards of right and wrong. I was taught things—but I know quite well really that they wouldn't have weighed in the balance against happiness. I suppose that's what is meant by an unprincipled person. Somehow I thought that he was going to feel like that too. I dare say," said Miss Marchrose, simply enough, "that it is because I have never been loved by anyone (except poor Clarence, whom you can hardly count) that I thought that. Such little things seemed to me to mean a great deal. I read indications into things—you know—and all the time they must have meant nothing at all."

"I don't think that altogether," Julian said, entirely against his saner judgment.

"What *do* you think?" she asked with a kind of listless curiosity.

"I can only give you conjecture. I know nothing at all, and you see, men don't talk to one another, much. In this case especially, of course, I have nothing whatever to guide me but my own conjectures."

"Tell me," she said.

"I think he was very much attracted by you," said Sir Julian, with perfect directness, and noted against his will the instant flush of brilliant colour that the words brought to her face.

"But Mark has ideals too, you know, as well as principles. If he ever contemplated eventualities, he knew that he had no right to ask you—to—"

"To ask of me what I was prepared to give," she finished the sentence calmly.

"Do you know what that would have involved, altogether?"

"Perhaps I do and perhaps I don't," she said indifferently. "The point is, that I was prepared to take my risks."

"In any direction?"

"In any direction," she assented, without vehemence.

"I see."

Hers might indeed be the daring of ignorance, but Sir Julian felt very little doubt that she had spoken in perfect accordance with fact, as regarded her own capabilities. One by one there filtered through his mind, and were rejected, the arguments that he knew himself entitled to use. What of morality, of Mark Easter's work, of his two children, of a future grey with unspoken possibilities for themselves and for others?

Her reckless impulse had not been put to the test; would never be put to the test.

Sir Julian let the rest alone.

"I don't know, quite, when I first realised that I—I had been making the people at the College talk," she said, and again she coloured. "It was only a few days ago that it began, and then I had that horrible feeling that everything was soundlessly working up to a crisis, and that sooner or later something must snap. You know?"

"Yes, I know."

"It was after Iris Easter's wedding, I think. And at first I was glad that it had come. Oh, you don't know, you can't imagine, what *fools* girls can be. How they can imagine and fancy and plan things, till it all seems true, and they try to go on into real life with the romance that they've been living in their dreams and fancies. And it doesn't come true. Mine didn't come true. Even if I was wrong and absolutely wicked even to let myself imagine what I did imagine, it was just as real to me as if things had been all right. It meant just as much to me as it does to a girl like Iris Easter, who knows that the man she cares for can ask her to marry him."

"Perhaps it meant more," said Sir Julian.

She gave him a glance of gratitude out of her shadow-encircled eyes.

"But when the people at the College suddenly began to watch—and talk—and look at me—then I thought that it was going to—to—well," said Miss Marchrose desperately, "to give me my chance."

"Tell me what happened."

"Nothing happened. Only, you see, at the end of twenty-four hours I saw that he was—well, just frightened. He didn't want there to be a crisis. He never had wanted it."

Sir Julian, who was Mark's friend, involuntarily paid tribute to the truth of her description. Mark had been afraid.

No wonder that Miss Marchrose had capitulated, after all. The citadel for which she had been prepared to stand siege had been only the flimsiest of castles in the air. The cause for which she had held that no casualties could be too heavy had no existence outside her own imagination.

She spoke again.

"So, though I know I've been crying, in a little while I shall be glad that he's gone. Nothing can ever be worse than the last few days. They're over now."

"They're over now," repeated Sir Julian. "Do you want to stay on at the College next week, or had you better not go back on Monday at all?"

"I don't know," she said, in a bewildered way. "Mr. Fuller has been extraordinarily kind to me. And, anyhow I shall be gone before Mr. Easter comes back. I told him that yesterday."

"You saw him, then?"

"He came to my office to say good-bye to me."

She waited a little and then said, with something that was half a laugh in her voice, although the tears had welled into her eyes again:

"He said, 'Good-bye, Annie Laurie.'"

"Poor Mark!" said Julian in a low tone.

Presently he made her walk, afraid of the sunless spring afternoon for her.

"Where are you going to, when you leave?" he asked her.

"London, I suppose. I can get another post there and this won't affect my references," she answered, unconsciously using Alderman Bellew's phrase.

"Let me know if there is anything that I can do for you," said Sir Julian rather hopelessly, neither thinking that there was likely to be anything that he could do, nor that there was much probability of her applying to him.

She made reply with candour.

"I think you've done everything that you can do, Sir Julian. I'm—I'm not trying to thank you. Will you leave me here, when you go back?"

"I can take you to the farm, or wherever you want to go."

"I would rather stay here a little while longer, by myself. Then I shall be all right," she said, like a child.

He left her.

"Perhaps," said Sir Julian to himself, as he climbed the sand slopes with long strides, "perhaps I ought to have said 'Good-bye,' 'Remember,' or 'God bless you,' or something like that to her. But whatever the rights or the wrongs of her point of view, her sincerity is worthy of respect. And I will mock her unhappiness with no catchwords, poor child."

As he went towards Culmhayes in the gathering dusk, he met a frantically-bicycling figure violently urging forward a machine that was devoid of lights.

"Fuller!"

"Sir Julian?"

Fairfax Fuller came to attention, as it were, with a promptitude that nearly sent him over his handlebars head foremost.

"You had better not go through Culmouth at that rate and without a light, surely?" said Sir Julian mildly. "Can I give you a match?"

"Are my lamps out?" enquired Mr. Fuller negligently.

Sir Julian felt convinced that they had never been lit, but he handed the Supervisor a box of matches without observation.

"Thank you, Sir Julian. The fact is," said Fuller, with an air of candour, "that I'm upset and I hardly know what I'm doing."

"What's wrong?"

"This resignation," elliptically said the Supervisor.

"My dear chap, I'm very sorry about it, but we've got to make the best of it. I've told Miss Marchrose that we accept her resignation from a week yesterday."

Mr. Fuller groaned.

"May I ask, Sir Julian, whether you have any idea where the girl is now?"

"Isn't it Saturday afternoon?" was Sir Julian's rather pointed reply.

Mr. Fuller brushed aside this suggestion of the liberty of the individual.

"I'm uneasy about her. I tell you quite frankly, Sir Julian, that I didn't like her looks this morning. One never knows."

"She strikes me as level-headed enough, you know, Fuller."

Mr. Fuller bent down and examined his rear light, but Sir Julian knew very well by the mere set of his shoulders that he remained, and would continue to remain, entirely of his own opinion.

"I think that's all right now. Just as well not to run any risks, perhaps," easily observed Mr. Fuller, once more preparing himself to bestride his machine. "Good evening, Sir Julian."

"Good evening."

He watched the red glimmer of Fuller's rear light shoot away into the dusk, and then descry a sudden curve.

"By Jove!" said Sir Julian.

Mr. Fairfax Fuller, guided by some unexplained instinct, had swept away from the road and taken the path that led down to the sea-wall. The incident, for reasons which he did not seek to analyse, rather amused Sir Julian as he went on his way.

His thoughts remained occupied round the subject until he entered his own house, to find it in possession of the two most unwelcome guests possible, in the persons of Miss and Master Easter.

"Daddy went away at lunch-time and we're all alone," proclaimed Ruthie with pathos. "And Sarah said, she said—Sarah said, to come and see if Lady Rossiter wouldn't like to invite us to tea."

Sir Julian had his own opinion to the amount of liking bestowed by his wife upon the suggested festivity, but evidently she had fallen a prey to Sarah's unblushing design for dispensing for a while with the society of her charges.

"We'll all sit round the table and have nursery tea," said Lady Rossiter, brightly endeavouring to make the best of a situation that, from the Rossiters' point of view, left much to be desired.

"Have any of you heard from Auntie Iris?" enquired Julian.

"She wrote to Daddy, and she sent her love to us. She didn't say anything about that baby," remarked Ruthie in a tone of regret.

Sir Julian felt that Edna could have dealt with Miss Easter's tendency to call a spade a spade a good deal more fully had he not been present. He could almost hear the few strong, tender phrases in which she would have bade the child refrain from the public consideration of such matters of eugenics as now appeared to be engaging her attention.

Proceedings varied but little when Mark Easter's children were entertained at Culmhayes. Sir Julian began by indifference, proceeded to annoyance, and ended in a mood but little removed from infanticide. Edna remained forbearing throughout, but became less maternal and more repressive as the necessity for repressment increased.

Ruthie monopolised the conversation with as much determination as ever; Ambrose whined quite as much as usual, and surpassed himself in the degree of stickiness to which he attained; and the *séance* ended with the usual violent quarrel between the two and their eventual expulsion from the room and from the house—Ruthie rampant and Ambrose in tears—and the inevitable valedictory wish expressed by the host that they should never be permitted to return.

Edna said, "Poor motherless children," in a tone that sounded rather more evidently exasperated and less compassionate than she had intended it to sound, and Sir Julian retired to the smoking-room.

He remembered presently that Edna probably knew nothing of the complete victory signalised by Miss Marchrose's resignation from the College staff; but he realised that the episode, in all essentials, was already past.

That which he termed "atmosphere" was dissipated, and he knew that it was almost as an afterthought that Edna, that evening, asked him whether Miss Marchrose was going.

"Yes, she is."

"At once?"

"I don't know. I've left her to settle that with Fuller."

"She must go before Mark comes back. It's far better so."

"I think probably she will."

"Julian, I've been thinking about her. And it seems to me," said Edna, "that we must help her. God knows, I can judge no one, least of all to condemn, but I think that her weakness and recklessness are going to make life terribly, terribly hard for her. And I, for one, can't see her drift away like that without one effort to help."

The depth of Sir Julian's disapproval for the suggested scheme of philanthropy left him bereft of speech. Finally he observed:

"In my opinion, Edna, you have done rather too much already. Leave her alone."

"What do you mean? Julian, you carry your mania against officiousness too far. Indeed you do. What are we here for, unless it is to help one another?"

Sir Julian shrugged his shoulders.

"I knew the character of this woman before she ever came here—I couldn't help knowing it—I saw her trying to wreck Mark, as she nearly wrecked poor Clarence. I believe that I have saved Mark—and I thank God for it, very humbly, and very proudly. As for her, I hold no brief against her. I condemn no one, and I seek only to help her. ... If she cares to turn to me now, all the love that I *can* give that poor, struggling, feeble soul is waiting for her."

"I don't think she will ask you for it, Edna."

Sir Julian thought of many things. For a moment he wondered whether he should say them aloud. Then the habit of apathy that had possessed him for a number of years asserted itself anew, and he did as he had almost always done—he left things alone.

The episode was past.

He told himself so again, with a faint sense of surprise that already it should rank as an episode merely.

There had been no calamity, and, as Edna had said, nothing had been put into words.

He revised the collection of infinitesimal ripples that had momentarily disturbed the atmosphere common to the little groups of people with whom he was concerned.

Almost each one had contributed vibrations in a greater or lesser degree.

Miss Farmer, Miss Sandiloe, young Cooper—each and all of them had tittered a little, wondered a little, talked foolishly.

Auntie Iris—for the life of him, Julian could not feel as angry with pretty, ridiculous Iris as he thought that her folly deserved—Iris, too, had played out her little comedies, her childish attempts at directing the hand of fate.

Old Alderman Bellew—Julian gave only an instant's half-amused recollection to the dogmatic condemnations and assertions of old Alderman Bellew. He had merely found it easy to follow the lead given him, after all.

On the thought of Edna's many activities Sir Julian dwelt not at all. Somewhere at the back of his mind lingered the echo of her specious gospel, her creed of "giving out."

For himself, he preferred to think that the trend of events had been in no way deflected by all that Edna had done and said.

The whole had been fated to remain an episode, devoid of climax.

XX

Nevertheless the last word remained to be spoken, and it was destined to be heard by Sir Julian when he made casual enquiry of Fairfax Fuller on Monday morning.

"Have you settled the day that Miss Marchrose leaves us?"

"Yes, Sir Julian."

"Well?" enquired Sir Julian, after a moment, as his subordinate appeared quite indisposed to make any further communications.

"She's not coming back here at all."

"Is that with your sanction?" said the surprised Julian.

"I talked it over with her on Saturday evening, Sir Julian."

"Then you did find her?"

"Down by what they call the sea-wall."

Fuller, his dark face marvellously heated, looked full at his chief.

"I've asked the girl to marry me, Sir Julian," he remarked.

Some weeks later, Julian wrote a letter, and addressed it to Miss Marchrose in London.

My dear Pauline Marchrose,

Since you ask for my opinion, I send it to you for what it is worth, admitting that, as you say, I stand committed to a certain degree of officiousness already. That, however, is not the word of which you made use. Thank you, on the contrary, for the expressions that you have selected.

I am glad that you are marrying Fuller. He is a good fellow through and through, and the other side of his bull-dog tenacity is a very real and dependable loyalty. I think that that loyalty will be of great service to you. And don't think that you are relinquishing the abstract ideal of which we spoke one afternoon down by the sea-wall. You were never false to your standards for a moment, and to recognise defeat is not always an implication of weakness. It may, as in your case, denote the courage of a perfectly sincere outlook. Humbug is the only thing to be afraid of. You have eliminated that, and Fairfax Fuller is not prone to illusion or self-deception. Besides, your intercourse took place at a time and in circumstances which admitted of the luxury of sincerity. For that, and for the fact that Fuller knows something of the extent of his incredible good fortune, I send you my congratulations and I wish you luck.

Sir Julian paused for a long while.

The episode was over. His letter was a postscript merely.

"Are you coming upstairs, Julian?" said Edna's most forbearing tones, full of fatigue.

"Is it late?"

"It's nearly twelve. It's the servants that I'm thinking of. I hate keeping them up."

"It's quite unnecessary to keep any of them up. I am perfectly capable of putting out the lights in the hall without Horber's assistance."

"I shall not ring for Mason. I never do ring for her if I'm later than eleven o'clock. After all, it's a very little thing, when once one realises that a maid is a sister-woman, when all's said and done...."

All was so far from being said that Julian, taking up his pen again, slowly added the final sentence to his letter, unconsciously adjusting his speed to words that struck upon his hearing and penetrated hardly at all to his thoughts.

"I believe so much in *little* things, in the immense power of a thought, of a kind glance, of a smile ..."

If the Colonial scheme materialises rapidly, as I think it will, I shall send Fuller out. It is largely owing to his management that we have the funds

in hand to extend the branches of the College, and I can see both you and
him as pioneers, in the near future.

"Sometimes I think that when one has not received very much oneself, it only makes one readier to give. One knows the lack—"

Keep up a very good courage—but that I believe you will always do. You have got your scale of relative values clear, and, once that's done, you can afford to accept truth. Nothing else matters.

"Perhaps one would be less tired at the end of the day if one gave out less, but after all, it's all part of the great, wonderful, Divine plan.

"Have you finished writing, Julian? 'Jorrocks' is on the table."

"Yes, quite finished," said Sir Julian, and first signing his name, he sealed his letter.

Afterword

The opening revelation of *Tension* is that Auntie Iris has written a book. And not just any book, but one with a title which brilliantly satirises the vogue at the time for novels that looked unflinchingly at love and relationships: *Why, Ben! A Story of the Sexes*. In reality, many such novels remained at least partly flinching – not least because of the obscenity laws that remained in place for another few decades. Readers of Delafield's best-remembered work, *The Diary of a Provincial Lady*, may be reminded that the unnamed diarist is, at one point, invited by Lady B. to meet 'the author of *Symphony in Three Sexes*'. She writes:

> Hesitate to write back and say that I have never heard of *Symphony in Three Sexes*, so merely accept. Ask for *Symphony in Three Sexes* at the library, although doubtfully. Doubt more than justified by tone in which Mr Jones replies that it is not in stock, and never has been.

Lady Rossiter and Sir Julian are equally doubtful about the contents of *Why, Ben!* and we never learn much about its plot or characters, and only a little about its theme. The hints that we do get are largely filtered through Iris's devoted fan and eventual husband, Mr Garrett, who says Iris has 'shown extraordinary courage in attacking a problem which could only present itself to thinking minds'. He adds that the novel is 'an extraordinarily powerful study of man's primitive needs', and Iris later recounts his review that *Why, Ben!* 'has simply gone straight back to earth [...] I always think there's something so pure and strong and passionate about the soil. That's why I gave Ben a rural setting.'

'Gone straight back to earth' is possibly a reference to Mary Webb's novel *Gone to Earth* (1917), one of the more popular in the vogue for 'rural novels' in the 1910s and 20s that Stella Gibbons satirised so mercilessly in *Cold Comfort Farm*. While Webb still has her admirers, *Gone to Earth* requires a stomach for such lines as "Where you bin? You'm stray and lose yourself, certain sure!" said a girl's voice, chidingly motherly. "And if you'm alost, I'm alost; so come you whome [sic]." Iris's novel isn't directly quoted, and Delafield resists giving the reader an extended satire of the rural nature of *Why, Ben!*; nor does she detail its investigations into 'man's primitive needs'.

Lady Rossiter has locked up her own copy of *Why, Ben!* 'on account of the servants', whom she tries to tempt with 'copies of Ruskin and Stevenson, in the rather cheaper editions'. Her maid, Mason, is instead reading Mrs Henry Wood's *East Lynne* – a sensation novel from the mid-nineteenth century in which, appropriately enough for the plot of *Tension*, a Lady is led to a life of misery and immorality because she incorrectly assumes adultery. Lady Rossiter's misinterpretation of reading tastes is also used, early on, to show her inability to understand her husband. She jokes about Sir Julian's fondness for 'Jorrocks', a cockney grocer invented in the 1830s by R.S. Surtees, noted for his vulgarity and good nature, when, in fact, Rossiter is reading *En Route*, an 1895 novel by the French author Joris-Karl Huysmans about the protagonist's conversion to Catholicism.

Iris's novel certainly has a mixed reception, and *Tension* refers to 'an astonishing harvest of press-cuttings, variously indicating surprise, disgust and admiration at the startling character of "Why, Ben!"' There is an echo of this in *The Provincial Lady Goes Further*, the second in the *Provincial Lady* series, published more than a decade after *Tension*:

'Singular letter from entire stranger enquires whether I am aware that the doors of every decent home will henceforward be shut to me? Publications such as mine, he says, are harmful to art and morality alike.'

The 1920s was, in many ways, a confusing period for what was or wasn't permissible in literature. Innocuous books like *The Diary of a Provincial Lady* might well have been targeted for censure, even while relatively explicit books like E.M. Hull's *The Sheik* (1919), in which a woman is kidnapped and repeatedly raped in Algeria, were runaway bestsellers. In non-fiction, too, the reading public was getting greater access than ever to overt writing about sexuality, including women's sexuality. Marie Stopes' *Married Love* is the most remembered, if not the most radical, of the many contemporary marital guides aimed at women who were not yet married (selling 750,000 copies between 1918 and 1931). Formerly, as Mary Scharlieb wrote in 1915's *The Seven Ages of Women*, it was 'by no means uncommon for unfortunate brides to say that they had been shocked by learning after marriage the facts of married life'. By the 1930s, R. Edynbry's *Real Life Problems and Their Solution* could advocate a woman 'hold[ing] her husband and sharing his ecstasy'. The 1920s bridged this gap.

Similarly, the 1920s also saw an increase in discussions of 'free love'. As a female character in her forties notes in Rose Macaulay's 1921 novel *Dangerous Ages*, 'Polygamy. Sex. Free Love. Love in chains. The children seemed so often to be discussing these.' By 'children', she means women in their twenties. In *Tension*, Iris Easter can't ask her friend to be a bridesmaid for the same reason:

"Oh no! She doesn't approve of marriage, you know. She thinks it is a mere servile bond for the woman," explained Iris glibly. "In fact, she's a tremendous advocate for Free Love. She's furious with me for marrying at all."

Sir Julian glanced at Mr Garrett, wondering how he regarded

the rather stupefying gospel preached by the chosen friend and companion of his bride.

The young man appeared more thoughtful than dismayed.

"In a general way," he remarked detachedly, "we moderns are all in favour of abolishing the present rather archaic marriage laws, and re-establishing the whole thing upon the basis of a purely civil contract; dissoluble after a term of years at the wish of either or both of the contracting parties."

'Free love' has covered a fairly wide range of doctrines since the term was coined in the early eighteenth century. Broadly, free love seeks to separate the rule of state or church from personal relationships – chiefly the idea that it should be acceptable to have sex outside of marriage, including adultery, though it later incorporated a broader philosophy of anti-authoritarianism and radical social change. In the 1920s, it was usually used to mean extramarital sex.

The idea of free love had become more widely known in the late Victorian period in the UK and was preached by many intellectuals of the period including writers H.G. Wells, George Bernard Shaw and Olive Schreiner. The impact on the broader public, or at least on their behaviour and decisions, was pretty limited. These discussions did little to alter the stigma attached to unmarried mothers or female adulterers, though there was, unsurprisingly, much less moral censure for unmarried fathers or male adulterers.

By the 1920s, it was more fashionable to discuss these ideas in bohemian circles (though equally unlikely to have an impact in less privileged echelons), and Bertrand Russell was a leading proponent. His most noted work on the topic of free love was 1929's *Marriage and Morals*, which was met with much outcry and the decree that Russell was 'morally unfit' to teach. Thomas Herne's *Love, Courtship and Marriage* from 1922, part of Camden Publishing's 'Sexual science series', gives an opinion that probably met with wider recognition from

■ ■ ■

the general public. In questioning 'whether Free Love is a better ideal
than Marriage', Herne doesn't look at philosophical or theoretical
arguments, but reality in the context of society. If, he asks, a man 'gets
tired' of a woman he is not married to, 'what becomes of the woman?
She has no protection at all. If she has a child, she has misery and
shame. She is an outcast.'

One of the ironies in *Tension* is that, even with the presence of
the author of *Why, Ben!*, there is no expectation that the themes of
it and similar novels will have any bearing on the lived morality of
anybody in the community – including Mark Easter, estranged from
his alcoholic wife. Even Iris herself, when the topics of marriage and
sex are raised with actual application to herself, 'looked as though she
were undecided whether to blush or to look extremely modern and
detached'. When it comes to the central tension in the book – the
rumour that Mark Easter may commit adultery with Miss Marchrose
– the debate is whether or not it is true, rather than whether or not
it is moral. Almost nobody gives serious weight to the idea of 'free
love' – even Iris has moved on from the idea that 'it would be such a
beautiful thing for them to defy conventionality and be happy in spite
of everything – a *grande passione*'.

> "In those days," Iris continued, with an effect of great remoteness
> in her manner, "I thoroughly and completely believed in Free Love
> myself. Of course, I was younger, then."
> "Only by two months," Sir Julian gloomily reminded her.

Readers who have previously enjoyed the company of the Provincial
Lady will see echoes of the same ironic wit in *Tension*, albeit echoes
that came 10 years earlier, but there is less flippancy. In the *Provincial
Lady* books, the enraging Lady B. can usually be dealt with by politely
smiling and thinking murderous thoughts. Lady Rossiter is more
determined in her pursuit.

She is one of Delafield's greatest creations in a type to which she often returned: those with no self-awareness. Sometimes Delafield spears these characters as figures of fun; here, she shows how malevolent they can be. Lady Rossiter is a monstrous, if pitiable, character who truly believes that she is doing right. One of her maxims, 'her favourite touchstone in conversation', is, "Is it kind, is it wise, is it true?". With impressive mental acrobatics, she is convinced that her efforts to destroy Miss Marchrose tick all three boxes. The reader can only watch as Lady Rossiter uses every weapon at her disposal to make life unbearable for Miss Marchrose, all the while remaining within the accepted moral behaviour of her period and position. Sir Julian's views are more sympathetic – but he is too fundamentally weak to stand up for what is right in the face of what is easiest.

Another of Lady Rossiter's favourite things to quote is 'There's so much bad in the best of us, / There's so much good in the worst of us'. As the narrator notes, 'she never finished the quotation, except by the smile, because she knew it to be at all times easy to trip over its inversion and repetitions, and thus risk the transition from the sublime to the ridiculous'. There are many variants of the rest of this quotation, all of which are along the lines of '… that it ill behooves any of us to find fault with the rest of us'. The source of the quotation is contested, with Edward Wallis Hoch, a Governor of Kansas in 1905–09, being the most likely candidate. More significantly, for its use in *Tension*, is how consistently and thoroughly Lady Rossiter disregards her own advice. To take another example, her claim that 'Love is what matters most, always' is contradicted by almost everything else that she says.

Ultimately, *Tension* is not about the tension between adultery and chastity, or marriage and free love, or between Mark Easter and Miss Marchrose, but rather the tension that Lady Rossiter creates with her rumour-mongering and 'desire of drawing attention instantly to the failure of a fellow-creature in subscribing to the recognised code'.

■ ■ ■

Delafield's skill in the novel is showing the polite face of vicious and unstoppable hypocrisy – and that, for most people, the recognised code was far more powerful than any attempts in the 1920s to expand the boundaries of love.

Simon Thomas

Series consultant **Simon Thomas** created the middlebrow blog Stuck in a Book in 2007. He is also the co-host of the popular podcast Tea or Books? Simon has a PhD from Oxford University in Interwar Literature.